ALLIED
OPERATIONS

BY

TRACY TAPPAN

ALSO BY TRACY TAPPAN

The Choose A Hero Romance™ reading experience
JUSTICE
Keith Knight's Story
Brayden Street's Story
Pete Robbins's Story

Wings of Gold Series
Military Romantic Suspense
BEYOND THE CALL OF DUTY
ALLIED OPERATIONS
MAN DOWN

The Community Series
Paranormal Romance
PREY (free novella)
THE BLOODLINE WAR
THE PUREST OF THE BREED
BLOOD-BONDED BY FORCE
MOON-RIDERS
HALF-MOON RISING

For more information, go to www.tracytappan.com.
Sign up for Tracy's author updates and find out about
FREE books today!

Who's your favorite type of romance hero?

A devoted gentleman…a hard-charging leader…a reckless
bad boy…?

How about *all three*?

Now's your chance to have 'em all!

Destiny waits for each of these men with Justice Hayes,
master thief, star athlete, and the first woman to survive
SEAL training.

"THE most powerful reading experience I've ever had!"

*"WOW. Just wow! This was a totally unique romance, and I
loved every page. I was hooked from the first word."*

<u>JUSTICE</u>
A Choose A Hero Romance™ Novel

<u>Congratulations to Trish Jones for winning the birth date contest to honor her father, Army Sergeant Pat Tomaro</u>.

Pasquale Frank Tomaro

Pat won the Purple Heart for an act of incredible bravery during the Korean War. He was on point one night during a blackout/radio silence, and his battalion suddenly came upon a cliff they couldn't see in the dark. He flipped his jeep on purpose to stop the vehicles behind him from going over, and ended up sliding down the cliff and getting pinned under his jeep. He was paralyzed as a result, and doctors told him he would never walk again or have children. But Pat eventually proved them wrong. In his later years, his right leg was amputated due to vascular deficiency, but even that never held him back from living his life to the fullest.

He passed away eighteen years ago, but not a day goes by

that his daughter Trish doesn't miss him. "He was my hero! He never let the PTSD he suffered from conquer him, and was the best daddy to me and my sister. I know he remains with me in spirit, watching over and protecting me, because that's the kind of man he was."

** To honor Sergeant Pat Tomaro, his birthday, **November 27th**, has been chosen as the birthday of a naval aviator in this book, Lieutenant JG Steve "Jobs" Whitmore.

"They say if you stay in this business long enough, you will lose a friend. I guess that's true. I'm no hero. Just an average guy doing a tough job. My friend and copilot is a hero. He gave everything he had for something he believed in. I will miss him."

Mark "Clutch" Eoff, USN, Retired

Mark "Clutch" Eoff, crash survivor

To the men and women who've given their lives doing a job they believe in.

Note to readers: Pilots use technical jargon and a dizzying array of acronyms and slang when they talk and think. For the sake of storytelling, I've toned down much of this lingo, but it would be impossible to portray naval aviators realistically without it. The terminology shouldn't trip you up in the story, but a **glossary** has been provided in the back for those who are interested in exact definitions.

PROLOGUE

KYLE ROLLED OVER on the mattress and slowly lifted his eyelids. Rumpled sheets, empty bed… Quieting his breathing, he homed in on sounds. Nothing. Only silence. No one was messing around in the bathroom. No one was *anywhere* in this hotel room.

Except for him.

He closed his eyes again, but not before confirming there wasn't a carefully folded note deposited sweetly on the pillow next to his. *She left me without a single word…* And he was an idiot. Not just any sort of idiot, but on a level with a lobotomized Mr. Magoo, or Mr. Bean after ten years of glue-sniffing. That was him, Kyle "Mikey" Hammond, Lieutenant, United States Navy—on the idiot scale of one to ten, he was the googolplexian. Because here he was again, lying in bed with a broken heart. Repeat: *again.*

Then a familiar sound drifted to his ears…

The Universe *tsking* at him.

Kyle shifted onto his back, locked his hands behind his head, and gave the ceiling a hard stare. If he could stand up and defend himself to the Universe—not that the Great and Powerful U would even listen to any more of his yadda, yadda, yadda—he would cite "extenuating circumstances" for this, yet another round of cyclical stupidity, and claim he'd never experienced his ex-girlfriend, Sienna, like he had late-morning yesterday.

In the little over six years he'd dated Sienna Kelleman—starting in his junior year of high school and ending shortly after he'd gone to flight training in the Navy following college—he'd always had to scramble like a dog on all fours for every meager bestowal of attention he received from the gorgeous, though mean as a hissing cat, blonde. But yesterday, when both of them were heading down the tiled corridor of San Francisco General Hospital, Sienna made the first move *ever* toward him. She slipped her hand in his and gripped it hard, as if she needed—no, was *relying* on—his strength and support. *Him*, the guy she'd always complained was a man she could never rely on.

"I'm really nervous," she whispered.

He shot her a startled glance. "You've never met him?"

"No," she'd returned in a choked whisper. "Not even the day he was born."

The way she'd looked at him then... Her expression, her tone... He'd never known callous, demanding, impossible-to-please Sienna Kelleman could be vulnerable.

A lump pushed into Kyle's throat, and he squeezed her hand back while they walked toward room 254 of the pediatric ward.

A couple, clearly a husband and wife, waited for them by the door, introducing themselves as Stanley and Marie

Coleman.

The man was dark-haired with a prominent widow's peak, and he wore glasses. He was of medium height and slender. The woman was short and a little plump, with a face that was probably jolly and apple-cheeked when she wasn't so pale and scared-looking.

The lump in Kyle's throat grew. He would guess his face didn't have much blood left in it, either.

Mr. Coleman gave Kyle a long, intense inspection, and his complexion paled a whiter shade than his wife's. Finally, he spoke. "Thank you both so much for coming. The doctors are waiting this way to take a sample of your bone marrow." He gestured down the hall.

Kyle hesitated. "But…" Was this how it worked? "Aren't we going to see the boy first?"

Mr. Coleman frowned. "Do you think that's wise?"

The Universe spoke loudly and clearly directly into Kyle's ear. *It is probably the worst idea ever created by man.* But Kyle chose to do what he always did when he didn't like the answer. Not listen. He glanced at Sienna.

Her eyes were pooled with tears.

Screw it. Kyle drew himself up. "We want to see him."

Mr. Coleman paused some more.

But what could the man say? He needed Kyle and Sienna's help.

A bored-looking orderly lumbered by with a crash cart. *Chogga-chogga-chogga*…one of the wheels was lopsided.

"All right," Mr. Coleman conceded. "But we haven't told Brodie he's adopted yet. Please," he directed at Kyle, "say you're a colleague of mine from work." Mr. Coleman led them inside the room.

It took every particle of willpower Kyle could muster to walk normally—not to stop dead in his tracks at coming face to face with his own son—to keep a normal expression—not to stare in appalled horror at all of the tubes running out of the seven-year-old boy—and to keep his jaw levered in place—not to let it drop all the way to China, because Brodie Coleman, with his sandy-colored hair, blue eyes, and bone structure that could've been formed from a plaster cast right off Kyle's own features, looked exactly like Kyle. Not just a little bit, not even much like Sienna, but *exactly* like Kyle.

It was a total earthquake moment.

Considering how much seismic activity had been turning his life ass-over-fuck lately, that was no small thing. Case in point *one*, half a dozen hours ago Sienna had confessed that the sex-capade she and Kyle enjoyed right before he left for flight school had gotten her pregnant. *Two*: her anger over the unwanted pregnancy was the reason she'd broken up with him. *Three*: she'd given up their son for adoption. *Four*: Kyle was never supposed to have known any of this. And whopper number *five*: he never would have known if Brodie Coleman hadn't become gravely ill with cancer, and Kyle and Sienna, as the boy's biological parents, needed to donate bone marrow for his treatment.

"Hi," the kid said.

Weird how one simple word could feel like a punch straight to the gut. "Hey." Kyle let go of Sienna's hand to step forward and offer his palm to Brodie. "I'm Mr.

Hammond."

The kid reached out and shook Kyle's hand. "Nice to meet you, sir."

Polite words, a firm grip. This was a good boy. As Kyle stepped back, emotion stung the backs of his eyes, and for an absurd moment, he wanted to kiss Sienna for giving up Brodie. The boy was a better kid than if Kyle had been given the job of rearing him. Kyle probably would've raised him into a surly, hate-the-world-and-everything-in-it kind of person who spent his days shooting at stuff with a BB gun.

"I'm Sienna." Sienna moved forward and set her hands on the upraised bed rail. "We're going to get you out of this bed real soon."

"Definitely," Kyle agreed in a voice that felt strangled. "Get you back out to doing… uh…" He forced a smile. "What do you like to do? Sports?"

"Yes, sir."

"Which ones?" *Please don't say baseball, please don't say—*

"Baseball."

Kyle's stomach cramped. Baseball was his sport. *So he's like me in that way, too.* Or…you know…maybe… "I bet your dad taught you, right?" Kyle felt his smile start to fray. *Actually, I'm your dad.*

Brodie's eyes flickered toward Mr. Coleman.

Mr. Coleman shifted his feet. "Brodie and I practice the cello together."

The…cello?

"What instrument do you play?" Brodie asked him politely.

Kyle raised his brows. "Me?"

"I told Brodie," Mr. Coleman jumped in, "that the man coming to the hospital to help him is a visiting musician for the San Francisco Philharmonic."

So that's what Coleman does for a living. He plays the cello in a professional symphony. "Yeah…" Kyle put all his weight behind getting some words passed his throat blockage—violin, flute, the kazoo, bagpipes, a fucking squeeze box—but he couldn't do it. *I'm a naval aviator, and I'M YOUR DAD.*

"The trumpet," Sienna answered for him.

"Mr. and Mrs. Hammond are only here for one day," Coleman added pointedly.

Kyle nodded, the movement pressing down on his throat-lump. *That's right, one day to see my sick-as-a-dog biological son, and then out the door I go.*

A nurse entered the room wearing purple scrubs. "Time for lunch," she singsonged, like they were at Magic Mountain, instead of the pediatric oncology ward.

"No." Brodie threw a desperate glance at Mrs. Coleman. "Mom, please…"

"Brodie—"

"Eating makes me throw up."

"You have to try and keep your strength up, sweetheart."

Tears started to run down Brodie's face. "But, Mom," he whispered.

Kyle's knees went slack, and his belly watered down. He whipped around and took two short steps for the door before it hit him, what he was doing. *Leaving…*

The memory came at him in such a violent rush, it

snapped the bones in the back of his neck, making it so all he could do was bow his head. Kyle had been the exact same age as Brodie, also in a hospital, having just come into the ER with a broken arm from falling off his bike.

His mom showed up ten minutes later, lines of strain on her face...not for Kyle's injury. No, he recognized that expression of hers well enough. It was because Kyle's broken limb was too much for his father to deal with, so Matthew had taken off again. For weeks? Months? Who knew? Kyle, his mother, and younger brother sure as hell never did. The last time Matthew Hammond had found the door, he'd been gone for two months...and all it'd taken was Kyle's birthday to roll around, requiring Matthew to buy a present for his oldest son, or maybe blow up a few balloons. It didn't take much responsibility to be placed on the old man's shoulders for him to take a powder.

Exactly like Kyle was doing...

Jesus, no. Somehow getting his brain to command his muscles and tendons to act, Kyle turned back around. He stood in place, his throat full of sand. A couple of months ago he'd been in a Colombian jungle, fighting three drug-running *soldados* for his life. He'd been stabbed twice, nearly got his forearm broken, and was strangled until his eyeballs had partially mushed out of their sockets. And he'd go back there right now, *in a second*, do it all over again, rather than watch his kid cry.

Mr. Coleman came to Kyle's rescue, ushering everyone toward the door. "Let's give Brodie some privacy," he said quietly.

Kyle nodded, like, *'course*, that'd been his plan all

along.

It WAS NEARLY eight o'clock at night by the time Kyle and Sienna arrived at the downtown Travelodge, located only two miles from the hospital. He'd let Sienna do the talking at the front desk, and when she ordered one room instead of two, he hadn't argued. He started to catch flak from the Universe, but he was beyond numb, so the U got a one-fingered-salute. He couldn't stand the thought of being alone right now anyway, and Sienna probably felt the same.

The room was clean but small, consisting of not much more than a television on a dresser, a bathroom, and a queen-sized bed, the bedspread a collage of differing beige shades of nondescript.

Kyle tossed both his bag and Sienna's into a corner of the room, then sank down heavily next to her on the foot of the mattress.

Outside, an eighteen wheeler's horn blared, then faded to nothing on the 101 freeway just south of the motel.

"You must be tired," he said. Last night Sienna had taken a red-eye flight from Virginia to San Diego, reaching Kyle's place in the early morning hours on Friday to drop her multiple bombshells. Soon after that they'd both hopped on a plane for San Francisco, met their kid, and finally each of them had gone under local anesthesia to endure having a hollow needle thrust into the back of their pelvic bones.

"And sore." Sienna grimaced as she carefully shifted her rump on the mattress. "Are you?"

"A bit." But who cared? He would've endured a lot

worse—*anything*—if it meant a chance to save Brodie. "I went to the cafeteria while you were finishing up and bought a couple of to-go sandwiches. You hungry?"

"I guess." He heard her swallow. "Brodie looks just like you." He felt her watching him. "Is that...was that weird?"

Kyle remained facing forward, placing his hands on his knees. His spine felt very straight. "Yes," he whispered.

"Seeing him cry..." She sniffed. "God, it made me want to...to hug him..." Her voice caught. "B-be his mother."

Jaw twitching, Kyle stared at the on-off switch on the television set, a bunch of tight fists gripping his belly. What was a man supposed to do with an upset woman? He had no training for it. Sienna never got emotional in front of him, and other women...he just banged them.

Sienna laughed wetly. "I wouldn't have made him eat lunch."

Kyle managed a stilted smile. "Me either."

She exhaled slowly. "It made me think...how our lives might've been different, if...maybe I'd kept him."

Not for the first time the thought squirmed its way inside Kyle. Dully spoken, necessary words came out of his mouth. "We're not good together, Sienna. Brodie is better off with the Colemans." Kyle still had all of his teeth, thirty-two, wisdom included—for all the good those did him—and they all pressed together simultaneously. *No! No! I want my kid!*

Sienna's fingers brushed over his forearm. "You could've been my greatest love, Kyle," she said softly. "It's just...you're so..." She trailed off.

Pain pushed his eyes closed. "You don't need to say it." She'd already said it yesterday. *This is exactly why I never ended up with you, Kyle. You're so undependable. Just like your father. I saw how depressed your poor mother was her whole life. Do you think I wanted to end up like that?* His jaw quivered.

Sienna pulled her hand back. "You were going to leave Brodie's hospital room today, weren't you?"

His throat jerked. Heat flashed up the back of his neck. Snapping his eyes open, he rounded on Sienna, all sensation leaving his lips. "I'm extremely fucking shell-shocked right now, Sienna. Do you think maybe you could not jab a sharp stick into me?"

A starter pistol went off in his head. *We're off!* The act of yelling would ignite their regular pattern—her yelling back, him yelling some more, until their raging would land them in bed, having rough, clawing, I-hate-your-guts/love-your-guts sex.

But it was a day of belly-twisting, soul-shocking firsts. Sienna just lifted her hand and palmed his cheek. "Okay."

He went utterly still. He even stopped breathing for a couple of seconds. Emotional Sienna was as much of a mind-bender as Nice Sienna. What to do...?

So he pushed her down on the mattress and had sex with her—gentle, not rough—their fingers entwined, gazes locked, sore hips gently rocking together...

And now, here it was morning, and Sienna was gone. Without so much as a light shake of the shoulder to wake him to say goodbye...as if everything they'd been through hadn't meant a single damned thing to her. *As if?* Ha. It was for fucking sure the cryogenic bitch hadn't made even an iota of space for him in her heart.

Kyle sat up on the edge of the bed, rigidly shoveling anger into the smoking hole in his chest. *Why* did he keep doing this shit to himself? Fists pressed to his thighs, he actually cocked an ear to the Universe, waiting for an answer.

Unfortunately, he got one.

Go blow your "extenuating circumstances," Kyle. You said it yourself: you're the googolplexian of all idiots.

CHAPTER ONE

April, seven months later
Jebel Ali Club, Dubai, United Arab Emirates

S AMANTHA WAS GOING to sleep with the next man who walked into the club. *Absolutely. It's happening.* Gripping her gin and tonic in a tight fist, she peered from her position at the bar through the dim light at the front door. Her stomach fluttered.

But no sexual liaison entered.

She gave her drink an erratic stir with the swizzle stick. He would come in, though, eventually, and when he did and she secreted him away someplace private, there wouldn't be any kind of *I've never done this before* utterances from her. *No.* Even though she never *had* indulged in a one-night stand before, such a phrase sounded regretful, and she wasn't going to allow herself to feel remorse over this. Death was a real possibility on the mission she was undertaking tomorrow, and she'd be damned if she was going six feet under before she'd first had six inches *in*. She hadn't had sex in over a year, and this might very well be her last chance to have it, so she was going for it.

The door swung open, letting in a burst of unintelligible chatter from the Ibn Battuta Mall outside, plus a whiff of the scents she associated with Third World nations: everything musty and underused, like opening the lid of a chest that'd been stifled in an attic too long.

She straightened on her stool as a man entered the bar…wearing a turban. *Oh, boy.* She slouched back down. A great deal of choosiness probably wasn't a luxury she had time to indulge, but her instincts told her that making whoopee with a local wouldn't be the best of ideas.

She sipped her drink, her tummy still trying to run away and hide behind her spinal cord. No one else came in. *Slow night.* Or was it? She usually flew directly into Karachi—the most populated city in Pakistan—when she had an assignment in Pakistan, so she wasn't familiar with this club.

The place was a strange combination of exotic—the walls were painted an outlandish red color—plus ordinary—several pool tables were in the back, and twinkle lights were strung around the ceiling. She'd chosen the bar for its proximity to Jebel Ali port, where US Navy ships regularly anchored. An illusion of safety came with being close to something American. She'd even left off wearing a headscarf, or hijab, tonight, although she was still covered from neck to toes, dressed in boots, long pants, and a long-sleeved shirt buttoned down to her wrists and up to her chin. April temperatures in this part of the world already reached into the high seventies, occasionally the eighties, but any less clothing would earn her too many hard stares in this heavily Muslim nation. Besides, she believed in respecting other countries' traditions.

She caught her breath when the door opened again.

Two men strode in, and...short hair and clean-shaven equaled military men. *Bummer.* No surprise, though, considering a Navy ship currently sat in port. But she would be reporting to that very ship tomorrow first thing at oh-my-God-o'clock to kick off her mission. Wouldn't it be dandy to show up to her meeting with the commanding officer and *know* he had a mole on his unit?

So no locals, no military men. Where did that leave her? Stopping this nonsense and going back to her hotel? Her small backpack was slung over her knee, and she moved it onto her lap. She gulped down the rest of her drink.

The door opened.

She spun on her stool to see. And her heart lurched.

The newly arrived man was dressed like an American in desert-colored clothes and boots right out of an Army surplus store. So not a local. He had short hair, but not excessively so, and moreover, he wore a closely cropped beard. So not military either...unless he was special forces, but that was doubtful. From what she understood, special operatives never traveled alone. So who? Maybe a journalist. Wouldn't that be a hoot?

The man stopped just inside the door and scanned the room with a practiced eye. His focus skimmed past her, then skidded back and locked on. The look in his eyes turned decidedly intimate, as if they already shared something personal, and his lazy smile had *Gotcha!* written all over it.

In other circumstances she might've taken umbrage at his presumptuousness, but, well...she *was* here to get *got*.

He crossed the room, aiming straight for her without

any pretense at subtlety. Drawing up next to her, he braced an elbow on the bar.

Had he purposely placed his forearm in such a way to showcase how well-defined his muscles were? If so, he was a player of the highest caliber. He definitely gave off that kind of an air, oozing confidence like his sweat was made out of liquid gold, good-looking and knowing it. Her hormones took notice of his T-shirt hugging the muscles in his arms and chest, and her body heat rose. So...

She favored him with her most brilliant smile. *Gotcha*! back, buddy.

He chuckled at her expression. Visions of her legs wrapped around his waist were probably already dancing through his head. "Gin and tonic?" he inquired, indicating her drink.

"Yes."

His smile broadened. "My very own drink of choice."

She fluttered her lashes and gushed, "How marvelous!" Okay, she didn't really do that. But...truth was, she wasn't sure how to respond. In a normal bar situation, yes, but this was the *abnormal* situation of flirting with a man she had no interest whatsoever in having a relationship with, just sex, and, *hmmm*, maybe that was kind of freeing. "Then when you buy yourself one, you can get me another."

"My pleasure," he said in the smoky tones of a consummate seducer. As he turned to grab the bartender's attention, she caught sight of a long scar along the line of his left jaw, like white railroad tracks traversing through the field of his beard. Whatever injury had necessitated those stitches had been a nasty one.

He pointed to her drink, raised two fingers to the bartender, then sat down on a barstool, angling his body toward her, his elbow still on the bar, his thick thighs spread wide.

She picked up her glass and pretended to peer at the watered dregs of her drink when she was actually lowering her focus to the crotch being presented to her—openly, for her inspection, of that she had no doubt. She took a sip and smacked her lips. Maybe tonight would be *more* than six inches in.

The bartender dropped off their gin and tonics.

She handed the bartender her old drink and took a sip of her new. "So," she said to her impromptu date, "if you were going to try to seduce a woman in a place like this, what would you say to her?"

To his credit, he pretended to give her question serious thought, when she suspected the reality was that he was operating off a well-worn, and probably extremely successful, script. "If it were you?" he began.

Who me? No, not me.

"I wouldn't unload a bunch of flattery on you about the amazing color of your eyes or the awesome shape of your thighs in those pants."

"Oh?" *Why not? It might work...it was sort of a little working now.*

"Nah. That would come across as trite to someone like you."

"Like me?"

"Smart."

She rolled her eyes. "You have no way of knowing such a thing. You just met me."

"Sure I do." He gestured at her head. "From your haircut. It's no-nonsense."

She ran a hand through her short hair. She wore a pixie cut, long in front, with right side bangs swooping onto her brow, but cut very short in back. Occasionally she blew her hair dry for added fullness, but most days she merely ran her fingers through it as she walked out the door. She'd started out life as a dirty blond and had never done anything to change that fact. So, yes, no-nonsense was reasonably accurate.

"You look like a woman who has more important things to do than spend hours in front of a mirror. A busy woman." Devils danced in the depths of his eyes. "And smart."

"I'm not sure if that's actually a compliment." Did not spending time in front of a mirror really mean she looked slovenly? "But I'm going to choose to take it that way."

His brow furrowed as he crunched on a piece of ice. "How else would I mean it?"

She waved it aside. "So what would you do with this theoretical smart woman, then? Talk politics with her?"

He guffawed. "Politics ain't sexy, honey. No, I think I'd encourage her to seduce me."

She exhaled a disbelieving breath.

Shrugging, he took a sip of his drink and licked his lip.

"Okay. How?"

"I'd be straightforward." His voice was starting to take on a Southern drawl. "For example, if it were you, I'd say: hey, if you were trying to seduce a man in a place like this, what would you say to him?"

She burst out laughing. "No fair!"

A glint darted through his eyes. "C'mon now."

"All right. *Hmm...*" She panned the room, then aimed her chin at the two military men who'd come in earlier, now seated at a small table. "I'd take a page out of their book and say, 'hey, baby, I'm going out in the field tomorrow to hunt terrorists, and I don't know if I'm going to make it back'." She leaned forward, close enough to catch her date's scent—something indescribably masculine—and set a hand on his thigh. "Don't send me out there a lonely woman," she said in a husky tone.

He eye-locked her for the space it took a vein in his neck to pulse twice, then his focus slipped sinuously to her mouth. "And my response would be..." He came to his feet, taking her hand off his thigh and holding it. "Let's go get some air."

CHAPTER TWO

"**A** POOL!" SAMANTHA exclaimed when they stepped outside onto the bar's back patio. And Olympic-sized, too, of all the amazing things.

Artificial turf ran the length of all four borders, and lawn chairs were neatly lined up on the right and left. An eight-foot-tall wall of solid cement surrounded the entire patio, the interior side of which was dotted with palm trees.

Her date's eyebrows soared. "Wow, who would've guessed something like this would be at the back of a dive bar?"

She stepped to the edge of the pool and knelt, setting her backpack at her feet as she swished her fingers in the water. Perfect temperature for a dip. "I haven't been in a pool for several weeks." Between all the preparations for her Pakistan trip, she'd been too busy.

"You make it sound like a long time. You swim often?"

"Very." She smiled to herself. There was nothing like the feel of being buoyed out in space, noises dampened by water to shut out the rest of the world, her arms pulling through resistance as she pushed for faster and faster speeds.

"Do you want to go in?" Her date stepped up to her

side, the toes of his boots jutting over the edge of the pool.

His feet were enormous…a sight which probably should've encouraged her to check out his package again. She didn't, though, the first inklings of nerves overtaking her. This man had brought her out here to have sex. She'd come out here with the same objective sitting squarely on her agenda. But planning to have sex with a stranger and actually doing it were starting to feel like two very different things.

"'Course we'd have to skinny dip," he added in a wicked tone.

She angled her head to peer up at him. From down here, the scar on his jaw looked even nastier. Had he been sewn up by his next-door neighbor? A reporter buddy who just so happened to be drunk at the time. "Oh?" She arched a single brow. "And then what?"

A slow smile spread across his face. "We could race each other. There are lines demarcating lanes, after all."

"I'd kick your ass."

He laughed.

She stood up and stared at him.

His laugh cracked off. "What? Really?"

"I'm afraid so. When I was seventeen, I was an alternate for the women's breaststroke on the 2004 US summer Olympic team. I even went to Athens, Greece."

His eyes briefly flashed wide. "Holy shit. That's incredible." He sounded genuinely impressed.

Which brought a chuckle rippling out of her. "You want to hear something even more incredible?"

"Definitely."

"I can hold my breath for over three minutes, occasionally close to four."

"All right, we're staying out of the pool." He picked up her backpack and took her hand. "I wouldn't be looking my best in there...not next to you." He led her to the farthest corner of the building, and in a smooth, expert move that spoke of long practice he spun her into the shadows against the wall.

He was against her in the next moment, his hands grasping the circumference of her waist, his head bent to her throat. His gin-and-tonic breath was hot and promissory against her flesh, his beard a soft, teasing burr as he kissed a path from the place where her neck met her shoulder up to where her jaw joined with her ear.

Her belly churned. *Samantha, what are you doing?* She conducted another quick check of the outdoor tables and lounges. Deserted. She couldn't even really hear music coming from inside the bar. Crickets chirped and that was all.

Her date stepped back a little, his lids hooded. His fingers flickered down the front of her blouse, and before she knew it, her shirt was gaping open from her neck to her navel.

She dragged her tongue across her lips. That was...quick.

He tucked his hands inside her shirt, smoothing them from her waist to her spine. His fingertips rode over the gentle knolls of her vertebrae, slowly making their way up to her bra. With another impressive, nearly nonexistent flutter of his fingers, he unclasped her bra. The garment sagged off her chest, and his palms rounded up to cup her.

She stiffened. A man she'd talked to for less than thirty minutes was feeling up her naked breasts. She couldn't... Forcing a deep inhale, she closed her eyes. *Stop it. Get in the game.* The whole reason for doing this was to have a last hurrah! If she couldn't enjoy it, what was the point?

Her date made a low sound when her nipples beaded under his teasing thumbs.

She wasn't particularly large-breasted, lagging back to the low end of a B-cup. She could tell she didn't quite fill his palms, but...he didn't seem to mind. He was giving her breasts a thorough going-over, all the while rumbling deep, pleased noises over them, especially every time he encountered the perky crowns of her breasts.

At least her nipples were enjoying this.

Samantha! Get going. Seizing a fistful of hair at the back of his head, she urged him toward her for a kiss. A kiss was everything. If he couldn't kiss well, she was out.

Damn, this man could kiss.

He started out slow and easy, which was absolute perfection, his lips meeting hers in a gentle massage, his tongue no more than a coy, sweet friction over hers, feeling a little cold from his icy drink. Her hand relaxed in his hair, her fingers winnowing through the soft strands. He tasted like he smelled—masculine, but in a way that she couldn't quite put her finger on. Almost like...this man could control something of incredible and lethal power. Maybe he was a lion tamer.

The kiss deepened, becoming wet and slippery, a little wild. Could he taste how she felt...like desire edged with desperation? Like a part of her wanted to cry, the other part of her bay at the moon? She locked her arms around his neck.

He embraced her tightly, pressing his body—quite a lot of muscles—against her as he sucked on her tongue.

She moaned into his mouth, an indication—heretofore unknown to her—that he should clutch her butt and give it a good squeeze.

Her pants came undone.

She stopped kissing him on a swift exhale. How did he manage these things so effortlessly? Did he work part time as a secret agent when he wasn't lion taming?

He pushed her pants and undies down, and...*Okay. So. We're doing this now.* Seeing as she was naked from the waist down and all.

He released her to tug a wallet out of his back pants pocket and extract a condom.

She stared fixedly at the square foil. Condoms were for having sex. They were going to have sex. Sex was going to happen. Here tonight, by this pool with—

"Do you want to take your shoes off?" he asked in a roughened voice. He ripped open the package.

She blinked down at her pants sagged around her knees. *Right. A girl can't exactly spread her legs like this, can she?* She went into a crouch, studiously ignoring the sight of his jutting member. If he did, in fact, have a mole on his unit, then *oh, well.* She wasn't going to find out. As she untied first one of her boots, then the next, only her peripheral vision registered him taking care of safety matters by unrolling the condom over IT.

Bootless now, she straightened and kicked her pants

aside.

He waited while she transferred moisture from her mouth down to her crotch, then he grabbed her by the waist and hiked her up.

She helped by giving a little jump and flinging her legs around him.

With a grunt, he seated her directly down onto his member—first shot, perfect bull's eye, bingo!

Her mouth opened on a gasp. He was *definitely* more than six inches. And—yow!—as he started to thrust inside her, she gritted her teeth. Felt like twice that.

She grasped his shoulders and clamped her jaw harder. She wasn't incredibly prepared. The condom had some lubrication on it, but still... "Could you, uh, not go quite so deep?"

He kept pumping, but eased up, receiving credit for not being a selfish jerk.

She gazed out across the pool. The stars visible over the cement wall bounced in front of her vision. She blew out her cheeks. What was taking so long? She felt a shudder run through him, and the noises he was making started to sound strained. He was on the verge of coming, so...

Oh, God. He was delaying for her.

He earned more credit, but, unfortunately, his efforts were wasted. She wasn't going to climax. Not crammed against a wall at the back of a bar in Dubai. Not with a man who didn't inspire a single feeling in her. She nearly sighed. She should've known better. A woman couldn't change her spots just because she willed it for a night. Time to chalk this one up and head back to her hotel for a bath. Although apparently she'd have to dust off her acting skills first.

"Yesyesyesyes," she panted into her date's ear. "Oh!" She squeezed her vaginal muscles rhythmically around his member, gasped out another couple of *Ohs* for good measure, and was rewarded with a mistake-ending orgasm from him.

He jammed himself deep inside her on a last thrust and grated a sound of pleasure behind his teeth.

She hung in his arms, fighting the urge to squirm while she waited for him to pull out and set her down. A breeze drifted by, cooling the sweat on her skin and rippling the pool water. *Well, done is done.* She clearly didn't excel at one-night stands, but she did have considerable skills at forgetting unpleasantness…smoothing things over, taking care of matters so everything and everyone remained unruffled. And she'd promised herself, *no regrets*, right?

There was one saving grace. He wasn't in the military, not with a beard. She had that much, at least.

Earlier…

HANDS TUCKED INTO his pockets, Kyle strolled into the Jebel Ali Beach Hotel, and, after glancing around a bit, chose the Captain's Bar. It was the least ritzy of the places he saw, located outside on a patio right on the water. It had a roof made from thatching, like a Tiki hut, and the tables and chairs were built of whiskey-colored wood with off-white upholstery on the chairs. During the day the view of the Persian Gulf and the Jebel Ali Port must be spectacular. Now at night there was nothing much to enjoy except the occasional faint breeze bringing in the scent of the sea.

Only a quarter of the ten well-spaced tables were full, and Kyle easily found an empty one in a corner.

By himself.

He exhaled as he sat. *It's lonely at the top* was something he totally understood now that he was the OIC, or Officer in Charge, of his own helicopter detachment. Boundaries could too easily be crossed if he went out drinking and partying with the men he led, especially since he was the same rank as both his maintenance and operations officers. He needed to be careful about maintaining his position—super-careful, if he wanted to prove himself in a job that had dropped into his lap by luck.

Mostly OIC positions went to lieutenant commanders or, if it did go to a lieutenant, a Super JO like his aviator buddy, Eric "LZ" O'Dwyer. But the LCDR slated for this deployment had broken his wrist a week prior to setting sail, and when no one else had been available to step up, Kyle was able to grab this career-enhancing opportunity.

But that left him with a short list of men he could hang out with on port calls—mainly, other leaders. On a ship, that meant the department heads, but so far Kyle wasn't jumping for joy over the higher-ranking ship guys he'd met. The Navigation Officer had six kids who were his sole topic of conversation, the Chief Engineer was always pissing and moaning about all the time he spent in the boiler room, and the Supply Officer was a teetotaler. There was the chaplain—*hahahaha!*—and the XO, but he was a dick.

So, here he sat, *alone*, nothing better to do than wander around inside his own head. Never a good thing for him.

Exhaling again, he glanced around for a waitress—he needed a drink—when out on the water a ship's running lights grabbed his attention. A vessel was driving by: a massive vessel. He saw the number 70 lit up on the ship, and his stomach balled.

It was the aircraft carrier, *USS Carl Vinson*—the very carrier he'd visited a week ago to get handed the most high-risk mission of his career.

First thing when you get back to your ship, write your letter…

COMPRESSING HIS LIPS, Kyle searched the bar again, this time looking for a target of sexual opportunity. The hell if he was going to sit here and brood about how the next few weeks were going to play out. The hell if he was going to sit here *alone*.

Tonight had just become about getting laid.

CHAPTER THREE

One week ago.
The Persian Gulf, thirty-five miles from US Aircraft Carrier,
USS Carl Vinson (CVN-70)

J AW SQUARED, KYLE stared out across the blue
landscape of sea as the steady *chop-chop* of the
helicopter's rotors battered his nerves. Usually the best
sound in the world, this afternoon the noise of the
spinning blades signified forward movement toward
something bad, so it was as annoying as fingernails hard-
scraping his balls.

He didn't know exactly *what* the bad was, just that
nothing good ever came from a measly lieutenant like
himself being summoned to stand tall in front of the one-
star admiral in command of Carrier Strike Group One.
And not any ol' one-star. As a cherry on top of the bad,
the admiral was Robert Kelleman.

Sienna's father.

There weren't many men who made Kyle want to
stink his pants, but Admiral Robert Kelleman was one of
them.

His morose thoughts were interrupted by his copilot,
Lieutenant Junior Grade Steve "Jobs" Whitmore.

Whitmore, nicknamed Steve Jobs because he was a
brainiac and technical Whiz Kid, was all about precision

flying. Kyle had never seen a new pilot fly with such textbook accuracy, but for all his book intelligence, Jobs ran a little low on street smarts—and he looked it, with a face like the Beav's and likewise the kind of innocent attitude straight off a 1950s sitcom.

Kyle was going to use this cruise—Jobs' first—to take the kid under his wing, show the eager Padawan the real world of aviation.

"Sir," Jobs' voice crackled into Kyle's earpiece. "We're approaching the *Vinson's* air space."

"Roger that." Kyle clicked the trigger on the stick in his right hand to change over to outer cockpit communications.

Any time a pilot flew near a US aircraft carrier, he gave plenty of warning of his presence or soon found a couple of fighter jets flying up his pooper.

"Red Crown," Kyle said, using the call sign for combat control of the Aegis Cruiser in charge of protecting the twenty-mile radius of airspace around the carrier. "This is Lone Wolf six-five on your one-zero-zero, thirty-five miles at five hundred feet, squawking two-five-one-four, inbound for a thirteen-hundred overhead."

"Roger that," combat returned. "Proceed to starboard D. There's one in the pattern."

Kyle confirmed, then briefly closed his eyes. Only thirty-five miles left to figure out what the hell he could've done in such a short amount of time to dick up his career.

Kyle's helicopter squadron, the HSM-75 Wolfpack, had only been on station in the Gulf a little over two weeks. While the Wolfpack CO based on the carrier, four of the squadron's helo detachments were posted on smaller ships in the strike group. Kyle was aboard the *USS Bunker Hill*, a Ticonderoga class cruiser.

Would this be this be his home for long? Was he about to get canned from his OIC job, then sent off to clean yardarms for what little would remain of his naval career?

The muscles in Kyle's jaw began to burn under the pressure he was exerting on his teeth. *Shit.*

They arrived ten miles out from the *Vinson*, and Kyle switched radio frequencies to contact air traffic control on the carrier. "Tower, Lone Wolf six-five, entering starboard delta."

"Negative," the tower crackled back. "Cleared to land directly on spot three."

Jobs turned to gawk at him. As inexperienced as he was, even Jobs knew that a helicopter—which sat just below belly button lint in importance to a carrier, especially during jet flight operations—was almost never cleared directly to land. Rather it was sent to fly in an endless, boring circular pattern, known as starboard D, off the right side of the ship until the Air Boss—the officer in charge of all air traffic around the carrier—deigned to allow the bird to land.

Not Lieutenant Kyle "Mikey" Hammond. *No, siree.* Apparently whatever wrench Admiral Kelleman had up his ass that needed to be pulled out and thumped on Kyle's head was awful enough to earn the Wolfpack helicopter immediate clearance.

What did you do? silently rang off Jobs.

Kyle's face heated. "Roger that," he gritted to the

tower. "Crossing the wake." He banked the helo across the ship's wash. "Cleared to land, spot three." He clicked back to inner cockpit comms. "Take it from here," he told Jobs. "You've got the controls."

The young pilot needed experience operating around a carrier. Kyle wasn't turning over the controls because his fingers were experiencing a weird pins and needles thing. *Nuh-uh.*

"I've got the controls," Jobs confirmed.

Kyle lifted his palms in the air to verify he was "hands off."

Jobs pushed the helo's nose forward, gaining speed to catch up to the carrier, then leveled off as he drew adjacent to spot three. He flew form on their landing zone, fifty feet from the deck, waiting for the LSE to direct them on board.

"I've got the LSE in sight," Kyle said. "He's signaling slide right."

Jobs edged the helicopter over, hovered above spot three, then set down like he was placing a baby chick on a bed of feathers. Jobs was an impressive stick—Kyle would give the kid that.

With the blades still turning, Kyle yanked the helo door open, unstrapped, and leapt to the tarmac.

Kyle's maintenance officer, Lieutenant Pete "Bingo" Robbins, jumped out of the back of the helo and took Kyle's place in the right seat.

Pete had earned his call sign "Bingo"—which was aviator speak for the lowest fuel required to return to base—by flying below fuel minimums on two missions in his career to date. *Operational necessity* had warranted the break in safety protocol on both occasions, but Kyle was still going to keep an eye on Robbins.

Kyle saluted his bird, and the helo lifted off.

Jobs and Bingo would now fly over to starboard D and hang out there until Kyle was done. Kyle didn't know how long his meeting with Admiral Kelleman would last, but to shut down a helicopter on the busy flight deck of an aircraft carrier would only get the helo's rotor blades folded back and the bird shoved away into a dusty, out-of-the-way corner.

And Kyle had no doubt that he'd want to get off the *Vinson* fast after his meeting with Kelleman.

Something about needing to lick his wounds after having his nuts filleted and barbecued.

Across the runway a dozen or so jets were parked around the "island"—the part of a carrier that stuck up from the starboard side of the flight deck—with crew climbing all over the aircraft, fueling and pre-flighting. An F/A-18 Super Hornet sat in ready five, preparing to launch, heat waves emanating from its jet engines.

Kyle received clearance to cross the flight deck, and he hoofed it over to the island, ducking through the personnel hatch.

His Wolfpack CO was waiting for him. "What the hell did you do, Mikey?"

A sting of blood hit Kyle's cheeks. "Skipper." He saluted his commanding officer in greeting, then tugged off his flight helmet. "I have no idea, sir. I was hoping you could tell me."

His CO mulled that over for a moment, his lips twisted, then just chopped a hand down the passageway.

"Let's go."

Let's go—as in, you and me, together. Kyle had the weird urge to hug his boss. Whatever deep kimchi Kyle was in, his skipper wasn't going to make him face it alone.

Kyle followed his CO down the passageway, periodically angling his shoulders sideways to let other sailors pass, all of them moving with speed and purpose. The passageways of the *Vinson* were like a New York City street.

Home to over six thousand men, the average United States Aircraft Carrier was the size of a city, and it had many perks the smaller ships didn't. There was a large geedunk, a barber—not just some solider who cut hair as collateral duty—a well-stocked medical clinic, a dentist, and more. The extra square footage and larger population probably should've given Kyle a sense of more space, but it always had the opposite effect. Carriers made him feel claustrophobic.

He and his skipper reached the admiral's stateroom, knocked, and were ordered to enter. Kyle's boots sank into plush carpet as he navigated through a sitting area populated by a leather couch and two deep-cushioned chairs. Aiming for a large mahogany desk where the admiral was seated, he—

"I need one-on-one time with the lieutenant." Admiral Kelleman said to the Wolfpack CO. "You're dismissed, Commander."

Aw, hell. 'Bye, Dad…

As the door shut, Kyle came to back-breaking attention in front of the admiral's desk, latching his focus onto the collection of *see how great I am* plaques on the wall, instead of on the man himself.

Kelleman was one hundred percent cold metal: iron jaw, steely eyes, gunmetal hair, hard body.

Fuckfuckfuck... Sweat ran down Kyle's butt crack, of all places, and his armpits were having a pool party.

"Stand at ease, lieutenant."

Kyle assumed a wider stance and tucked his hands into the small of his back.

Kelleman sat back in his chair, although the pose was anything but relaxed. "I assume you're aware of the current hostage situation?"

Kyle blinked once. That'd come out of the ass-end of space. "Yes, sir."

Two days ago, the extremist militant group, Jaish-e-Mohammed, or JEM, kidnapped four American engineers, three men and one woman, who'd been making repairs in northern Pakistan on the Mangla Dam. JEM was demanding that four of their guys—known terrorists—who were imprisoned by the US be released in exchange for the hostages.

"This is the Bergdahl situation all over again." Kelleman said, referring to the newsworthy Bowe Bergdahl, an American soldier who'd been held captive in Afghanistan, and then swapped for five senior Taliban prisoners in Guantanamo Bay.

"Yes, sir," Kyle said.

Kelleman's upper lip curled into a sneer. "Give in to one militant group, and the next assumes it's a free-for-all. *This* is why we never negotiate with terrorists."

And to add to the stink, many believed that the American adage *Leave No Man Behind* shouldn't have applied to Bergdahl. He'd been charged with desertion of his post in eastern Afghanistan and accused of being a traitor.

"But the White House botched it and *did* submit to the Taliban's demands." Kelleman's voice was frost on ice. "So now the current administration will be damned if they'll give in to JEM. A rescue operation is in the works, classified top priority—OPERATION PRIDE, if the name tells you anything. A SEAL unit is prepared to deploy on my command."

"Yes, sir." Kyle was starting to sound like a parrot. But he couldn't think of anything else to do except keep *yes, sir'ing* until he knew the full story.

Was he in trouble for something or not?

"To save the hostages, we first have to *find* them. That's where a journalist from the *LA Times* by the name of"—Kelleman glanced at a paper on his desk—"Max Dougin comes in. JEM wants media coverage in order to spout their rhetoric, so Dougin is being pulled in to help. He's a foreign correspondent, an expert on Pakistan, and fully up to speed on the covert nature of this op. While the US government strings JEM along with empty negotiations, Dougin will conduct a false interview with JEM, the actual objective being to discover the hostages' whereabouts."

"Yes, sir."

"I'm assigning you to protect Max Dougin, Lieutenant."

Some of the starch left Kyle's spine as he sagged into his waistline in shock. *That's* what this was about? An assignment so far out of his usual mission parameters it wasn't even in the same hemisphere? He was an expert in *maritime* warfare, which usually required, you know, *water* to perform, not a whole lot of desert.

"I need someone I know and trust to be my eyes and ears on this operation," Kelleman stated. "That's you, Hammond."

Kyle immediately snapped straight again. "Sir, yes, sir." Had the prestigious Robert Kelleman just said he *trusted* Kyle?

"It's imperative that this rescue goes off without a hitch." Kelleman glanced down at the paper again.

Kyle didn't get the sense he was reading it.

A clock set in the middle of what looked like a ship's wooden wheel sat on Kelleman's desk and *tick-tocked*.

Kelleman looked up again, his voice lower than before. "My nephew is one of the hostages."

Kyle's belly jerked. *Oh, crap.* "Sir—" He hesitated. "I'm sorry, sir."

Kelleman didn't react. "You met him once when you were with Sienna, during a barbecue at the house. Todd."

Heat pressed outward from Kyle's checks. He was blushing, *laugh-your-head-off-at-me blushing*, over the mere suggestion that the admiral remembered Kyle once being at the Kelleman house. "Yes, sir." Unfortunately, Kyle didn't recall Sienna's cousin Todd.

Kelleman's steady stare never wavered. "Once Dougin has located the hostages, I want you to report to me— *directly* to me. I need to make sure this rescue op gets underway fast. There's no time to lose. Clear?"

Kyle felt the significance of the mission bear down on his shoulders. Here was a chance for him to prove himself to a man who'd never given Kyle any indication of liking him, who'd never uttered anything even close to, *Hey, call me Bob*, a man who, for all Kyle knew, assumed Kyle had knocked up Sienna, then done the douche-bucket thing and bailed on her. Because the idea of Sienna shining a complimentary light on Kyle by telling her father that she'd kept Kyle in the dark about the baby was laughable.

No felt like an impossible answer to give, even though taking on this mission would also provide him with plenty of opportunities to fuck up and cost Todd his life. And that would drop a heavy weight on Kyle's shoulders too. "Clear, sir."

"Very good." Kelleman shoved aside the papers on his desk. "First thing when you get back to your ship, write your letter."

Here was another topic coming at him from the back forty. "My letter?"

"A *final* letter," Kelleman clarified without emotion, "to your loved ones."

Kyle's pulse changed rhythm.

When military personnel went on a life-threatening mission, they were supposed to leave behind a letter to be read *in case of*.

And going on an assignment that dealt with a volatile, dangerous, and unpredictable terrorist group obviously qualified, but...who would Kyle even leave a letter for? His father? Ha! Sienna? Just as much of a joke. His mother? He wouldn't want to burden her with it. His younger brother, Andy? Maybe. Eric? Like he wanted a fellow aviator to be reminded of his own mortality.

Kyle fisted his hands at the small of his back. *This has*

been such an awesome stroll into the emptiness of my life, Admiral, thank you. "With all due respect, sir," Kyle said. "If this mission is as life-threatening as you suggest, then should a journalist be a part of it? Why don't I just fake the role myself?"

Kelleman shook his head. "Dougin has interviewed other terrorists in the past, and JEM has asked for him by name. So we don't have a choice. Dougin is our sole contact with JEM, the only means we have of getting intel about the hostages." Kelleman's expression hardened. "You're to treat this as an allied operation between the Navy and the *LA Times*, Lieutenant. We can't do this mission without Dougin. Understood?"

"Sir, yes, sir."

"JEM has forbidden any US military involvement," Kelleman warned, "so you'll be playing the role of a news cameraman. Max Dougin is expected in Jebel Ali in no more than a week, so you don't have much time to go lax on the grooming standard and change your appearance. Start growing your hair out today, Hammond, and get a beard on your face, quick."

CHAPTER FOUR

Present time.
Port of Jebel Ali. *USS Bunker Hill* (CG-52) Ticonderoga class
cruiser part of Carrier Strike Group One

*N*O *REGRETS.* SAMANTHA repeated the phrase to herself
the next morning, soon after she was escorted into a
room that looked like a cross between a conference room
and a dining area on the *USS Bunker Hill*—a Navy
cruiser currently anchored in the port of Jebel Ali.
Straight ahead of her was a rectangular table large enough
to seat twenty people, surrounded by just as many cloth-
covered chairs. On the wall to her right was a flat screen
TV, keeping company with an assortment of nautical-
themed pictures and banners, and to her left was a
sideboard with a tall silver urn, coffee cups, and a basket
of pastries.

The ship's commanding officer, dressed in blue-and-
gray camouflage, stood near the head of the table.

Another man stood next to him.

For the briefest second, Samantha didn't recognize
the second guy. He was wearing a flight suit—and she'd
been so convinced he wasn't military—and the narrow
look he was aiming at her was so unlike the warm,
charming way he'd treated her in the Jebel Ali Club.

But, yep.

Hair the color of wheat or sand, eyes the blue of a Caribbean Sea…

He was last night's *oops*, no doubt about it, beard and all.

She groaned internally. The *one* time she'd indulged in a casual hookup—*one, one, one!*—and she'd landed herself in the exact situation she wanted to avoid: running into the penis-mole-bearer the next morning. Although in a literal sense, she had no idea if this guy's unit had a mole on it, or a tattoo, or a palm tree growing out of it, seeing as she'd forgone any close inspections of his organ.

Main thing—extreme bad luck was not how she wanted to start out a dangerous assignment.

Worse and worse, there was only one reason Lieutenant Carbuncle would be in this room with the ship's captain; he was her pretend-cameraman partner. *Glory Hallelujah!* She was stuck with him for the duration of this assignment. Another groan rose in her throat. She would've let it loose, along with a fair amount of eye-rolling, if she'd been okay with letting down appearances. But she wasn't. She was *woman who has it all together even when living her own personal Gong Show.*

The young lieutenant who'd escorted her into the "wardroom" announced her. "Max Dougin."

She strode toward the ship's captain, crossing an insignia of the *USS Bunker Hill* woven into the carpet, and shook hands with him. "Nice to meet you, sir."

He gawked at her, providing her with ample opportunity to shake Roger Ramjet's hand, too, but…she kinda wasn't ready to face him. "Do you mind if I have some coffee?" She proceeded to the silver urn.

"I was under the impression you were a man," the CO said to her back.

An unnecessary clarification: his gawking had made that obvious.

She offered up a reassuring smile while she cranked out a stream of coffee into her cup. "It happens on occasion." Her bio was deliberately written to leave her sex nebulous. People would have to dig further to find out she was a woman. Sometimes people didn't.

The CO frowned. Clearly he wasn't happy about his peons failing to brief him thoroughly enough. He recovered quickly, though. "I'll call ahead to the aid station where you're going and make sure they change you out of the men's quarters to a private tent."

From the side of her vision, she saw Flash Gordon's eyebrows slant. *What a shame we won't be sharing.* Or? *Hoorah, a private tent! That could work out good for me too.*

"That would be nice. Thank you, sir." She took a large swig of her coffee, then topped off her cup. A morning person, she was not, and the sun had just been rising over the bow of the *Bunker Hill* when she crossed the gangplank.

The CO gestured at *Oops.* "Lieutenant Hammond is the officer in charge of the flight crew assigned to work with you."

She finally turned toward Hot Shot. *A pleasure to meet you, Lieutenant.* Hmm, that didn't exactly fit, did it? "Great," she said, not entirely erasing the flippancy in her tone.

The lieutenant's eyes snapped a brilliant, glittery blue.

"When do we take off?" she asked him.

"As soon as we're done pre-flighting. We can head out to the hangar now, if you're ready."

"I dropped off some luggage and equipment with the officer at the gangplank when I boarded. I'll need to swing by and get it."

The lieutenant shook his head. "He would've already loaded it onto the aircraft."

"Okay." She gulped her coffee, then set down the mug and grabbed a Danish. "Let's do it." She started for the door with a teensy hesitation in her step—did she really just say *do it*? She followed the lieutenant into the corridor.

Ten feet down the hallway, his arm shot out in front of her, his palm slapping against the bulkhead to block her path.

She stopped, her spine pressing back against the wall. Steam hissed through a pipe beside her ear.

Ramjet was very close, his wide body hemming her in.

Well, here was a surprise. Outside of the forgiving dimness of the Jebel Ali Club, he was actually very attractive. Nothing that would land him on the big screen, but still compelling. His eyes were more startlingly handsome than she'd realized, so pale a blue as to be almost silver. His nose was a sharply inclined slope, his mouth, exquisite, and his beard shadowed a jaw that was square and could be quite stubborn, she'd bet, but right now was angled at her in a way that projected an aura of animal maleness.

A trickle of heat skipped along the skin of her belly. This was what was compelling about this man. More than his looks, it was his raw magnetism.

"Max?" he inquired, almost making her name sound like an accusation. "Is that short for Maxine?"

"No. My real name is Samantha." She dropped her focus to the colorful patch on the left side of his chest where his own name was displayed: LT. Kyle "Mikey" Hammond. Her throat pinched off with an emotion that felt like guilt. Shame on her for not bothering to know this man's name prior to letting him...sow her fields.

"I was a young reporter," she said, "first day on the job, and I paraded into the newsroom and said to everyone, 'Hello, my name is Samantha. Not *Sam*—that's a man's name—but *Samantha*.' To pay me back for being too big for my britches, everyone started calling me the most masculine three-letter name they could think of: Max." She shrugged. "It stuck."

He laughed. It was a deep, rich sound, and crinkled the corners of his eyes. "I like that. Although I can't imagine you ever being 'big for your britches.'" His gaze roved down her body. "You're too dainty."

She edged her brows together. No, she wasn't. She was 5'5", which was hardly short. She had a swimmer's body, though, with slender muscles, and she supposed that lent itself to the illusion of her being smallish.

"You know," Hot Shot went on, "when you first came into the wardroom, I wasn't too thrilled by the idea of having a female along."

"Keep the woman in the kitchen kind of guy, are you?"

The sides of his eyes creased again. "Sure. Go with that. But now...let's just say this cruise won't be the usual bore." His mouth curled into a smirk.

The arrogant son of a gun looked like he thought she should be honored by his offer to be his deployment sex toy.

She took a slow bite of her Danish. Best to chew when using her mouth to speak wouldn't produce anything nice.

SHE WAS FINISHING up the last of her Danish when Kyle Hammond led her into the ship's hangar, a place that looked like a garage nourished on growth hormones. It was stocked to the high rafters with all the necessary accoutrements for the care and feeding of Navy helicopters: tools, hoists, chains, tire chocks, oil cans, etcetera, tossed together with a potpourri of nose-wrinkling odors, like grease and fuel, and others she didn't recognize. One helicopter was inside the hangar, across from the door, its long rotor blades tucked back like a sleeping pterodactyl. Another helo was visible outside through the open hangar door, crouched in a white-painted circle on the flight deck and secured in place by chains.

She stared at the closest helo, suddenly feeling *dainty*, after all. She'd ridden in news helicopters several times, but these Navy birds were gigantic in comparison, gray beasts of prey emanating power, menace, and the potential for massive destruction.

She cut a glance at Hot Shot from beneath her lashes. She knew what he smelled like now. A man who could control one of these things.

Two other men wearing flight suits were lounging in the hangar, but livened up when she and Kyle entered.

Kyle introduced the men. "This is my copilot, Jobs,"

he said, indicating a young man who'd just arrived off a Nickelodeon television show, jug-eared, stars shining in his eyes, and with an embarrassment of freckles. "And my AW, Tarzan."

"What does AW stand for?"

"Aviation Warfare Specialist," Kyle translated. "Tarzan monitors the anti-submarine warfare computers and radar in back, and he mans the M50 machine gun. He's also a certified search and rescue swimmer. Pretty much a jack of all trades."

"Wow." She smiled at Tarzan.

He was a stocky, compact fellow with dark hair nearly down to his shoulders, a beard, like Kyle—although Tarzan's was thicker—and a tattoo on his body, at least to judge by the snaking ends of some creature curling up the left side of his neck.

She held out her hand. "Hi, I'm Max."

He grinned at her and shook her hand.

She was used to her name earning lots of smiles. But this time she wasn't alone in the strange name department. "Why are you called Tarzan? Are you a yodeler?"

He chortled. "No, ma'am. The call sign has to do with the type of skivvies I wear. Which I'd be happy to show you"—he winked—"if the lieutenant here gives his permission."

"Denied," Kyle drawled.

She rounded on Kyle. "What about you? Why are you called Mikey?"

"Story time's over." Kyle turned away.

Tarzan chortled again. Apparently he knew.

She'd find out, too. Unearthing secrets was one of her

reporter superpowers.

Kyle grabbed a small plastic book bound with metal rings. "Let's get this show on the road." He moved to stand in a circle with his men.

They began their pre-flight routine, talking in a language all their own, acronyms being bandied about like IFF, ADIZ, IMC versus VMC emergencies. Procedures upon procedures were discussed, maneuvers, tactics, ordnance... It was head-spinning. She'd never heard pilots of news helicopters talk like this.

She kept her gaze on Kyle. His face was in profile to her most of the time, giving her an even better look at the nasty scar on his jaw. Had he been sewn up on the battlefield, maybe by a corpsman with a hand shaky from combat fatigue?

What a fascinating enigma this Kyle Hammond was. In the interval of a heartbeat, the silky flirt had disappeared and in his place was a professional speaking on a level of expertise she never would've believed the smooth operator could manage. A point lost for her. She was usually spot-on when it came to reading people: another reporter superpower.

"Now the passenger brief," Kyle said to her. "This is for you, so listen up."

She nodded.

"If there's an emergency, you'll hear it over the ICS."

"What's the ICS?"

"Our Internal Communication System. You'll be wearing a modified helmet called a 'cranial' with headphones and mic."

She nodded again.

"If you hear the words *mayday, mayday, mayday*, stay off comms." Kyle crossed his arms over his chest. "If we have an emergency requiring a water landing, you'll hear *ditch, ditch, ditch*. Immediately prior to the helicopter going in, pull the black-and-yellow handle on the passenger observation window to jettison it, then hold onto your seat. We'll land as carefully as possible, but even so, the aircraft will flip over quickly. Do *not* try to exit until the cockpit is completely filled with water. Otherwise you'll get shoved to the back, and it's where you'll undoubtedly stay."

She hid a grimace. That sounded pretty unpleasant.

"Once we all make it to the surface, we'll check each other for injuries, link ourselves together, and I'll coordinate a rescue operation on the handheld PRC radio. Understand?"

"Yes."

"In the event of an emergency ground landing, don't exit the aircraft until all violent motion has stopped or we tell you to do so. Once clear of the aircraft, meet at the twelve o'clock position—or where the nose of the helicopter used to be—and we'll plan our next move. Do you have any questions?"

"Nope," she said. "I'm ready."

He paused, studying her.

Well, why shouldn't she be ready? He looked and sounded like he knew what he was doing.

One corner of his mouth twitched. "All right." He instructed her to stay in the hangar until his AW escorted her to the helicopter, then he turned to Jobs and Tarzan. "Let's pre-flight the aircraft. I'll take the tail and rotor head."

The three men trotted onto the flight deck.

She watched them climb all over the aircraft for the next fifteen minutes. She had nothing better to do other than study Mister Enigma himself, so she put her feelers out and took in data about who Kyle Hammond really was: the man he acted around his men or the man he was with her? Maybe he—

She nearly jumped clear of her boots when a high-pitched whistle blasted from the ship, immediately followed by a voice booming from a loudspeaker. "Flight quarters, flight quarters, all hands man your flight quarter stations!"

As the loudspeaker continued to announce things she didn't entirely understand—*smoking lamp is out topside?*—she saw several men dressed in floatation coats jog onto the flight deck. A couple of them unchained the helicopter, while another guy hooked a cord up to the side of the aircraft. Jet engines *whirrrrred* to life. The rotor blades began to turn, faster and faster, until they were steadily hard-thumping the air.

The noise grew deafening, and she pressed her hands over her ears.

Tarzan appeared at her side and dropped the 'cranial' helmet on her head. Taking her by the arm, he led her across the tarmac.

Her pants slapped her legs and her shirt billowed behind her.

The AW helped her into an aircraft seat and strapped her into a five-point restraint, then he plugged an electrical cord into the back of her helmet.

"Tower," she heard Kyle's voice in her ears, "request green deck for takeoff."

"Roger," an unfamiliar voice crackled back. "Winds are three-five-zero at fifteen knots, pitch two, roll four, RAST open. You have a green deck, cleared for takeoff."

The big beast lifted slowly. The body of the creature shuddered. Cords dangling from the roof swayed. And then the ship dropped far, far away...

CHAPTER FIVE

*T*URBULENCE. KYLE CURSED silently. Dammit, passengers hated jerky rides.

Granted, catching bumpy air currents in an H-60 Romeo-class Seahawk helicopter was better than riding out rocky air in an MH-6 Little Bird or a TH-57 training helicopter, but it a helluva lot worse than surfing rough swells on a commercial airliner.

An Airbus would be a little bit of rock 'n' roll.

A helo was slam dancing in a mosh pit.

"I'm going to descend," Kyle told Jobs. "Try to find smoother air."

Luckily, they were on the last leg of their journey. It'd been a long one, requiring two stops for fuel, one at a supply ship in charge of UNREPs, and the second at a Pakistani air force base. Their mission was taking them to Azad Kashmir, deep into the northeast part of Pakistan near the border of Kashmir, India. JEM's main base was rumored to be in India's southern Kashmir and Doda regions, and so it'd been arranged for the American journalist, Max Dougin, to make contact with JEM from Azad Kashmir.

Max. Kyle nearly snorted. It felt like he'd been hit in the middle of the forehead with a ball-peen hammer when Max Dougin strode into the *Bunker Hill's* wardroom as a female. No, he hadn't been happy to discover her sex. Bad enough he was being made to babysit a journalist on a dangerous mission without that person being a woman. Call him old-fashioned, but he tended to worry more about women than he did about men, especially a woman with no combat training.

But what could he do? As Admiral Kelleman had pointed out, they couldn't find the hostages without Dougin. She was the person JEM would allow into their inner sanctum.

So Kyle had bright-sided it.

They'd had fun last night, right? She'd come. He'd come. Why not go for more, liven up this deployment?

The suggestion had earned him a whole lotta blank-face from her.

Not that he'd expected her to immediately pull her old Girl Scout uniform out of mothballs and play *want to sample my cookies?* with him. What he *had* expected was for her to flirt back. She'd been forward enough last night, making him instantly rejoice in his decision to take a taxi from the proper Captain's Bar to the livelier Jebel Ali Club.

But she hadn't flirted at all. Not even a wink. Just a lot of unperturbed blank.

To start only a slight flicker of a single eyebrow had acknowledged that she even recognized him for who he was. And he'd *never* encountered a woman who didn't react in some way to a run-in with him after a one-night stand—a quiet gasp, a little blush, an excited thrill leaping to her eyes at the prospect of a do-over.

Had last night been so meaningless to Max Dougin

that she'd already set it aside? If so, he was impressed. He didn't think so, though. She wasn't a pro at the ol' fuck-'n'-shuffle. He knew woman, and the moment he stepped into the Jebel Ali Club, he got a bead on her. She was a woman on the prowl for a little out-of-the-ordinary adventure.

He'd been happy to accommodate.

He was happy to continue to accommodate, as he'd made clear. Although, frankly, if it wasn't for all the months of deployment-induced sexual deprivation stretching out ahead of him, he would've passed on a second helping of Max Dougin. She wasn't his type. He was a tit-man. Full-bodied women with long hair were his preference, and Max was angular, with a pointed chin and sharp cheekbones. Not only that but the bones in her shoulders, at the base of her throat, and at her hips thrust out in rigid relief against the sleekness of her muscles. Okay, he'd give her that—she was pleasantly lithe. He'd been telling the truth last night when he complimented her thigh muscles.

And her eyes.

They were downright incredible. Her irises were dark indigo at the outer rim while a lighter shade of blue surrounded her pupils. The combination gave the impression of her eyes being lit up. Which was really cool, and…back to the subject of tits… He had to give hers mad props. While on the small side, they were soft and supple.

"Sir," Jobs' voice came through his earpiece. "We're thirty miles from our destination."

They were flying to an aid station located just outside

the tiny town of Saaneh, approximately twenty miles east of the Mangla Dam and very near to the Indian border. The aid station had been set up by an NGO, or nongovernmental organization, called International Humanitarian Medical Relief.

IHMR specialized in offering medical care in times of crisis. They'd been one of the first on the scene in Haiti after the 2010 earthquake, and they spent a lot of time all over Africa. IHMR recently landed here near Saaneh because hostilities had flared up between Pakistan and India, two long-time enemies.

IHMR had deemed that Pakistan was on the losing end of most of the skirmishes, so they established their aid station on the Pakistani side.

"Roger that," Kyle said to his copilot and banked left, flying between the two ranges of jagged rock where the aid station was located. He aimed for a dirt area near the motor pool—which consisted of one mini-sized bus—located at the northern tip of the camp. A landing zone had been cleared there large enough to accommodate three helicopters.

From the sky, Kyle could see that a perimeter fence of huge rolls of bailing wire surrounded the entire camp, landing pad included—the kind of fence which stopped human incursion, but not bullets. To the south of the landing pad was the motor pool—one jeep and one bus—and next to that, a rectangular-shaped structure about one hundred fifty feet long—or half the length of a football field—constructed of wood and desert-colored canvas. The roof was painted with a large red cross. So it must be the main medical tent.

Kyle came in on final approach, his helo blowing up twin tubular waves of sand from either side of the aircraft as he set down the wheels on the landing zone. Normally the Pakistani government wouldn't have allowed a US military aircraft to land in their country, but due to the current hostage crisis, they'd granted special permission for a team of journalists to be dropped off.

Kyle checked his sight lines, scanning for threats. Strange thing about the terrain in this part of Pakistan, it wasn't strictly desert. A patchy mix of green grass and arid sand, trees peppered throughout, made up the landscape—like the countryside couldn't decide what it wanted to be.

Kyle didn't spot any troublemakers, so he shut off the engines. The rotors slowed, then stilled.

He swung out of the cockpit.

Max hopped out too, and he sent her off to settle into her private quarters while he and his men erected a tent of desert camouflage netting over the helo. After that, he left Tarzan to do the Daily and Turn inspection on the aircraft, and he and Jobs headed for the main medical tent.

A road from outside the aid station led inside through the only gate and continued to the front of the main medical tent, where it curved around like a U-shaped drop-off driveway. A dirt circle about ten yards in diameter sat to the right, or south, of this U. A flag pole thrust up from the center of the circle, flying the IHMR logo: a medical symbol—which was two snakes winding around a winged staff—with two human hands clasped in a handshake, one light, one dark, just above it.

A Pakistani sentry was posted between the flag circle and the road. He managed to look bored while still maintaining a rigid posture. The noises of a working camp filled the air: the occasional voice raised to a shout, hammering off somewhere, the steady flapping of the IHMR flag in the breeze, the *tacka-tacka-tacka* of something mechanical running—sounded like a second-rate generator.

At medical, Kyle checked in with Dr. Farrin Barr, the IHMR physician in charge. Dr. Barr was in her early thirties, of medium height, and came from Middle Eastern or Arab ancestry if her black hair, off-white skin, and almond-shaped dark brown eyes were taken into account. Attractive, if exotic was a man's type. It wasn't necessarily his.

The resident corpsman, however, was.

HM3 Katherine "Kitty" Hart was every man's fantasy girl-next-door darlin'. She spoke with a sweet Southern accent, had big blue eyes, a heart-shaped face, and chestnut-colored hair, which was wrapped into a tight bun at her nape—a decent-sized bun, so she probably had *long* hair. She was on the short side but packing a nice set of curves.

Maybe he'd take a run at her if Max didn't pan out.

This thought woke up the Universe. The Big U butted in with a lot of finger-wagging and bullshit about how screwing one woman while on a mission with another, who he'd also screwed, was the quickest way to crash and burn the op. Oh, and—*tap, tap on the shoulder*—fraternization between officers and enlisted was illegal.

For once, he must've listened, because the idea of bagging the corpsman didn't entirely appeal.

"Meals are served at oh-seven-hundred, twelve-hundred, and eighteen-hundred," Dr. Barr was telling him and Jobs as she led them into the post-op ward. "Water is rationed here, so take military showers."

The sharp scent of antiseptic pierced Kyle's senses, and he stayed by the door with a whole lot of *get me the hell outta here* going through his brain. Too many of his worst memories involved hospitals.

Dr. Barr gestured at the line of twenty immaculately made beds stretched down either side of the tent, so forty in all. "We haven't been too busy, lately. Thank goodness."

IVs dripped down to three men in post-op beds.

"There's only been light skirmishing. Still, the border is volatile. Anything outside the wire should be treated as a hot zone." She picked up a clipboard and glanced at it. "If we get incoming, you'll be expected to help with the wounded. We're a small outfit. Any questions?"

"Anyone else American military besides the corpsman?" Kyle asked.

"Two Seamen orderlies have been lent to me off the *USNS Mercy*," the doctor answered. "Other IHMR employees are civilians, including a secretary, a supply administrator, an anesthesiologist, and two cooks. The two men who do the laundry are Pakistani locals, and the guards are all Pakistani military."

Kyle nodded.

"I've assigned you and Lieutenant Whitmore to tent eight. Your enlisted man can bunk with my two cooks in tent nine. There is a barracks building here, but it's only for the Pakistani guardsmen. I'm in tent seven, if you need me. Anything else?"

"No, ma'am."

Dr. Barr started to turn away, then, "Oh. The woman you arrived with, Max Dougin—she wanted me to pass on to you that she'd like to see you when you're done with me. She's in tent ten."

"Roger that," Kyle said.

He and Jobs strolled outside and were met by Tarzan. The three of them strode to the south edge of the flag circle, where a footpath led to the rest of camp. Ten to fifteen tents were stacked along this main path at precise intervals. The tents were of various sizes, but all built of the same wood and canvas semi-permanent material as the main medical building.

Boots stirring up dust, the three of them passed the supply tent and the latrine, at which point Kyle's senses got smacked with the caustic smell of urine cakes. They continued past the barracks, the showers, then the mess hall.

Kyle caught a distinct hamburger aroma.

He dismissed Jobs and Tarzan to grab evening chow and headed on toward a row of smaller tents—living spaces for personnel.

Tent number ten was about five by five. The door was wood, and Kyle knocked on it, entering at Max's call.

She was unpacking her equipment bag, just setting a laptop on her cot when he entered.

A second cot was on the opposite side of the tent, an olive-green sleeping bag slumped on it. A small stand of shelves set next to the tent wall stored the miscellaneous junk—books, brushes, framed photograph, toiletries bag—of the person whose living space this was.

Glancing over her shoulder, Max noticed him studying the other bed. "It turns out I'm sharing with Kitty."

Kyle moved further into the room. "Dr. Barr said you summoned." He grinned. "Changed your mind about partying with me already, have you?" He reached for his belt, as if he was going to undo it.

She flipped open her laptop and booted it up. "This is going to be a *very* long assignment if you keep doing that."

She didn't sound perturbed. Only amused with him. So glad he could be of service. He half-curled his lip into the vague consideration of a sneer, annoyance with her warring with respect.

"Actually—" She pulled a cell phone out of a small backpack. "I'm finishing up your fake bio online and need a picture of you to upload. You appear too military in the photos I found of you on your Instagram page. And, *ahem*, you were always with a different woman."

He cocked a brow. Did that bother her? Difficult to tell. Which added numbers to his annoyance percentage. Her ability to play it cool continued to be world-class. "What can I say?" He hitched a single shoulder. "I'm a sociable kind of guy."

She raised her phone to him. "Smile," she instructed.

He deepened the crooked lean of his mouth.

She clicked the camera on her phone. "You're Richard Sagget from CBS News."

"Whoever you want me to be, honey."

Not a twitch out of her.

"I'll call you *Dick* for short," she said.

Ah-ha! There was the perturbed he'd been looking for. "Oh, Max, better not. It would be like a mating call for me. Let's go with Rick."

She guffawed softly as she connected her cell phone to her laptop.

"Whoa, I made you laugh," he said, oddly triumphant. "That's the first I've heard you laugh since...hell, since you seduced me last night with, 'hey, baby, I'm going out in the field tomorrow to hunt terrorists, and I don't know if I'm going to make it back.'"

He paused, poised for a blustering correction about *him* being the one to seduce *her*, not the other way around. None came.

She just placed her laptop on her knees and started *clacking* away on the keyboard.

"What a line, Max," he went on, still trying to bait her...to see what her amazing eyes would do when she got riled. "Did you think—?" He stopped. *Hold up.* He frowned suddenly, a funny feeling building in his stomach. "Holy shit." It was a day for ball-peen hammers to the forehead, because another cracked him a good one. "You weren't kidding with that line, were you?"

Clackity-clack...clackity-clack...

"Max?" he snapped.

She stopped typing but kept her focus on the computer screen and didn't speak.

He set his hands on his hips. "Are you actually afraid of dying on this mission?"

Another infuriating pause. "Does it matter?"

"Hell, yeah."

She looked up at him, her eyes unnaturally dim.

Which was enough to make a man want to hurl himself on a grenade for her.

"Why?" she asked.

"Because…" *Because, dammit, I'll be with you, and I want you to believe I can keep you safe.* "Because I need to know if you have intel I'm unaware of."

"Nothing that would affect your part of this mission."

He scowled at her. "Maybe you could clue me in so I can form my own opinion."

She exhaled a sharp breath. "All right. Have you ever heard of Daniel Pearl?"

Ah, shit. "He was a journalist." *Now a dead one.* Kyle ground his teeth, crunching sand. Didn't take a genius to get where she was going.

"Yes, a journalist, like me. In 2002, he was captured by a terrorist group and decapitated." Max set her hands together in her lap, one palm cradling the back of her other hand. "Jaish-e-Mohammed killed him. The same terrorist group I'll be dealing with on this assignment."

He glowered at her, words piling up on the back of his tongue again. *I'm not going to let anything happen to you!* Words he had no right to speak.

You're so undependable, Kyle. Just like your father.

"Look, I'm no novice at this." But despite the assurances, she looked tense. "I've interviewed Pakistanis from army generals and top officials in Intelligence to some of the deadliest leaders of the Taliban and other terrorist groups. Honestly, if this time I was genuinely here to interview JEM, I wouldn't be so worried. But I'm not."

She ran a finger along the top edge of her computer screen. "My job is to find out where JEM is holding four American hostages so that I can help rescue them. If they discover the double-cross, then my head will, quite literally, roll. Yours, too, in all likelihood. Both our lives depend on how well I negotiate with JEM." She smiled dimly. "No pressure, right?" She dropped her hand to her lap again.

Kyle stood there, fuming, a storm of blinding white whipping up inside him. *Unbelievable.* She was worried about taking care of *him*? He bent at the waist and peered under her cot.

Max's brows drew together. "What are you doing?"

"Searching for my balls. I'm pretty sure they rolled off somewhere under there when you chopped them off just now." Exactly what he needed in his life: another woman doubting him.

"No offense to your male ego." She raised a palm. "But it's not like you can go into this situation loaded for bear. You're a cameraman, Kyle. You're in as much danger as I am."

"Yeah, I'm clear on that." *First thing when you get back to your ship, write a final letter to your loved ones…* "But I'm in the military. It's my job to put my life on the line for others."

"In this case, it's my job, too. JEM asked for me by name."

She sounded so damned reasonable, he itched to reach out and squeeze her cheeks until her tongue lolled out, make her stop saying annoying shit. "Fine," he bit out. "Whatever." Lips tight, he stepped to the edge of her cot and glared down at her. "Just get on the satellite phone and arrange the damned meeting with JEM." *I've got your six* should've left his mouth. But it didn't.

You were going to leave Brodie's hospital room, weren't you?

Growling, Kyle spun on his heel and hauled ass out of her tent.

CHAPTER SIX

A T OH-EIGHT-HUNDRED THE next morning, Max put on the type of clothes she usually wore while on assignment in Pakistan: dark jeans, suede boots, and a long-sleeved shirt, this one light blue, that buttoned all of her flesh away under cover. She wrapped a dark blue hijab around her head, leaving only her face and hands exposed.

She supposed Kyle was right—she could be pretty no-nonsense when she wanted to be. Besides a quick brush of her hair and teeth, dressing was all it took for her to get ready for the day. Kyle was wrong, however, in his assumption that she didn't spend hours in front of a mirror because she was too busy, or smart. It was because time in front of a mirror would eat into her precious *sleep*.

She headed down the camp's central path, her camera bag slung over her shoulder. Despite a few jumping frogs in her belly, she was ready to walk the tightrope with JEM. *One foot in front of the other, and keep your emotions out of it, Max: just cold, unbiased reporting.* She knew how to do that.

Ducking into the mess tent, she stuffed two sausages into a pancake, and proceeded to eat it like a burrito on her way to meet Kyle. Who needed a sit-down breakfast when that would also take away from sleep?

When she arrived at the motor pool, Kyle and baby-faced Jobs were already there, both men frowning at a stubby and unwieldy bus—a makeshift ambulance.

"I guess an armored Humvee," Kyle murmured, "would've been too much to ask for." He had a large black rifle propped on his shoulder, and he was dressed in his desert-colored gear again: khaki cargo pants and a brown shirt.

Jobs was equally bland.

Kyle turned to her, hesitating over the sight of her wearing a hijab—at least to judge by how he was staring at it.

Well, her hair hadn't been covered at the Jebel Ali Club.

"We're ready for you to brief us," Kyle said.

Us? She slashed a look at Jobs. "What? He's going?"

"Affirmative. The more muscle on this operation, the better. You told your JEM contact you'd be bringing your *crew*, right?" Kyle gestured at Baby Face. "Jobs will be our driver."

Superb. More lives to be responsible for. She jerked her chin at the rifle. "What's with the weapon?"

"I *am* going into this thing loaded for bear."

She cut a look at him as she set her camera bag on the hood of the small bus. "You're not supposed to be military," she reminded him.

"Tha's right, sugah," he returned in a Southern accent. "I'm just a little ol' cameraman, packin' some downhome heat, is all."

"JEM's not stupid." *Boy,* was it difficult not to roll her eyes. "Are you packing any more heat?"

One of his eyebrows inched upward.

If he grabbed his crotch and shook it at her, she was going back to the mess tent for more coffee.

"A knife in one boot," he answered, "and a Beretta nine-millimeter strapped to the other."

She looked at Jobs. "And you?"

His boyish smile shaved another ten years off his face. "Same. Well—" He gestured at Kyle's rifle. "Minus the AK."

She exhaled, long enough and loud enough to make her feelings patently clear. "Terrorists can be a little jumpy about such things."

Kyle shrugged. "We'll leave the weapons on the bus." He swung the rifle off his shoulder and placed it on the hood of the ambulance next to her camera bag. "This is non-negotiable for me, Max. You can stand there and waste time arguing or brief us on the mission."

Max was a big believer in picking her battles, and this one didn't seem like it was worth the effort. She would have to trust Kyle to be careful.

"Okay. Here's the skinny." She unzipped the camera bag and pulled out a map, spreading it open on the snub-nosed hood. "JEM has arranged a rendezvous point for us here." She stuck her finger on the dot marking the town of Charhoi.

Kyle stepped up next to her, put his own finger on the map's legend, then glanced at where she was pointing. "That's ten klicks from our current location. Normally about a ten-minute drive, but considering we'll be traveling along a winding dirt road by lumbering ambulance, we should plan on twice that."

"That'll still work."

"Do you think the hostages are at Charhoi?"

She pulled out a thermos from her bag and unscrewed the top. "I'll dance the Macarena for you in a bikini if they are."

A smile entered Kyle's eyes. "I'll take that to mean 'highly unlikely.'"

"You can take it to mean 'no way at all.'" Although she'd brought the GPS tracker with her on the extreme off chance that they were. She offered Kyle the thermos. "Want some coffee?"

He gave her a look of mock offense. "And share saliva with you?"

She caught back another eye-roll and drank a couple of gulps of warm coffee. "You and I will go through all the motions of giving JEM their sixty seconds of fame. When it comes to the hostage exchange, I'm going to insist on proof of life. So plan on a second meeting with JEM."

"Roger."

"During the proof of life inspection, I'll slip this small GPS tracking device to one of the hostages." She pulled the one-inch doohickey out of her camera bag and showed it to Kyle and Jobs. "It'll pick up where the hostages are taken. Our CIA contact who's manning all the high-dollar sensory equipment will let us know their location and provide us with satellite imagery of the strike zone."

"Then it's time to send in the cavalry?"

"You've got it."

Kyle glanced at Jobs. "Any questions?"

Jobs shook his head. "I'm good."

Kyle folded the map. "Mount up."

Max packed away her thermos and the GPS tracker while Jobs took the driver's seat. Kyle hopped into the passenger side and propped his rifle between his spread thighs.

She climbed in back.

The ambulance was equipped with four fold-down stretchers, two attached to each wall, stacked one on top of the other, all currently stowed. Medical supplies were kept in metal boxes secured to the backs of the two front seats. The interior of the ambulance smelled like the inside of the Smithsonian: well-scrubbed, but old.

Max unfolded the bottommost stretcher situated behind the front passenger seat, and sat, placing the camera bag at her feet.

The engine came to life with a dieselly grumble, and they took off, driving past the main medical tent and the pole flying the IHMR flag, then passing through the aid station's gate.

Trees, still green in April, hugged the border of the road. The foliage was dense for the first part of their journey, but after about five minutes, began to dwindle.

"Actually, I do have a question," Jobs said. "What if JEM refuses the proof of life request?"

Kyle turned around to look at Max, looping one arm over the back of the seat.

He really did have the most extraordinary biceps. "They won't," Max said. "Not if they want their buddies out of Guantanamo." She squinted at the road ahead. *What is—?*

"Shouldn't we still have a Plan B ready to go?" Kyle

asked.

Oh, no. "Are those what I think they are?" She pointed at the two small dust clouds approximately three miles in front of them on the road.

Kyle whipped back around.

Like ghostly tumbleweeds, the boils of dust were rolling toward them.

"Vehicles," Jobs confirmed.

Kyle also squinted. "Is it JEM's practice to meet a contact along the way?" he asked without looking at her, his ominous tone right out of Edgar Allan Poe.

"I don't know." This was her first time dealing with JEM. "But I wouldn't think so."

"Then are those a couple of fertilizer farmers with their morning shipment of petrified donkey patties?" Kyle pulled his pistol out of his pant leg.

She gripped the stretcher on either side of her thighs.

"I see two jeeps, and..." Kyle leaned forward. "Weapons," he hissed. "Turn around!" he ordered Jobs.

Jobs pitched the ambulance to a near stop and cranked the steering wheel hard to the left.

"Not an exact three-point turn, Steve! Jesus!" Kyle barked. "Do a fucking u-ie."

Jobs hit the gas again. The ambulance lurched into motion, continuing left.

Max's lungs emptied of air in an icy rush.

Jobs' delay had allowed the jeeps to get too close.

She saw a man in the lead vehicle stand up and point a rifle at them. "Watch out!" she yelled. *My God, who are these people*?!

Snarling a string of curses, Kyle stuck his pistol out

the passenger-side window.

The ambulance completed its left-hand turn, the jeeps wheeling by...

And through the kick-up of dust, Max saw lightning flash at the end of the enemy rifle snout. *Bam!*

And *bam!* back—Kyle had fired at the same time.

The standing man in the jeep folded in half, gut shot, while a bullet zinged past Kyle's chest and whacked into Jobs' arm.

Jobs shouted and drove off the side of the road into a wide, clumsy u-ie.

They jolted and jounced over the uneven earth. Max held on tight to her stretcher, but her butt still did a lot of bouncing. All the while, she kept her attention on the bullet hole in Jobs' arm. It didn't seem so...then a generous stream of blood dumped out of it. They hit what must've been a canyon-sized pothole—she was sent flying off her seat. She crashed into the opposite wall and splatted onto the metal floor. *Ow.*

Gasping, she clambered back into her seat.

The ride smoothed out somewhat as they returned to the road and headed back the way they'd come...putting the two enemy jeeps behind them.

"Floor it!" Kyle yelled at Jobs.

The ambulance picked up speed.

Max got up and staggered to the rear of the ambulance where there were two round windows. She peered out one.

The lead enemy jeep was still very close, so close she was able to see the driver's face. "Oh, my God," she breathed. She knew who—

The driver pointed a pistol at her.

She yelped and instantly dropped down, landing hard on her butt just as a hail of glass blew inward.

Kyle came charging back. "Stay down!"

She did as he ordered, scooting over on her rear to make room for him.

He stood to the side of the broken window, his back to the wall, rifle held vertically in front of him. A beat passed, then he rotated forward, planting his booted feet wide and sticking his rifle through the glass-less window. He fired two rounds in quick succession.

From her place on the floor, Max saw Kyle's thigh muscles flex rigidly against the fabric of his cargo pants as he braced himself against the recoil.

She heard tires skidding, a rattle of dirt and pebbles, then the repeated *bumpity-crunch* of what could only be a large metal object rolling over and over.

There went one jeep.

"Dammit!" Kyle turned around and hurried forward again. "Jobs, the second jeep is pulling alongside your three o'clock. Maintain speed while I—"

Kyle's shoulder slammed into the left wall of the ambulance while Max skidded sideways on her butt in the same direction.

Jobs had chosen that inconvenient moment to slump over the steering wheel in a faint. The unmanned ambulance was now careening hard right, going too fast into a too-tight turn. The right wheels lifted off the ground and the bus tilted into a perilous angle.

Max tumbled farther along.

The two right-hand stretchers slapped down, clapped

back up, then down again, drumming against—

The ambulance *ka-whomped* to the ground on its left side.

Max flew up, her knees hitting the right wall—now the ceiling—as the first aid boxes exploded open to release twin streamers of white gauze. An IV bag splattered apart like a water balloon dropped off the Empire State Building. Max fell back down, her hand automatically shooting out to brace her fall. Lightning streaked through her wrist.

She lay where she landed—on the underside of the folded-up cot nearest the roof—trying to catch her breath. She blinked through a haze of grainy dust and a white powder cloud that was probably talc. Over the thunder of her heartbeat, she heard the ambulance let out a long sibilant hiss. The stench of transmission fluid suggested that the dying radiator wasn't the only engine part wrecked in the accident.

Outside, tires spit sand as the remaining jeep ground to a halt. Two men spoke in Urdu. She couldn't understand what they were saying—she knew only the rudiments of the Pakistani language—but the low, intense tones made one thing perfectly clear.

The two men were coming for them.

CHAPTER SEVEN

THE MOMENT THE ambulance passed through its final death throes and came to a complete stop, Kyle lurched onto one knee.

He first checked on Max, squinting through a gently shifting interior fog.

She was in the process of sitting up—so essentially okay. He called out anyway, "Are you hurt?"

"No."

Good. Next, he assessed himself.

His planted knee felt wet, but, *no*, it wasn't bleeding. When he glanced down, he saw that he was kneeling in a puddle of what looked like a mix of saline from a busted IV bag and coffee—Max's thermos had rolled out of her bag and broken. Coffee was now leaking from a long fissure along the side.

His mouth, however, was definitely bleeding—he tasted the blood. He went in search of the injury with his tongue and—he winced. He'd bitten his damned tongue during the tumble.

He'd kept hold of his rifle, though.

A man only had to lose his weapon one time in a dangerous situation for his hand to learn how to clamp shut around anything with bullets. For Kyle that lesson had come from a downhill roll-a-thon on Isla Gorgona in

Colombia during a counter-drug op. He let go of his sniper rifle and landed weaponless into a threesome of badass soldados. After almost dying because of that, he promised himself *never again*, so it was nice to know his reflexes had honored the vow.

Okay, then. Other than somehow getting a pile of sand down his pants, he was fine.

He hurried in a crouch toward the front of the bus and clambered into the front cab to check on the kid. Besides the shot-up arm, Jobs didn't look much the worse for wear. He'd avoided potential bumps and bruises by wearing his seatbelt—points to the kid—and being unconscious when they'd rolled had kept Jobs' neck nice and floppy, so he probably also escaped a case of whip-lash.

So everyone made it through the crash basically fine. Question was: were they going to stay fine?

Kyle peered through the fractured windshield. Out-side, he saw only desert. No bad guys. He leaned back into the main part of the ambulance and pawed through the first aid debris, finding a roll of gauze and medical tape for Jobs.

"Trouble's coming," Max whispered.

He snapped his head up. *Voices.* He heard them now too. He went back to the first aid debris and found a tongue depressor, using it to push the passenger side outer mirror into a different angle. It gave him a visual of the road.

There was the enemy jeep, parked about three hun-dred feet away, and—*Fuck.* "They're mounting a machine gun."

Max paled. "They're going to pepper the ambulance with bullets." And them along with it. "I can't imagine they're happy with you for destroying their other jeep."

He shot her a glance. She was speaking in a strange monotone. When she'd talked about Daniel Pearl, she'd been tense. This was something different. It wasn't much, he'd give her that, merely a little quiver of her eyelashes, but it was fear, nonetheless.

Footsteps moved closer to the ambulance, and Max's eyes darted back over to him.

"I'm a woman," she said in a low tone. "If they capture me, it, uh…it won't go so well."

And she wasn't referring to being decapitated.

Kyle climbed into the back of the bus again. "Reckon I oughta blast any such notions outta their no 'count tango heads then." Despite his play at lightening the mood, his own mood was anything but cheery.

He was remembering Max naked at the back of the Jebel Ali Club, how the bones of her hips thrust out against her flesh, how fragile she'd looked. As small as she was, any abuse—any at all—would break her.

Holding his AK in a tight fist, he did a quick-check out one of the rear round windows. *Shit.* He didn't have a shot. "I can't get good aim at them from inside the ambulance, so I'll need your help."

He watched her throat move with a swallow, and the muscles in his chest went cement on him. She wasn't wearing any makeup, same as last night, making her look very young, but with the headscarf on, framing her small face, she also seemed incredibly vulnerable.

The footsteps moved away again.

"I'm going to open one of the back doors," he said, "and once I do, I want you to start shooting at those assholes with this." He held out his Beretta. "Stick only your arm out, okay? Not your head or any other part of your body. I don't want you getting hurt, and it's not like you have to hit anyone. Just drive them to take cover, so I can get into position behind the ambulance. All right?"

"Yes."

"Do you know how to shoot a pistol?"

"I assume one pulls the trigger."

Haha, funny. "Yeah, well, I wasn't sure if I could trust a bleeding-heart journalist to know her ass from a hole in the ground when it comes to guns." He handed her the Beretta. "Be careful. The safety's off."

She nodded.

"The Beretta carries a fifteen-round magazine," he told her. "I put one in the bad guy's belly, so you've still got plenty."

"Should I save one bullet for, uh...myself?" Her face was white. "Just in case."

His heart almost reeled out of his chest. "What the fuck, Max? No, dammit. That shit is only from the movies. Don't kill yourself if they capture you." He almost wanted to pull a *Last of the Mohicans* speech on her—*You stay alive. No matter what happens, I will find you...* But the point was moot. If Max was taken, Kyle wouldn't be able to find her. Because he'd be dead.

No way was it happening otherwise.

"Are you ready?" His voice sounded gruff.

She nodded again, then positioned herself at the bottom edge of the ambulance.

CHAPTER EIGHT

KYLE UNLATCHED THE rear bay door closest to the ground and let it bang open to the desert floor. Dust puffed up. He gave Max the go-ahead signal, and she stuck her arm around the edge of the ambulance and started pulling the trigger.

Pop! Pop! Pop! Lightning flashed at the Beretta's snout. Burnt gunpowder choked the air.

AK tucked in close to his body, Kyle rolled out of the ambulance, got his feet under him, and ran, bent over, around the ambulance for cover.

The enemy returned small arms fire, several bursts from a rifle and a pistol. No machine gun yet, thank God, but still… *Please, Max, tell me you ducked back inside.*

Squatting down, Kyle braced his shoulder against the side of the ambulance—actually the roof—and concentrated on slowing his breathing and evening out his heart rate. He'd need every sniper skill he'd learned in his short stint in the Marines for this. The AK was reasonably accurate at a little over a thousand feet, and the enemy was about three hundred feet away, so he was within range. Hard part was him not being able to lie on his belly and take his sweet time aiming. He'd only get a split second to pop-the-weasel out of hiding and do his thing.

He took a last, even inhale of breath. *Okay.*

Go time—

Switching knees, he spun into the open and brought the rifle up, stock butted against his shoulder. He lined up on his first target through the sight, applied even pressure to the trigger, and snapped off a shot. The instant smell of nitroglycerin and graphite was familiar and oddly comforting.

The round tore into the head of the man who was working at mounting the machine gun. The bullet frayed off a chunk of skull, leaving behind shards of ragged bone and stringy ribbons of meat. These flailed like loose party streamers as the man fell over like a dead weight—because that's exactly what he was. *Dead.*

Kyle ducked back into hiding. His breathing and heart rate were still calm, even though that'd been mondo gross. *One more asshole to go…*

The jeep engine roared to life.

Well, whaddya know.

Looked like the gross factor was too high for asshole number two, and so he was bugging out. Although it was a good bet he was driving off to get more of his buddies to come back and help. *While I've got two lives depending on me and a KIA mini-bus… Sorry, dude, but you're dead, too.*

Kyle stood up, sand cascading off his knees, and—

Blam!

He shot out a rear tire before the jeep could drive too far out of range. Then—

Blam!

He picked off the driver with a single bullet to the neck. The body wilted out of the doorless vehicle and ragdolled to the dirt. The jeep came to a rolling halt and stalled out, five hundred feet away now.

Kyle lowered his rifle and scanned the area. No one else was around. He wouldn't have minded a peek through a magnified sniper scope to confirm his solitude farther out, but he was shit out of luck on that score. At least he knew the bad guys from the first jeep wouldn't be sneaking up his back door. They'd been totaled along with their jeep.

Edging over to the back of the ambulance, he stooped over and peered inside the one open bay door.

Max was in the front cab, straddling Jobs and looking at—

Ah, hell. She'd watched the whole evolution in the passenger side mirror.

She dropped down to meet his eyes. Her expression was bilious.

He straightened. *Fuckity fuck fuck.* He ground the heel of his hand into his eye, moving sand grains around his cornea. He heard boots slopping through first aid rubble, and then Max was standing in front of him.

"That was…um. Wow." She cleared her throat. "You're an incredible shot, Kyle."

The sound of his name on her lips tumbled his stomach into a ball. It was as though he could actually feel her tongue lightly pressing the back of her upper teeth on the L. He fiddled with the action of his AK. He didn't know what to say. "I seem to be making a nasty habit of killing people on deployments." *Oh, beautiful. Nice decision.* While he was at it, why didn't he confess how many times he'd been fool enough to boink an ex-girlfriend whose favorite pastime was treating him like her royal ass-wiper?

He glanced at Max.

She nodded almost imperceptibly, like a subtle message of understanding and solidarity. *Good ol' Max. Got your shit back together already, do ya, so you can be here for me? Gosh.* If she'd been a buddy, he would've slugged her good-naturedly on the arm. Too bad her nod was a lie. Because no woman understood him.

Not many men did, either.

Hell, he himself was without clue. Like this whole killing thing—he didn't understand why he couldn't muster any feelings about it. Just tiredness, same as when he'd taken out two Colombian soldados—maybe three, if another had gotten himself particle-ized along with a generator Kyle blew up. Probably the numbness was a sign he was heading for a case of PTSD a bunch of psycho-quacks would love to write papers about.

Wordlessly, Max handed the Beretta back to him.

Equally mute, he slid the pistol into his boot holder. Propping his AK against the ambulance, he trudged back inside and moved Jobs from the front cab. It was an awkward maneuver to pull off with a completely flaccid body, but he managed to get Jobs outside and to lie him down on a spot of soft sand. "Can you wrap up his arm?" he asked Max, handing her gauze and medical tape. "I want to see if the radio still works." If it didn't, they had one helluva long hike back to camp ahead of them.

Jeep number two was a no-go—the spare-tire holder was empty.

Luckily, the radio was operational. He asked the aid station to send someone to pick them up, suggesting that they might want to bring a contingent of Pakistani guardsmen along with them.

When he went back outside, Max was seated with her back propped against the ambulance, her camera bag next to her. She jerked her chin at Jobs. "Our boy's sleeping like a baby." His arm was also neatly wrapped.

Kyle half-smiled.

"Camera's busted." She gestured at the bag. "But fortunately not the GPS."

Kyle grabbed his AK and sank down next to her, setting the weapon beside his leg.

"I suppose that's sort of good news," she mused. "The camera is mostly for show, whereas the GPS is necessary to the operation."

He arched his brows. "You still consider this mission a go? Didn't a bunch of JEM shit-sticks just try to kill us?"

"Those men weren't JEM." She plucked her thermos out of a pile of supplies she'd hauled outside. "I recognized a man in the lead jeep as one of the aides to Rizwan Akhtar, agency director of ISI."

Inter-Service Intelligence? Was she fucking kidding? "Are you telling me Pakistani *Intelligence* just tried to take us out?"

"It makes sense, actually. ISI has always covertly backed the Taliban, much to the US government's disapproval. One of JEM's key leaders, Asmatullah Moavia, split from JEM in 2007 to join the Taliban, and since then JEM and the Taliban have been rivals." Unscrewing the top of the thermos, Max peered into the empty interior and sighed. "Crud, I wanted more coffee. Anyway, if JEM manages to get some of their key players out of Guantanamo with this current hostage exchange, then they'd up their power. ISI clearly wants to stop that from happening."

By killing us? "Unbelievable," Kyle bit out. "Bad enough we have to deal with a bunch of unpredictable terrorists, now we're up against all of Pakistani Intelligence."

"Worse, this is going to set us back with JEM. Once they hear about this attack, they're going to get skittish." Max picked up an energy bar and opened it, tugging the wrapper down halfway like the husk on a corn cob. "Think about it. Only JEM and our little group knew the particulars of this meeting. How was ISI able to attack us exactly on this road at this time, if not for a spy inside JEM?"

"Crap," Kyle said. *More time in custody for Kelleman's nephew while this foul-up gets figured out.*

"I'll contact JEM when I get back to camp, see how this plays out. We'll go from there. Here." She gave him another energy bar. "I found these among the medical supplies. I haven't opened this one, so, you know, you don't have to worry about my saliva."

He smiled. Almost laughed. *Cute.* She was *real* cute. "Thanks." He tore open the bar and took a bite. "Ouch."

"What's wrong?"

"I don't have mad love for chewing right now." He grimaced. "I bit my tongue when we crashed."

"Really?" She chuckled.

"Did I just say I shit my pants?" He gave her a disgruntled look, although the truth was he didn't mind her chuckle. It was great to see her amazing eyes getting back to their regular amazingness.

"I jammed my wrist," she offered.

He lowered his brows. "You said you weren't hurt."

"It's not too bad. Mainly sore." She rotated her wrist for him to see. "We're lucky, actually. We could've been hurt way worse."

She was referring to the crash, but also she meant— she had to—what the bad guys would've done to them if Kyle hadn't logged in those kills. Her relief swept some of his malaise away. He'd saved Max and Jobs today. Nothing wrong with that. "Once Jobs is back on his feet, we can have him check out the camera. Dude can fix anything." He glanced down at his energy bar. It already had sand on it.

Max took a bite out of her bar. "Good. It'd be better not to go into a media interview, fake or not, with a broken camera."

Kyle tossed aside his bar and made a face. "Is it me, or does everything in this country taste like grit?" He scratched his beard, sending tiny grains of sand pattering down to his lap. "Dammit, I have sand everywhere. And I'm talking places I didn't even know I had."

"You want to see something?"

He looked at her.

Nudging her head covering aside, she stuck her pinkie finger in her ear, wiggled it around, then showed it to him. It was coated in sand.

A laugh exploded out of him.

She smiled at him, the bright blue color near her pupils lighting up.

Man, a guy could fall in love with Max Dougin based

on those eyes alone. All it would take was—He snapped the amused expression off his face. *Uh…not me. I didn't mean me. Just…you know, a guy.*

He turned away, watching a gusty breeze whisk up a top layer of sand and dance it along the ground for a few inches.

A companionable silence fell between them.

This was the strangest side of weird, ever. He didn't do *companionable* with women. If he wasn't hitting on a female, he was maneuvering himself into the best position to escape her. Far as he was concerned, women weren't constructed out of friend material.

All right. Enough of this shit. He was going to make himself want to screw Max, right the hell now. He ran a narrow gaze over her, and… Jesus, she might as well be wearing a potato sack for how sexless her clothes were. He could barely find her tits anywhere under her shirt, and her pretty hair was covered by the stupid scarf. All right, so her hair was pretty. It was short, yeah, but the color was really—

His stomach lurched. Red liquid was oozing from the upper edge of her headscarf. "You're bleeding," he told her.

Her head came around with an abrupt motion.

He gently pushed her scarf off and wadded it up, pressing it to her forehead.

She angled her eyes up toward his hand. "I don't even feel it." She reached up to take the scarf from him, and her hand settled on top of his.

Warmth raced down his arm and shot in tingling streaks through his chest. He released the scarf to her, but the warm feeling stayed. *Good.* He wanted to screw her now. Or...did he? Wait...what was this? It seemed like...

He pushed to his feet, brushed himself off, and took a couple of steps in the direction of nowhere. The muscles in his abdomen twitched.

You were going to leave Brodie's hospital room today, weren't you?

Yeah, anything ever gets hard or weird, you run, don't you, Kyle?

Throat tight, he peered off at the horizon. It was like a part of the country God forgot, nothing but endless barren earth. His discarded energy bar stood up in a pile of sand, the breeze ruffling the foil wrapper.

It was the only sound.

He shut his eyes, blocking out the apocalyptic view.

CHAPTER NINE

CORPSMAN KITTY HART stopped putting surgical instruments into a pot of boiling water to turn and check on bed three. Sure enough, the occupant was waking up; he groaned again. Flipping a stethoscope around her neck, she walked over. "Good morning, sir."

A pair of groggy hazel eyes peered up at her out of a heavily freckled face. The fellow might as well have been wearing a baseball glove and eating apple pie for how All-American Boy he looked.

When he'd been brought into the triage ward yesterday with a gunshot wound to his arm, his appearance had momentarily thrown Kitty. Here at the aid station, she and Dr. Barr exclusively treated Pakistani civilians caught in the crossfire of the war, many of those bearded, older men. And before she was sent here on temporary duty, she'd been stationed on board the *USNS Mercy*—that medical ship's mission was to offer humanitarian aid to foreigners.

Any American soldier who was injured in the European and African theatres was generally flown to Landstuhl Army Hospital in Germany. She'd all but forgotten what a wounded American boy looked like.

Correction: man.

Lieutenant JG Steve Whitmore, as his dog tags proclaimed him to be, might have a face that was a cross between Eddie Redmayne's and Peter Pan's, but his body was no narrow-chested, youthful thing. When she cut his shirt off yesterday, she'd discovered a nicely defined physique. Not as massively muscular as her ex-boyfriend, Shane's—but was that fair? Shane was a SEAL. *Still.* Nothing as pre-pubescent as his appearance would've led a girl to believe.

Poor fella. Face like his probably put him as bad off as a rubber-nosed woodpecker in a petrified forest when it came to getting a girl to give him some lovin'.

"I'm HM3 Hart," she introduced herself. "But you can call me Kitty." Smiling, she stuck the stethoscope in her ears. "I'm going to check your vitals, okay?"

Her patient kept blinking, but his eyes were gradually clearing.

She dipped the stethoscope beneath the front of his blue and white striped hospital gown and listened to his heart. Sounded good.

"I was shot," he croaked out.

"Yes, sir." She took his pulse. "You sure were."

"I…" He lifted his other hand and rubbed a palm over his brow, then noticed he was dragging an IV line. "Aw, man, I passed out."

Pulse was good, too. "You were badly wounded." Kitty tucked a thermometer in his mouth. "Put that under your tongue now." No new-fangled electronic thermometers for them here—only the old-fashioned stuff. "The bullet got lodged in your humerus." With anyone else she would've added, *that's the upper arm bone.* But Steve Whitmore was an officer, so he'd been to college. "It took a fair bit of work for Dr. Barr to dig it out." It'd been a nasty job, and the lieutenant would have a devil of a time recovering from it. In fact—"How's your pain?" She glanced at his IV bag. He was three quarters of the way through it.

"Okay, I guess," he muffled around the thermometer.

"I can give you more morphine, if you—"

"No." He took out the thermometer and handed it to her. "Thanks, but I don't want to sleep anymore."

Normal temperature. The lieutenant was coming along nicely.

He struggled to sit up, and she helped him, arranging pillows behind his back.

No automatic beds in this place either.

"What...? Um..." His throat moved with a swallow. "What happened after I passed out? Do you know?"

Kitty slipped the thermometer into the left breast pocket of her blue scrubs—left was always for dirty. Normally she wore camouflage BDUs when on duty, but not here, since American military personnel were a no-no on Pakistani soil. "The ambulance you were driving crashed. Flopped over on its side like a dead milk cow."

He paled. "Oh, no."

"Don't worry about it." Kitty wrote his vitals on his chart. "Lieutenant Hammond and Miss Dougin came out fine." They'd come into triage looking a mite stressed, that was for dead sure, anxious for the unconscious lieutenant, of course, but also as if they'd seen and done things that they wished they hadn't.

Kitty hung the clipboard at the end of the lieutenant's bed. "You hungry? I need to check with the doctor to see if you're cleared for a liquid diet, but then...oh. Here's Dr. Barr now."

Farrin was standing just inside the door marked *Authorized Personal Only* located at the far end of the post-op ward, her hands on her hips. She was glaring at the pot of boiling water that was in the process of sterilizing surgical instruments. "The autoclave is broken again?"

"Yes, ma'am," Kitty said. "Sorry."

Farrin *humphed*. "It's not your fault IHMR has given us only second-rate equipment for this aid station." The doctor strode down the aisle, the edges of her white lab coat flapping at the knees of her tan slacks. "How are you feeling, Mr. Whitmore?" she asked, stopping at Steve's bed and unhooking his chart.

"Embarrassed," he answered.

Kitty stole a swift peek at her patient, the bare honesty of his words giving her a start. Officers generally weren't so...open. Most she'd met were kind of stuffy.

Farrin glanced up from reading Kitty's notes.

"I passed out," Steve admitted and blushed.

Farrin *tut-tutted*, like it was a silly thing to feel bad about.

But Dr. Barr wasn't someone who easily found fault in another—the only person in the world Kitty had ever met with such a quality. Out of all the doctors Kitty had worked for in her four years as a corpsman, Dr. Barr was by far the best: competent, fair, tolerant, and friendly without crossing the boundaries of the boss-employee relationship.

Farrin wasn't too forthcoming about the more personal sides of her life—whereas Kitty pert-near wore

Farrin's ears off with her own tales, especially about her SEAL ex-boyfriend, Shane Madden, breaking her heart. If the doctor talked more, then maybe Kitty would've figured out why such a beautiful, smart woman was still single. Was there something in Dr. Barr's past? Kitty had an inkling there was.

The doctor unwrapped the bandage on Steve's arm and inspected his stitches. "You're doing well," she pronounced. "Isn't he, Kitty?"

"Fit as a fiddle, ma'am."

Farrin straightened, writing on Steve's chart. "Let's get some broth and Jell-O into Mr. Whitmore." She smiled at Steve. "Lucky you." Dr. Barr re-hooked the chart at the end of the bed. "Re-dress his arm, if you would, Kitty."

"My pleasure, ma'am."

Dr. Barr moved off to the next bed.

Kitty grabbed a roll of gauze bandage and white tape and set to re-wrapping the lieutenant's wound. The skin on his arm was as pale and freckled as the rest of him.

Lieutenant Whitmore watched her work, his attention on her hands. Oddly, a blush began to rise into her cheeks. There was something so...admiring in the way he looked at her. His focus moved to her face, and she could feel his appreciation deepen.

"You've got an amazing touch," he told her. "You make me feel better just rewrapping my arm."

More with the frank honesty. She taped off the gauze and dropped her hands into her lap.

The lieutenant's eyes were now clear as a Fourth of July day. His hospital gown had sagged off his right shoulder, showing part of his chest. It was bare and smooth, just a sprinkling of hair right in the crease of his pecs.

"Yes, well...I know what it's like to be hurt and not treated so nice." Maybe his kind eyes lowered her inhibitions, all his admiration loosening her tongue, because for some odd reason, she told him how she knew...

CHAPTER TEN

THE DISTANCE FROM the Plainview Cemetery to Covenant Hospital was only three miles, but the seven-minute ride there was excruciating. Every lurching movement of the horse-drawn hay wagon jarred Kitty Hart's forearm, sending the stars in the night sky whirling together in a blizzard of agony.

When her fellow high school seniors had hoisted her off the ground, she'd taken a single peek at her arm, seen bone sticking out, and thrown up. Drunk as Cooter Brown when she'd taken her flight off the top of the wagon, she was now sober as a judge. Plumb amazing how pain could do such a thing to a person.

Little wonder her parents had always threatened to take a switch to her if she ever touched alcohol. Things sure unraveled when a girl got herself schnookered. What had started out as a fun homecoming night hayride turned into this nightmare trip to the emergency room, and all because Kitty's boyfriend, Clete, had brought a jug of his pa's moonshine to the party—and this time she decided to try it. It only took a few swigs for her to think it'd be hilarious to hijack the reins of the wagon team and hightail it from the high school to the cemetery. She was a little vague on whether it'd been an accident or a planned idea to start running over headstones, but at some point, she hit an especially stubborn square block, and the wagon had stopped abruptly.

She hadn't.

So now here she was, sitting on paper sheets on an ER bed, her arm clutched to her breasts while she waited for the doctors to treat her—hopefully starting with a walloping dose of pain relief drugs. Clete was slumped half-asleep in the visitor's chair, his nose still red from his own liberal partaking of the moonshine jug. She should probably send him home to—

The examination room curtain was slapped aside, and Kitty's mother plowed in like a John Deere subsoiler. "You broke your ever-lovin' arm?" Shirleen demanded.

Clete jolted awake.

Kitty's father ambled in behind Shirleen.

"Do you not have the sense God gave a goose?" Shirleen's eyebrows, bushy as any man's, arrowed together.

Kitty dragged in a shaky breath. "Yes, I-I was just funning around, but then—"

"I. Beg. Your. Pardon." Her mother's face flushed a dark red. "I may not be the Queen of Sheba with jewels, a fine house, and shittin' in high cotton, but I sure as heck know I didn't raise no daughter of mine to be forgettin' to say 'ma'am' and 'sir' to her betters."

Kitty swallowed. "Yes, ma'am."

"And *you*." Shirleen rounded on Clete. "Nothin' but a no-'count pissant, lettin' this happen to Kitty. Skedaddle!"

Clete took off so fast, his boot soles left black skid

marks on the tiles.

"*Funnin' around*," her mother repeated Kitty's words with her ample bosom heaving. "Do you think you're at liberty to be gettin' arm broke with your father out of work so many months now?" She made a sweeping gesture of the emergency room. "We ain't got the money for this. We lost our insurance. You know that, girl." Her careworn hands landed on her rounded hips. "How could you be so stupid?"

"She's a dimwitted child," her father agreed. "Always has been."

Blushing painfully, Kitty clutched her arm tighter to her breasts.

"Let's go." Shirleen grabbed Kitty's good arm and pulled her off the exam table.

Kitty yelped, a sharp flash of pain enveloping her.

Her mother's rigid forefinger instantly appeared in front of Kitty's face. "You hush," she hissed. "This is your doin', and you'll take your up 'n' comin's without complaint."

Shirleen led the Hart family through the ER ward with all the charm and grace of a front loader.

Hospital staff gawked but did nothing beyond that. No one dared to stop Shirleen Hart when she was wearing one of her legendary scowls.

Soon the three of them were rattling home in their Chevy flatbed, Kitty barely choking back tears. She stared into the night through vision doubled by pain. What was going to happen to her arm now? Dread turned her stomach into Buffalo Springs Lake on a blustery day.

Her lips were numb by the time her mother was leading her into the dining room at home and forcing her to sit in a chair jammed against the wall.

"Get my sewing kit, Howard," Shirleen ordered Kitty's father. "And the aspirin."

"Mama…?" Ice filled Kitty's belly and froze her spine. "What are you going to do, Mama?"

"I'm goin' to set your arm myself, girl." Shirleen pushed up her shirt sleeves. "Did it to a calf once. Don't imagine I can't do the same here." She held out her hand to Kitty. "Now give me your broke arm."

Kitty cradled her arm closer. *No, please…* Tears streamed down her face.

"Give me your arm, I say!"

Kitty sobbed harder but offered her arm to her mother.

Shirleen grabbed Kitty by the wrist, planted a mud-caked boot on her daughter's chest, then yanked back hard.

KITTY JERKED WHERE she sat on the side of Lieutenant Whitmore's bed. Her fingers were trembling, and she'd unraveled the roll of gauze a bit during the telling of her story. Guess five years wasn't enough distance from that memory for it not to leave her shaky and feeling a tad sick.

Drawing in a deep breath, she pulled herself fully back to the present by focusing on the soft *clank* of surgical instruments butting around in the boiling pot.

She lifted her head to meet Lieutenant Whitmore's gaze, expecting to find an expression of shock or dismay on his face. But he surprised the heck out of her, because he was sitting rigid as a washboard, his face cherry red, looking like he wanted to cream Shirleen's corn.

Sighing, Kitty started to re-roll the gauze. "You have to understand, my ma was—"

"I cannot believe," he cut in sharply, "that your boy-friend didn't stay and look after you in the hospital."

Kitty glanced up, blinking. "What?" He was mad at Clete, not Shirleen?

The lieutenant's eyes blazed—an odd sight in such a pleasant young face. "If you were my girl, I would never leave you. And I wouldn't have let Shirleen do that to you."

Kitty just kept staring. *Not let Shirleen do…? Well, no one ever stopped Shirleen.*

Lieutenant Whitmore yanked his sagging hospital gown back in place. "Did Clete at least look out for you afterward?"

"Well, uh…" Kitty peered down at her hands. The gauze tangled on her fingers.

CHAPTER ELEVEN

MAX RIFFLED THROUGH the clothes she'd unpacked onto the shelves next to her cot, finding a pair of olive drab shorts, a short-sleeved maroon top, and flip-flops meant to be shower shoes, but today would relieve her of her boots. Her feet would probably be covered in dust in mere minutes, but, *oh, well.* The temperature was already in the high eighties, and it was only nine o'clock in the morning. She also definitely wouldn't be putting on a hijab.

She could change into something more conservative if she ended up leaving the camp today, which she seriously doubted she would anyway.

As suspected, JEM was very upset about the attack on the Americans. Yesterday when she talked to her contact via satellite phone, he'd told her all meetings were off until JEM found out what was going on. She assumed that meant unearthing their traitor, if there was one, and then doing God knew what to him—she didn't ask, and she didn't particularly want to think about it.

Once she was dressed, she propped the door to her tent open—if a breeze came by, she wanted it—then went over to her roommate's shelves. Kitty had said that Max could borrow any of her books.

She was reading the blurb on the back cover for *A*

Hundred Summers when Kyle strode inside.

"Any word?" he asked her.

He was dressed similarly to yesterday, and she grimaced at his long pants and boots. By high noon, he'd be melting. "No. But we need to give JEM a few days."

"*Days?*"

She angled the book back into its slot. "I told my contact that the US Government would be less inclined to negotiate as more time passed, hoping the veiled warning will keep JEM from lollygagging too much. But still." She shrugged. "I have no idea how long this will take."

"Shit." Kyle moved over to Max's cot and sat down. "I hate doing nothing."

"Me, too." She picked up a small, locally made purse off the top of Kitty's bookshelf and ran her thumb over the colorful Sindhi patchwork design. "But we don't have a choice. It's out of our hands."

Kyle gazed out the tent door. "Nothing to do around this Deliveranceville aid station, either." He hefted a large breath. "Gives me a hankering for a steel beach barbeque."

She laid the purse down. "What's a steel beach barbeque?"

He brought his attention back to her. "It's a like a picnic we have sometimes on the ship while we're underway. We clear the flight deck and put out barbeques, cook up dogs and burgers, maybe set up a basketball hoop in the hangar."

She smiled. She could imagine Kyle doing all of that. Maybe in a pair of shorts…? "Sounds fun."

He lifted a shoulder. "Kills time when we're not

working."

"I think there's a movie tonight in the mess tent," she offered.

His lips twisted. "Eleven hours from now."

She grabbed a deck of cards off Kitty's second shelf and held it up. "We could play gin rummy."

Kyle glanced at the cards, then his gaze moved up to her face, holding on her lips for two beats before meandering down her body. One corner of his mouth rose. "I think I've got a better way to chase off some boredom." He languidly stretched out on her bed, crossing his legs at the ankles and folding his hands behind his head. The pose displayed a set of wide lats and his beautifully formed biceps to perfection. Not to mention that his crossed legs enhanced the sizable bulge at his crotch.

"Let's have sex," he said.

"Because you're bored?"

"Because it's fun." His voice softened to a velvety rasp, a teasing light dancing in his eyes.

Hello. The seductive predator from the Jebel Ali Club was back.

This time, however, she knew what waited for her on the other end of Kyle's charm—the need to fake an orgasm followed by self-recriminations for sleeping with a man who didn't inspire a single feeling in her.

Although... The second part of that wasn't entirely true anymore. Beneath the smooth operator, she'd started to discover a man with a lot of heart.

I seem to be making a nasty habit of killing people on deployments... A look of pained confusion had flickered across his expression when he said those words—and *that* had inspired some feelings in her. Kyle also deserved credit for saving her from being captured by a bunch of ISI bad guys.

He grinned. "You're not going to start playing shy on me now, are you?"

"No. Just…" The *beginnings* of feelings weren't enough for her to sleep with him.

His grin turned into a knowing chuckle.

Sighing, she lay down the card deck. "I'm just not a casual hookup woman, Kyle. I never had a one-night stand before you, so…" She broke off. *Oh, drat.* She hadn't wanted to spill that.

"You *are* trying to play shy." His words were interwoven with continued laughter. "Look, honey, I *know* you had a good time with me."

Er…

"A guy can tell these things, especially a man like me whose equipment is…hmm, how shall I put it…?" His eyes suddenly narrowed down to tight slits. "What the hell?"

She startled. "What?" Talk about a weird mood change. "What's *what the hell*?"

"You did something with your mouth."

I did? "My mouth?" What had she done?

"You made a face," he accused. "You grimaced."

"I…"

His hands whipped out from behind his head and he shot up to a sitting position, his boots hitting the floor with a solid *wump.* "Did I hurt you that night?"

Mayday, mayday. Hard collision with his male ego imminent. "No. It was, uh, a little uncomfortable at first, but then—"

He slammed to his feet, his eyes on fire with a mixture of emotions.

Pissed off was a prominent one, but she was reasonably sure she also saw mortified in there.

"I know there wasn't a whole lot of foreplay involved in what we did," he snapped. "But...it's sort of how those things work, and I assumed you were okay. Why the hell didn't you say anything?"

"I did. I asked you to back off a bit, and you did. So, you know, it was fine."

"*Fine.*" He all but spat the word. He crossed his arms over his chest like he didn't trust himself not to punch a hole in the tent wall. "Did you fake?"

Um...

"Jesus! You did!"

She held up a placating hand. "No need to start searching for your balls under my cot, Kyle. I'm just someone who has to connect with a guy before I can enjoy sex with him—that's all."

He considered her for a long moment, his tongue moving around inside his mouth. "All right. Let's connect." He sat back down on her cot, so hard the hinges barked.

"Excuse me?"

He waved an impatient hand. "Whatever you do to connect, do it, so we can get on with it."

A laugh spilled out of her. He was being ridiculous. Yet...both the woman and the journalist in her were perking up over being given this free pass to puzzle him out. Who *was* the real Kyle Hammond? The supremely professional naval aviator, a gun-slinging, sharp-shooting rescuer of innocents, the man who'd chatted companionably with her next to a wrecked ambulance, or this shithead?

"We'll have to talk," she warned playfully.

"Yeah. Go big or go home, honey."

She came around to the front of Kitty's cot and sat down across from him. "Okay, so…" *Start in easy.* "Where are you from?"

"Virginia." He braced his hands on his knees.

Cool. "Me, too. Where in Virginia?"

"Norfolk."

She knew Norfolk. It was a large city, gritty in places. "Where?"

He paused. "The Young Terrace Projects."

The projects? Another point lost to her—Kyle had fooled her again. She hadn't guessed that about him. "A kid from the bad part of town, huh?"

A hint of impatience entered his tone. "I guess."

"We lived in Burke, close to DC. My parents are lawyers there."

That, apparently, didn't warrant comment from him.

"What do your parents do?" she asked.

"My mother's a waitress and my father…does odd jobs."

"Do you have any siblings?"

"One brother. Younger."

"I have a younger brother, too. He's a Marine, and he's the reason I know how to shoot a pistol." She formed her hand into the shape of a gun and popped her thumb a couple of times.

Once again Kyle just sat there, no commentary, no attempt at engagement, which was...*very interesting.* He was treating this like an interview. *No*—like he was brokering for power. And if this was how he connected with women, Max would bet her right arm he'd never had his heart involved in any relationship.

Let's see what he does when I start sharing. "When I was nine years old, I asked my parents for a baby brother for Christmas. And guess what? On Christmas Eve day, they brought home a five-year-old foster child, Kevin. He was so scruffy and adorable—his mother was trying to finish high school and couldn't raise him—and I fell instantly in love. My parents ended up adopting him permanently, so I wasn't an only child anymore. Cool, huh?"

Kyle hooded his lids, like he was bored. "Sure."

She smiled benignly. *I'm on to you, suckah.* He was leaning forward at the waist. Just a bit—it was subtle—but his body language projected that he was definitely not bored.

She pointed to the left side of his face. "How did you get the scar on your jaw?"

"I got cut," he said flatly.

She laughed. "That much is obvious. How?"

"Someone cut me."

My, but he was being a pill. "Ah. Who?"

"You interested in scars? I got another one—a monstrous one on my leg." Kyle stood up and unbuckled his pants, letting them drop to his ankles.

She skidded her focus past the front of his underwear and zeroed in on his left thigh, where—*good God.* Judging by the size of his scar, it was a miracle he still had his leg.

"But you've seen this scar already. Right, honey?"

She returned her attention to his face.

He winked.

"I haven't, actually," she said in a neutral tone. "I was too embarrassed to look at you closely the night we had sex."

His expression went blank. He didn't say or do anything. Clearly he wasn't sure what to make of her confession. Which part of it had thrown him? She didn't know. That she'd been embarrassed? Or that she'd engaged in one of the most intimate acts imaginable between two human beings with him and she hadn't even glanced at his parts?

"*Have sex*," he repeated on a drawl. "So very clinical, Max. How about bang? Bone? Bump fuzzies?" He smirked. "And those are just the B's."

"Diddle, doink, do it," she tossed back.

He stopped smirking.

"I'd offer you the F's, but that's too easy."

Brows down, he studied her for a long moment. It was like he was purposely trying to rile her, and he was a bit miffed that she refused to play along.

"You know," he finally said, "I was just thinking what a shame it is that we don't have a Jacuzzi nearby." The smirk came back.

Uh-oh.

"Considering how long you can hold your breath, you probably rock at underwater blowjobs."

A curious next move. She just smiled. "It comes with being a good swimmer. What about you?" She leaned back, bracing her palms on the cot's wooden frame. "Do you play a sport?"

"Baseball."

As soon as he said the word, the oddest thing happened: he blanched.

"Fuck this." He hauled his pants back up and refastened them with tight, jerky motions. "This is stupid." His boot heels ground into the grit on her tent floor as he wheeled and stalked out.

She straightened and stared at his retreating back. The man was beyond confusing.

Why in the world had *baseball* set him off?

Chapter Twelve

Plainview, Texas

IT TOOK A full week for Kitty's fever to break after her mother set her broken arm. The first three days, Shirleen dumped pill after pill down Kitty—aspirin, Motrin, Tylenol—but nothing worked against the infection raging inside her. Kitty finally got delirious—which she had no recollection of whatsoever, but then she supposed that was the definition of delirium. So Shirleen had no choice but to horse trade for some antibiotics.

She exchanged a ham hock from one of the Hart's recently slaughtered sows with Hal Tooley, a mechanic Kitty's father used to work with over at T J and D Auto, for some of the amoxicillin Hal's daughter was taking for an ear infection.

Today was the first day Kitty had made it out of her bedroom, two days after starting the antibiotics. She wore a bathrobe that used to be terrycloth, but now was thin cloth, the elbows completely worn out, and her broken forearm was splinted between a couple of cloth-wrapped two-by-fours and supported by a sling around her neck.

Kitty slouched on the sagging living room couch, sipping Campbell's chicken noodle from a chipped mug and watching *Family Feud*. All the contestants' faces were cut in half by a fuzzy horizontal line, but she could hear them okay.

She set her feet on the edge of the coffee table.

The coffee table was an oval piece of plywood set on a stack of empty oil cans that stank up their house like a garage. It was a smell Kitty was well used to, seeing as her father still seemed to ooze mechanic's grease from every pore even though he'd been out of work for over a year. But she'd caught other folks wrinkling their noses at it.

The Harts used to have a proper coffee table. But two years back, Kitty's older brother, Jake, broke it horsing around with friends one night, and Shirleen never got around to replacing it. Jake had been seventeen at the time, far too old for a whuppin', but Mama had given him one anyway; Mama's forearms were big as a wrestler's. Two months later, on the very day Jake graduated from high school, he lit out fifty miles south to Lubbock and started working at a garage there.

Kitty picked up the TV remote and switched the channel to—

The front door banged open, and Shirleen barged inside.

Kitty sat forward in a sudden motion.

It wasn't unusual for Shirleen to come home from work during her lunch break—Howard didn't tend to eat if someone didn't cook for him—but along with her manicurist smock, Shirleen was wearing an angry scowl.

Kitty's stomach bucked.

Shirleen planted herself in front of the TV. "Cemetery wants to charge us three hunnert dollars for those gravestones you knocked asunder." Her mother had a piece of paper in her hand, and she waved it now. *"Three hunnert dollars!*"

Kitty swallowed hard.

"Go set yourself in the dining room, girl." Shirleen pointed a domineering finger in the direction she wanted Kitty to go. "Your father and I need to talk to you 'bout this." Shirleen marched down the short hall to the master bedroom to wake Howard from his afternoon nap.

With a shaky hand, Kitty set her mug of soup on the coffee table next to an old bag of Jiffy Pop popcorn. A fly lifted off the bag and lethargically bobbed off to another location. She slowly hoisted herself off the couch, careful of her forearm, and shuffled into the dining room. Tears burned her eyes.

She hadn't been in this room since the night her mother set her arm, and seeing it again brought back a load of terrible memories. Those stories folks told 'bout falling unconscious when pain got too fierce…? Didn't happen. A body felt all the suffering, bones crunching back into place, the repeated jab of a needle and thread sewing the skin back together…lightning and fire and a thousand piercing spears, and endless sticky blood…

All of it.

Kitty moved to the dining table and eased herself into a chair at the head.

A moment later Shirleen barreled into the dining room, Howard in tow.

Her mother smacked the bill down in front of Kitty. "How in tarnation you reckon I'm goin' to pay that?"

"I'm sorry, Mama. I-I'll pay it."

Shirleen's voice rose. "Great day in the morning, *how*? Since you was stupid enough to get yourself fired from your job at KFC"—her mother gestured at Kitty's broken arm—"you ain't got no wages comin' in."

Kitty bowed her head and stared at the cigarette burns on the tablecloth. Jake was the smoker, always with a Parliament between his fingers as he gestured this way and that. He'd started smoking at fourteen, and now already at nineteen, his teeth were yellow as fly paper.

Shirleen planted her hands on her hips. "Cold, hard facts is, girl, your father and me can't afford you no more." Her mother exhaled coarsely. "We want you out of the house by week's end."

Kitty whipped her head up. "What?" Her mouth gaped open. "But...where am I supposed to go?"

"I called your brother down in Lubbock. He got a friend works with him in the garage there willin' to marry you."

Kitty widened her eyes. "Marry?!"

"You're nearly eighteen," Shirleen retorted. "Old enough to be gettin' hitched so you can be a husband's problem 'stead of our'n." Her mother's formidable finger stabbed the air in front of Kitty. "And don't be gettin' any fool notions 'bout tyin' the knot with Clete neither. That Randall boy doesn't have a pot to piss in now, and he won't amount to a hill a' beans later."

Kitty forced the question out of a tautly constricted throat, "Who, then?"

"Larson Holmes."

Bile burned up onto the back of Kitty's tongue. *Oh, Lord...*

"Jake says the boy knew you back when he was in high school and is sweet on you."

Kitty twisted her bathrobe belt around her index finger, pulling it so tight she cut off her circulation. Larson was known as "the weasel" because of his greasy hair and long skinny, rat-like nose. He stunk to high heaven, always with sweat rings under his armpits, and Kitty doubted he'd changed much since he'd graduated from high school.

She'd sooner eat a lizard every day for breakfast than let Larson Holmes ever lay a hand on her.

"I'll start makin' the arrangements." Her mother gave a firm, *that's-that* nod.

"Yes, ma'am."

Her mother marched out, her father shambling after.

Kitty just sat there, staring again at the table, which was really a holding place for a lot of junk: her father's tools—gathering dust—car washing supplies, also moldering from disuse, some of Shirleen's clothes, sewing supplies that made Kitty's stomach cramp, and shoe boxes full of papers and Howard's old Navy gewgaws, plus various whittling knives from when her father tried his hand at that hobby.

One thing the table had never been was a place where the Harts shared a family meal.

Kitty had planned for things to be different with her own family.

That would never come to pass in a loveless marriage to Larson Holmes.

Lord, what am I going to do?

Tears rose, blurring her vision of the dining table junk and—

Howard's Navy gewgaws…

She sat up straight.

That gave her an idea.

Kitty went into her bedroom and slowly, painfully pulled on blue jeans, a loose T-shirt, and cowboy boots, then snuck out the front door. She walked nearly a mile down Smythe Street to Highway 70. Turning left, she passed Jumbo Joe's Restaurant, the KFC where she used to work, then the strip mall where Hubbard's Pawn Shop and Sears Hometown Store were, finally arriving at the Dairy Queen.

Sweat was running down her back and temples. It wasn't hot out. She was hurting bad from the long walk.

She went inside the Dairy Queen, and, luckily, Mary Beth was working.

"Daaaamn, Kitty." Mary Beth eyed her up and down. "You look like you been et by a wolf and shit over a cliff."

Kitty smiled weakly at her friend. "Hey, Mary Beth, can I use the phone in back?"

Mary Beth snapped her bubblegum. "Your phone at home ain't working?"

"No. Mama just has a burr in her saddle right now."

"Shirleen could piss off the pope." Her friend gestured to the employee door. "Go on back, but don't dawdle. Joss is out for a five-minute smoke break, and if he finds you in his office, he'll get mad as a hornet."

"I'll be quick." Kitty dragged herself to the Dairy Queen's back office and sat down at the desk. Tucking the phone receiver between her ear and shoulder, she dialed Clete one-handed.

He picked up on the second ring.

"Hey," she said. "It's me."

"Hey."

"Remember how a spell back you told me there was a fella you talked to 'bout joining the Navy?"

"Oh, yeah. Fella down in Lubbock. Called *a recruiter*."

Sweat dripped off her chin onto the desk. "Do you think you could drive me out to see him?"

"What? Really?" Clete paused. "Shucks, Kitty, I don't think the Navy takes girls."

"Why not?" *Didn't they*? "Just come get me, Clete."

"*Now?*"

"Yeah, now." With the tip of her finger, Kitty smeared her sweat around on the veneer desktop. "I need to take care of this today. I'm in a fair bit of trouble here."

Silence came through the phone line.

"Clete Zachary Randall." She made her voice scolding, like his mother's. "I'm in this fix because of your stupid moonshine."

"All right, Kitty! Shit! Don't pitch a fit. I can take you tomorrow. My pa will tan my hide I don't get the chicken coop mended today."

Tomorrow! By tomorrow Larson Holmes could be here in Plainview, wanting to pick out a plate pattern with Kitty—no doubt one resembling a hubcap. "Never mind," she snapped and slammed down the receiver.

CHAPTER THIRTEEN

K ITTY HANDED STEVE Whitmore a screwdriver.

He met her eyes as he took the tool. He was standing on the opposite side of a table from her in the *Authorized Personnel Only* room, and most of the guts of the autoclave were spilled out in front of him.

After three straight days in bed in the post-op ward, Steve told her he couldn't stand the inactivity anymore. Could she find him some tools? She'd brought him the small toolbox kept at the front gate's guard outpost.

Steve set right in to fixing Miss Dougin's movie camera.

Now he was at work on the autoclave.

He'd exchanged his open-backed hospital gown for a pair of scrubs as soon as he started fixing things, and for this task, he'd also put aside his sling.

Kitty was eternally grateful for that. Of all the things she'd been forced to get used to as a corpsman—and now as Dr. Barr's surgical assistant—a sling still gave her the willies.

"I hate to side with your mother on anything," Steve said. "But in this case, I have to agree—Clete is a no-account pissant."

Kitty laughed. Even though she'd said the same phrase about Clete when quoting her ma, hearing Steve say it was funny. Just sounded weird coming from the lips of such a smart fella, and Steve was—inside and out and all the way through the middle—sharp as a whole bucket of tacks.

"I like your ex-boyfriend even less than I did before." Steve yanked a fistful of wires out of the back of the autoclave. "He didn't protect you again. You had to *join the Navy* in order to avoid marrying Larson Holmes. If you were my girl, I would've done anything to help you."

Kitty kept her eyes down. This protective side of Steve's always confounded her. The only soul in her past who'd ever said he'd protect her was her ex-boyfriend, Shane—but he'd never been around enough to do much of anything with her.

"How were you able to enlist, anyway?" Steve asked. "You were only seventeen."

"I couldn't right away—the recruiter wouldn't take me until I came of age. But I was only a month shy of my eighteenth birthday, so I moved out of my house, took the GED, then bought a case of Beanie Weenie and lived on that and water for a month in Mary Beth's back shed."

Steve glanced up. "You're joking?"

"Nope. I didn't have money for anything else. I'd given most of my savings to my ma and pa to pay for the cemetery damage." Kitty had been so hungry back in those days she could've eaten the north end out of a south-bound polecat. The sparse conditions didn't speed along her arm healing none either.

"My recruiter was a good man." Kitty skimmed her fingers over the top edge of the autoclave. "He saw I was in a bad way when I showed up to sign the enlistment forms, so he put me on the payroll, but tangled me up in paperwork for a couple of weeks so I could recover a bit before reporting for boot camp."

Lord, she'd never forget her shock when the recruiter told her she'd scored high enough on her Armed Services entrance exam to become a corpsman, *if* it was something she wanted.

She made him recheck her scores twice.

Steve shook his head as he picked up a frayed wire from the mechanical mess and inspected it closely. "I've just decided my life is boring."

"Oh, trust me, I'd trade plenty of the happenings in my life for a smidge of boring." Kitty looked down at her fingernails. "And maybe some better luck." *With men, 'specially.*

You don't talk to me at all, Shane! I've lived with you a year and I barely know you.

Pushing the memory aside, Kitty focused hard on her fingers. She had a hangnail. Best she get to trimming it, else it'd drive her batty with snagging on gauze all the time. "So, uh, you think your story of joining the Navy is dull?"

"I'll say," Steve said. "I was studying to be a mechanical engineer at Carnegie Mellon, then went on a helicopter sightseeing tour in New York and fell in love with the sensation of flying. But honestly…" He glanced up and smiled. "I also wanted the chance to be a hero." His smile slewed catawampus. "One look at my face and people don't exactly think 'heroic,' right?"

Kitty smiled. "I do."

Blushing faintly, Steve went back to sorting through

the autoclave's innards. "I'm getting a little hungry. Do you want to go grab lunch?"

"I guess I'd better." She glanced at her watch. It *was* getting on towards lunchtime. "Do you need help getting back to your bed?"

"Well, see…" He set aside the screwdriver. "I was kind of thinking we could go to the mess tent *together*."

She dropped her gaze. He looked downright adorable right now, what with a look of expectant hope in his eyes, plus his hair was all mashed up in back in a disarming bedhead cowlick.

But a *no trespassing* sign might as well be hanging from his officer's rank for how available he was to her. "I don't think that would be a good idea."

"Let me guess…" He stepped back and spread his hands. "You don't want to be seen with me like this? And here I thought chic hospital wear was in vogue right now."

She sniffed a little laugh. He sure could talk fancy when he wanted to. "The obvious answer is you're an officer and I'm enlisted."

"So? That doesn't mean we can't be friends."

"Actually, it does."

"I eat with Tarzan sometimes."

"That's different. He's on your flight crew."

"Well, it's too late." Steve stepped out from behind the table. "You *are* my friend, Kitty." He moved to stand in front of her. "You know, I've…I've never been able to talk to girls. Until you."

She gazed up into his sweet face and felt a smile building. Yes, they did talk mighty well together. Over the last three days she'd found herself at his bedside time and again, chatting about all manner of this and that.

"I think…" Steve paused. "I guess in the past I was always trying to figure how to get close to a girl…be able to kiss her or touch her or something, so right away I got tongue-tied. But from the first moment I met you, you *were* touching me. It evaporated a barrier." She heard him take a raspy breath. "I think you're amazing, Kitty."

She swallowed her heart back down her throat. Darn, she wished he hadn't complimented her. Her belly was now warming in a manner that always brought out a lot of stupid in her.

Sophomore year when she slept with Sam Faulk in the flatbed of his Dodge because he'd given her a lollipop on Valentine's Day and told her she was the nicest girl in tenth grade. He never talked to her again afterward.

Brady Collins said she had cute eyes, so she let him give her a poke from behind at the back of the gym, her cheek jammed up against the wall. He was rough, and her lady parts had been sore for two days after.

She sucked off Ron Divins in the boy's bathroom because he was the one person who hadn't gotten mad at her for earning the highest score on an English paper. When he climaxed, he'd grabbed her by the hair, jetted semen into her face, then laughed while he hiked up his pants.

When Clete Randall came around, she told him they'd have to go steady before she'd do any business with him. That was fine by him. She still made him wait two weeks after getting his commitment, so she'd be certain he wasn't fooling. They messed around a few times in those two weeks, making out and such. Every time he got his hands on her titties, he jizzed in his blue jeans. That should have clued her in on how the sex would go with him, and sure 'nuff, he came faster than green grass through a goose every time she gave him a poke, never getting more than two solid pumps in before making his baboon noises. She taught herself not to care. Clete didn't insult her, and that was the main thing.

She'd already set her standards fairly low by the time Shane Madden came into her life, so his interest in her completely blindsided her. *A Navy SEAL, liking me…?*

Her first job as a new corpsman had been as the medic in charge of taking care of trainees going through BUD/S. Her busiest time was the end of Hell Week. One after the other, the men who survived would show up on her exam table, their bodies traumatized in any number of ways. Shane had been so bad off, he had walking pneumonia.

There he'd been on her table, shivering uncontrollably, his legs swollen, his arms streaked with cuts. When she carefully took hold of his wrist to check his pulse, he looked up at her through eyebrows sodden with ocean water.

Somehow, as battered as he was, he managed a heartbreaker of a crooked smile. "Hello, gorgeous."

Gorgeous did her in. That's all it took to set her on a path to nowhere good *once again.* Their relationship had proved disastrous.

I want to know you care about me, Shane. Why can't you give me that?!

Kitty took a step away from Steve, tears needling her

nose. "I think you're amazing, too," she said quietly. "But it doesn't matter. We can't fraternize." *And I always think the wrong things about men.*

Her heart sinking into the pit of her belly, she turned and left.

Chapter Fourteen

K YLE WAS DOING his daily routine, lying flat on his back on his cot, his hands linked behind his head and his jaw jutted toward the ceiling as he brooded over *her*. Pain-in-the-ass woman was driving him nuts, sticking in his mind when he should've been able to banish her to the dungeons of his brain like he'd done with so many others. Max Dougin was nobody, just another skirt.

Okay.

Yeah.

So she was smart, brave, and cool as a fucking cucumber, which meant she wasn't given to irrational outbursts of yelling and name-calling, and hands to heaven in praise for *that*. She always seemed to know what to say to dump him on his ass with his head spinning, trying to figure out what his next move should be. Last thing he needed was a woman like that in his life. Right?

Well, actually…

He cut off the Universe's attempt to provide input and inserted his own answer.

Damn straight.

So for the last three days, he'd made every effort to steer clear of Ms. Max Dougin. When he unavoidably ran into her in the mess tent, he would nod a neutral *howdy*, then leave her to eat with HM3 Hart while he found a table with his men and tried not to bite off the end of his fork. Outside of mealtimes, he played ping-pong, read outdated newspapers, checked every bolt and screw on his helo over and over, waited for JEM to call, shook the sand out of his boots—and again!—and jerked off, not necessarily in that order, and *dammit all to crap and back.* He couldn't get Max out of his mind.

Who the hell did she think she was? No unmarried woman Kyle had ever wanted to screw failed to fall in line and get underneath him. All those others accepted the realistic truth: the female and male species never truly *connected.* Men faked intimacy to get laid, and women went along with the pretense so they had a good excuse to get laid. Kyle was willing to do his part and pretend with Max. But she—fucking cockeyed weirdo—wanted something *real* out of the impossible. If she would only—

His right ass cheek came alive, and he paused his internal rant to *What the fuck?* the series of gyrations going off in his back pocket. *Ah, his phone.* Messages arrived on his cell so rarely here in the middle of Sand Valley— Pakistan's Mobilink towers provided only spotty coverage—it took him an extra second to figure out what was happening.

Angling his body sideways, he pulled out his phone and checked the screen. He had three new messages.

His younger brother, Andy, was passing on the news that he'd received a raise at work. Andy had never gone to college like Kyle had, and he was now a welder in Chesapeake, Virginia.

Kyle's racquetball buddy, Tom, apparently hadn't heard that Kyle was deployed—Tom was trying to arrange a game at the North Island base gym...for last Wednesday.

The third message was—

Kyle's belly went sour. Teeth clamped, he hovered his thumb over the delete button for the message from Sienna. His thumb hovered, and...*fuck me.* He opened the message.

> What is WRONG with you Kyle? A MONTH AGO I asked u to talk to my cousin about joining the navy and u couldn't take 2 minutes out of ur stupid day to help him figure this out?! Now ur deployed and what is Michael supposed to do, huh???? Ur the most selfish inconsiderate man in the world. I hope u crash out there you prick!!!!

Oh, this was hilarious. *Bitch was calling* him *selfish.* Growling, Kyle shoved his phone back in his pocket. *Maybe I was gone on workups for the month before deploying, Sienna, you fucking battle-axe.*

He came off his cot in a burst of energy and stalked outside. He glared down two tents to number ten—Max's tent. Hell if he was going to let some pointed-chin, bleeding heart journalist ruin his record with women.

Head lowered like a charging bull, he took off, stomping his boots into his eternal nemesis—sand. The door to Max's tent was propped open, and he spied her inside, laid out on her cot with a book open in front of her face. He barged in with his hands already planted on his hips.

Battle ready? *Fuck, yeah.*

She tilted her head around the side of her book, saw who it was, then pushed to a sitting position. Her eyebrows arched high in question.

She wanted connection? He'd give it to her and then some, make her sorry for being an asinine realist. "You get ten questions, Max. *Ten.*" He raised the fingers of both hands to emphasize his point. "Ask anything you want to ask, then we're having sex. That's it." He sat down on HM3 Hart's cot and gestured Max to start. "Go."

Max's lips pursed and she eyed him with equal parts curiosity and amusement.

Kyle grabbed the edge of Hart's cot and felt wood splinter slightly beneath his fingers. He fucking *hated* that this woman was always looking at him like he was the world's most captivating specimen of dickified male, and she was oh-so-psyched to figure him out. Worse, he had the prickling, alarming sensation that she could excavate all kinds of secrets he didn't even know about himself. And the hell if he wanted that kind of exposure.

"Do you even like sex, Kyle?"

He stared a burning crater into her. What kind of idiotic question was that? "Everyone likes sex." He curled his upper lip, dialing up the dick-factor as he added some snark to, "Except you, apparently."

She just smiled patiently, which made him want to toss her headfirst down the latrine. The shout rang in his ears: *What does it take to rattle you?*

"Why do you have sex?" she pressed. "If not to share intimacy, then why?"

"Well, last I checked, Max, orgasms feel good. If you could stop analyzing the ethology of male-female bonding behavior long enough to shut up, maybe you could make the same discovery."

"Oh, I've had plenty of orgasms." She sighed a dreamy sigh and turned her eyes to the ceiling. "The best was with Brian Mulligan. He was on a swim scholarship at Stanford University, same as me, and, boy, did I fall cuckoo in love with him. It's what made it so good."

"Uh huh." How hugely, fucking annoying that she'd had great orgasms with another guy.

I asked you to back off a bit, and you did. So, you know, it was fine.

Kyle bared his teeth at her. *Fine!*

Or was it her having been in love with that Mulligan dildo that bothered him…

"Have you ever had sex with someone you cared about, Kyle? I mean, *truly* deeply liked? I'm telling you, it makes a difference."

He thought of Sienna, the only woman who'd ever been in his life longer than a week. He'd believed she was the one. As dysfunctional as their relationship was, he always imagined what was between them was love just trying to get better. But now, gazing into the bright blue halo of Max's eyes, he felt the wrongness of Sienna like choking hands around his throat.

He sneered. "You've used up half your questions," he informed her with malicious glee.

Max's chin tucked in. "How's that?"

"You asked me if I like sex; that's one," he said, ticking off her questions on his fingers. "Then two, why do I have it? Three, if not for intimacy, why? Four, have I ever had sex with someone I cared about? Then you confirmed with number five, 'truly liked?'"

She laughed. "I didn't know we'd started. Hmm, well,

okay. Would you like to have children someday?"

He rocked back on the bed like he'd been hit with a fast-moving fist. Heat slammed into his cheeks, then drained away as quickly, leaving him feeling slightly nauseous. *Damn this woman. Damn her!* "That's a question you ask a person you're thinking of marrying," he gritted out, "not just screwing."

"I think we've already established I don't *just screw.* Besides my one mistake, that is."

"Oh, so now I'm a *mistake,* am I?" He was back to squeezing the edge of the cot frame, more like clutching it.

She studied his expression.

He glowered at her.

"Make you a deal," she said. "I'll give you a blowjob if you exchange phones with me."

His eyebrows jerked up. *What the hell?*

She pulled her cell out of her small backpack and held it up. "I received some text messages a short while ago. I'm assuming you did, too. I show you mine, you show me yours, no more questions, and you get one of those impersonal orgasms you're so crazy about."

He showed her a full set of teeth. "You really know how to sell a guy on an idea."

"Is that a *yes?*"

CHAPTER FIFTEEN

KYLE DIDN'T ANSWER. Shoulda deleted Sienna's text.
*Just one reason—among twelve hundred others—
why you should press the delete key on your ex.*

Yeah, yeah, yeah, Universe, I get it. Fuck. Off.

"I'm not asking anything of you I'm not willing to give myself," Max added.

"Not necessarily," Kyle countered. "I could have something juicy on my cell while yours is merely filled with all the mundane details of your sexless life."

"True," she agreed, a note of humor entering her voice. "There is risk involved. So?" She jiggled her cell at him. "Yes or no?"

"Thing is, Max, you know *exactly* what's on your phone, don't you? No risk at all for you."

Her brows slanted. "Is that a *no*?"

He shifted. He was probably starting to look like a total chicken shit. "Well, hell," he drawled, "why not roll the dice?" He pulled his phone out of his pocket and handed it over. The text from Sienna didn't give away anything personal about him. Mostly, Sienna sounded like a haranguing bitch.

He took Max's phone and said in a purring Southern accent, "Hope you've got good gag-reflex control, sugah." He clicked open her recent messages.

Like him, she'd received three new ones today.

"Mom" texted a reminder about someone named Samantha—ah, that's right, Max was Samantha—needing to give a baby shower for Cousin Joanne, and don't forget to buy plane tickets back to DC in plenty of time.

Kevin—who Kyle remembered was Max's younger, adopted brother—said, *no*, he didn't want Max to do that! And, damn, if Kyle wasn't tempted to scroll back and find out what they were arguing about.

Finally, someone named Edward Aubrey wanted to know when Max was getting back to Los Angeles so he could have dinner with her. *Fucker.*

Kyle handed back her phone. "Who's Aubrey?"

A small smile touched Max's lips.

How fun it must be to play a game of peek-a-boo with his jealousy.

"My editor," she answered. "He wants to discuss another assignment." She handed back his phone. "Who's Sienna, and why hasn't anyone adjusted her medication?"

He rammed his cell away. "My ex."

"Oh? How long have you two been over?"

"Fuck if I know...about six years."

"*Years?*" She swayed back. "Jeez, Kyle, you're not very good at breaking up, are you?"

He narrowed his eyes. "I thought you said, I show you mine, you show me yours, and *no more questions.*"

"Hey, you opened the door by asking about Aubrey."

"Whatever." Kyle spread his legs wide and pointed at the floor between them. "Time to pay up. On your knees, pencil pusher."

Max rose.

He lifted his eyebrows at her in a mocking arc, his expression telling her that he totally knew she was going to back down.

Shock—she closed the door to her tent. Moving over to him, she lowered into a crouch between the vee of his legs and rested her hand lightly on his thighs.

His heart stopped, dropped, and rolled. She was actually going to do this?

"Take off your shirt," she said quietly. "I want to see your body."

His nipples snapped taut. Not from lust. He was scared of something here, scared shitless. He hooded his lids, hiding his eyes. "My dick isn't underneath my shirt, Max. For a woman who went to Stanford, I'd think you'd know that."

Her lips curved. "Do you know what I find fascinating about you?'

Everything, apparently, and *shut up.*

"It's really easy for you to drop your pants," she said. "How many times have you done that already in front of me? You can expose your dick, no problem. But you never take off your shirt. Because"—she leaned forward and gently placed a palm over his left pec—"it covers your heart."

Said organ thudded maniacally.

"It's either all of you or none of you." She dropped her hand back to his thigh and gave it a squeeze.

That explained his terror. There was no *all of Kyle* to give. His whole persona was smoke and mirrors, just a lot of strutting naval aviator over a black, bombed-out interior.

Her voice lowered to a whisper. "Off with your shirt, Kyle."

With panic dancing up and out of his throat, he grabbed Max by the upper arms and hauled her off the floor. Propelling her backward, he planted her on her cot, but stayed in close, leaning over her. "I can't figure out what's sadder about you," he snapped, a nasty edge entering his tone. "That you enjoy tearing people open and staring at their guts. Or that you analyze the hell out of a poor chump just to avoid directing your demoralizing powers of observation on yourself. What do you think you'd find, if you did, Max? Something you'd actually have to *face* and *feel*?"

Of course, she didn't react, pain-in-the-ass woman who—no, wait. She did. Her eyes widened, although it was more her pupils than the lids, which was why he'd almost missed it.

"Avoidance is why you became a journalist, right?" He chopped a hand out. "Always on the outside looking in, reporting about life, but never living in the true grit of it. Probably that's the same reason you're a swimmer—all around you there might be people thrashing about, but you just keep to your own lane, so fucking removed from it all. What happened to turn you into such a loner, Max? Huh? Did go-getting Mommy and Daddy spend more time at their lawyer jobs than with their precious daughter?"

Pay dirt.

Max's eyelashes quivered, just like they had in the back of the busted ambulance when she thought she'd been on the verge of capture.

Jesus, he should've known he was dealing with a fellow stray. Rich, poor, Black, white, lawyers, waitresses: shitty parents lived in every socio-economic strata.

He took a step back. "Here's an idea. Maybe instead of spinning your wheels figuring out everything yourself—*taking care of* everyone else—you could let someone else carry the load for a change."

"You don't think I want to?" she asked, her voice hollow and hoarse. "No one *ever* follows through."

He made fists of his hands, the old need howling to the surface of him; the persistent, soul-level need to be the kind of man who could shout *I can be there for you!* loud enough to shatter the front of her cell phone and the lens on her camera. Loud enough for someone, finally, to hear him, and believe.

But like the day she'd told him she honestly feared for her life on this mission, the words he wanted to say bunched up on his tongue, crumpled and died.

You're so undependable. Just like your father...

Ashes to ashes, dust to dust.

"Full heads up." His voice sounded detached, unfamiliar. "I'm not your follow-through person, either."

Her answer to that? Not bitterness. No disappointment. He only saw tender understanding on her face.

Fuck this shit. He strode out.

"Kyle!" Max followed him out of her tent.

He felt her palm on his forearm and stopped.

"I never got a chance to tell you..." she started breathlessly.

Stiffly, he turned and faced her.

"Thank you for saving me...the day in the ambulance...with ISI. Thank you."

He stared at her, at first blankly, then stunned.

She held his gaze, the uneven rise and fall of her chest emphasizing the fragility of the bones at the base of her throat, the delicate dip where her collarbones met.

His stomach clenched. As smart and brave as she was, she *did* need a whole man in her life, someone with his shit well enough together to make her feel like she could safely enter the fray.

He thinned his lips as regret laid a bitter hand on his soul. "You don't want *all of me*, Max," he lashed out. "No way. I'm only another poor, scruffy urchin you want to save, like Kevin, so you can feel better about yourself. So *stop* trying to connect to me." He gave the order tersely, then executed a military turn on his heel and gunned down the main road, his quick, choppy strides stirring up a cloud of dust that choked off his lungs and stung his eyes.

CHAPTER SIXTEEN

THE NEXT MORNING JEM called. This time, the terrorists wanted to transport Max themselves.

The deal was that at thirteen-hundred Max and her crew—which consisted only of Kyle now—would travel on foot to a designated cluster of squat trees out of firing range from the aid station's Pakistani guard.

There, Max and Kyle would wait for transportation to arrive.

It was twelve-thirty when they headed for the rendez-vous point, not talking while they clumped along in the sand together. She didn't know what Kyle was thinking, but she was having difficulty maneuvering around a giant warty toad of awkwardness.

Triumph should've been what she was feeling today, not clumsy and tongue-tied. Because yesterday she'd offered Kyle the chance for an easy blowjob, and he hadn't taken her up on it, just as, deep down, she'd suspected he wouldn't. Because deeper down she believed he really wanted something more with her, same as she wanted with him.

Yeah, funnily enough, she was no longer using the excuse of needing a connection with him to avoid a casual liaison or as a means to peel him apart. She was actually drawn toward the idea of a relationship with the sometimes-shithead/sometimes-not man.

Not only was Kyle Hammond a confident, professional naval aviator, a gun-slinging, sharp-shooting rescuer of innocents, and a man who could chat companionably with her, but he was also someone who could figure out the deeper parts of a person.

Boy, but he'd pegged her spot-on yesterday, as if he knew exactly what it was like to be a loner. He'd said things that on some level she already knew about herself; she *did* tend to stay on the outside of unpleasantness. But this was something she hated about herself—because failing to respond emotionally to certain situations made her sound subhuman. So she ignored it. Nice solution, right? Did wonders for her personal growth.

What she hadn't put together was why she was this way.

Did go-getting Mommy and Daddy spend more time at their lawyer jobs than with their precious daughter?

They had. So Max had learned to do everything for herself at a young age because that's what she'd been required to do.

Well, there ya go.

Come the day someone stepped up and helped, then maybe she could try to stop being that way. Until that day, she didn't see any reason to open herself up to more letdowns.

Kyle knowing all this about her wasn't exactly a thrill, so...awkward, awkward.

Sighing, she slung her backpack off and opened it. It was now emptied of everything except a notepad, a couple of pens, two granola bars, and a coffee thermos borrowed from Dr. Barr. She and Kyle had both left their phones behind, which put them a little short on comms. But it was better not to have a cell phone than to risk a terrorist getting his hands on it—cells contained too much personal information...as they'd both discovered yesterday.

I hope u crash out there you prick!!!!

Max's curiosity antennae had risen higher than ever after reading the text. What in the world led a man to keep a woman like that in his life?

Max and Kyle arrived at the cluster of squat trees and stopped.

Kyle set down his camera bag. His Beretta was back in its holster on his calf, and he was dressed again in cargo pants, T-shirt, and boots, all in shades of blah brown.

She was decked out in her full Pakistan-assignment clothes, but luckily it wasn't as hot as yesterday. The sky was ominous today, dark clouds glowering in the sky, the occasional dart of lightning dancing out of them, scenting the air with brimstone.

Kyle gazed at the horizon. "Well," he murmured, "we know what the Universe thinks about this mission."

Max didn't respond.

"You're awfully quiet today."

"Just focused." It was a half-truth. Pulling out her thermos, she gulped down some coffee.

"Have you ever considered taking your caffeine intravenously?" Kyle asked dryly.

She screwed the top back on. "I would if I could." Shoving the thermos away, she aimed her attention at the road. Her heart jumped over its next beat. Dust cloud.

Kyle saw it too. "Show time."

"Yep." JEM was coming.

A battered blue flatbed truck, dented in more places than not, with paint curling off the fenders, appeared out of the dust. There were two bearded men inside. The driver was bare-headed. The one in the passenger seat had on a white *taqiyah*, or skullcap—it looked like a straight-sided cloth bowl had been upended on his head. Both men were carrying rifles.

The truck pulled to a stop.

The skullcap man stepped out. He was wearing sandals and a traditional white *kameez* tunic over billowing *salwar* pajama bottoms. He leaned his rifle against the truck, then approached Max.

Without a word, he began to search her.

As a Westerner and a female, Max was little more than a second-class citizen to this terrorist, and the way his hands moved over her body wasn't exactly polite.

A scowl darkened Kyle's brow.

Skullcap finished with her and moved over to Kyle, first searching the camera bag. Max had left the GPS tracker back in her tent at the aid station, so Skullcap only found a movie camera, film, and various camera attachments. He then searched Kyle, and in two seconds he was yanking the Beretta from its hiding place. Raising the pistol high, he called out to his companion in a language Max didn't recognize as Urdu. Maybe Punjabi?

The driver climbed out of the truck and glared at Kyle. "What do you mean," he demanded in English, "by bringing a weapon?"

"We were ambushed the last time we were supposed

to meet you," Kyle answered in an even tone. "Carrying protection seemed like a wise precaution."

The driver narrowed his eyes for several beats. Finally, he nodded curtly at Skullcap.

The man tossed Kyle's Beretta to the driver, then he reached behind him and pulled something out of the rear waistband of his *salwar*.

Max's throat slammed closed when she saw what it was.

Two black hoods.

Kyle stated firmly, "No."

The driver gave Kyle a flat stare. "Then we go nowhere."

"Are you taking us to where you're holding the hostages?"

"No."

"Then there's no reason to blindfold us."

"We go to the safety of one of our compounds," the driver countered, "not for your eyes." He waited.

Max managed a discreet swallow. This was starting out nicely. "Let's get going."

A muscle flexed in Kyle's jaw.

The driver made a hard gesture at Skullcap.

Skullcap walked over to her.

She forced herself to stand still while he *whooshed* one of the hoods over her head. The moment her vision was stolen from her, her blood ripped through her veins at high velocity. The hood stank of someone else's fear and sweat—although the former might've been hers. Not the best smell in the world.

She heard Kyle growl, "Fuck."

Someone grabbed her arm and urged to walk in the direction of the truck.

Her waist hit a solid edge. She reached out and her fingers encountered the small metal knolls commonly found on the floor of a flatbed.

She was commanded to step, "Up!"

She did as she was told.

She heard Kyle climb in too. He settled next to her, leaning back against the side of the cab.

Her flesh icy, she scooted even closer to him.

"If they were going to kill us," he said quietly, "they would've done it already."

Maybe yes, maybe no. Daniel Pearl hadn't been killed immediately, so JEM could still have something in store for her and Kyle. But she didn't hear a gun being cocked or a beheading knife being unsheathed, so Kyle was probably right—for now at least.

The tailgate slammed shut, the truck doors closed, then the engine sputtered to life.

They pitched forward into motion.

As the truck gathered speed and the wind picked up, she caught a scent that was vaguely fecal. Chicken poop? Either this truck was generally used to transport fowl, or her hyped-up emotions were making her hallucinate smells.

"You okay?" Kyle asked softly.

She released part of the breath she was holding, the rest sticking in her constricted airway. Her pulse was rapid in her throat, but otherwise... "More or less."

He shifted slightly. "Not an optimal situation."

"It's not," she agreed. Her breathing made a *shish-*

shush sound against the hood. "I'm sorry."

"For what?"

"For getting you into this."

He snorted. "Just another day at the office for a Navy helo guy, so don't worry about me."

She lurched against the cab as they went over an uneven patch of road. "I thought we decided that I couldn't stop spinning my wheels worrying about everyone else."

She swore she could hear Kyle's lips snagging along the rough fabric of his hood as he formed a smile.

Thunder grumbled sullenly, like a giant's hungry belly.

Kyle found her hand and held it.

CHAPTER SEVENTEEN

THEY DROVE FOR more than an hour, and each minute that passed set Max's nerves more on edge.

She and Kyle were now far from home base, weaponless and without comms, and in the hands of a terrorist organization that had no compunction whatsoever about chopping off American heads. Didn't matter that she and Kyle still had their heads attached right now—the possibility still hovered. JEM might want media coverage to promote their cause, yes, but what if that amounted to blasting images all over the world of two more Americans getting their heads lopped off?

Not good. Any of it.

She had to hold onto the hope that JEM wanted to be interviewed. A headless journalist couldn't very well do that, could she?

The ride to their destination was bumpy—Pakistan's corrupt government didn't consider its infrastructure, like roadworks, a high priority—and by the time the truck finally stopped, Max's butt was sore.

From behind her hood, she heard conversation being exchanged between several male Pakistanis.

The tailgate slapped down. She was tugged out of the flatbed. Her feet hit the ground and her hood was jerked off.

Straightening her hijab, she blinked in the overcast light.

They were in a courtyard, surrounded by high, whitewashed stone walls that enclosed a wide area of dirt. Against the far wall was a two-story structure that was also made of white stone, but liberally decorated with stripes of blue tile, each corner of the structure rounded to resemble an attached tower. The roof was massively domed.

It was a Sufi shrine. She'd been to many.

Sufi shrines—each dedicated to a different Sufi saint—tended to be more tolerant and welcoming than many mosques, especially of women. Islamist extremists, however, considered Sufism to be in direct competition with their beliefs, and as a result, many Sufi leaders and shrines had come under threat or attacks from Sunni militant groups...like Jaish-e-Mohammed.

Clearly, this shrine had been overtaken by JEM.

"Looks like we've traveled south into northern Punjab," she said in a low tone to Kyle.

He was standing next to her, his hair mussed from the hood.

This is weird. She'd thought JEM was primarily located in India's southern Kashmir and Doda regions, not—

Kyle hadn't responded.

She glanced at him.

He was staring in a fixed way across the open area of dirt, an expression of black rage on his face.

She followed the direction of his gaze to where a group of armed Pakistani men were training. Their rifles *cracked* every time they practiced shooting a "person"—

human-shaped gunny sacks stuffed with hay that were hanging from upright poles.

She moved to stand directly in front of Kyle.

Skullcap and their driver were still talking to a couple of other men near the nose of the truck and so hadn't seen Kyle's expression yet.

"Kyle." She tugged on his arm. "Look at me."

His ferocious eyes lowered to hers.

"You need to wipe that expression off your face."

His upper lip quivered toward a sneer. "Those assholes are training to kill Americans... military men...*my* friends."

"I know. But you're not a Navy pilot today," she reminded him. "You're a cameraman, chasing a hot story. I need you to get in the game. Now."

His chest moved with a deep breath, but his dark fury remained.

Thunderheads roiled in the sky above him.

She gestured across the compound. "Do you think those young men could've been recruited to this training camp if their country hadn't betrayed them? They have no jobs, no hope for a future, probably little to no education or money. They've been let down time and again by a corrupt government and a culture that gives everything to the rich and well-connected and nothing to the poor."

A full sneer twisted Kyle's mouth. "You're *defending* what they do?"

"Of course not. I'm only saying there're two sides to every story."

His silver-blue eyes pierced through her. "Well, you're

way nicer than I am, Max, because the hell if I'm getting on the *understanding* boat about a bunch of terrorists."

"I'm not asking for your compassion. I'm just asking you to chill out."

She heard footsteps behind her. One of the Pakistani men was coming over.

Her anxiety skittered. "Please, Kyle…start pretending."

A relieved breath escaped her when Kyle's face morphed from black hatred into something closer to intensity…something that could pass for the expression of a jacked-up TV cameraman.

Their Pakistani driver appeared in front of them. "Go." He used his rifle to gesture them toward the Sufi shrine. "Abu Majid is inside."

They started for the two-story building, their driver dogging their footsteps.

The report of rifles across the compound sounded again, and a muscle flinched in Kyle's cheek.

Tension sat in a tight knot beneath Max's sternum.

Their threesome stepped inside the shrine. Walls of shocking white framed a man wearing flowing robes intricately embroidered with mauve, hunter green, and gold thread at the cuffs and collar. A dark beard reached down to the middle of his chest and a white turban covered his hair, several inches of fabric left to dangle over one shoulder.

On Abu Majid's right were two benches on either side of a rectangular table that was laden with plates of unleavened lavasa bread and an etched metal teapot surrounded haphazardly by eight or so turquoise teacups.

A few cups were half filled with a light pink drink, undoubtedly Kashmiri chai.

On Abu Majid's left was a small round table set beneath an arched wall enclave with a candle tucked inside it. On the table sat a closed laptop and a satellite phone.

Behind Abu Majid was a cadre of half a dozen men, heavily armed, dressed in the baggy pants and the black, high-top, "Cheetah" sneakers favored by terrorist fighters. Some were wearing *kufiyas*: a triangle of fabric held in place on the head with a braided circlet, same as a sheik might wear. Their eyes were narrow and mean in the way of experienced, hard-bitten soldiers.

Seemed like a totally unnecessary presence of force for a press meeting.

If this *was* a press meeting.

The knot in Max's chest went cold. Something wasn't right.

Their driver spoke to Abu Majid and held up Kyle's Beretta.

Abu Majid passed cool eyes over Kyle, then his gaze landed on her.

Her spine clenched. She suddenly felt like she was in a scary movie, a skeletal hand wrapped around her ankle, pulling her down to some unknown horror.

She kept going with the whole *pretend* plan, inclining her head to Abu Majid in a show of respect. "Good morning, sir, I'm Samantha Dougin from the *LA Times*, and this is Rick Sagget from CBS News. I'll be doing the written article on Jaish-e-Mohammed, and Mr. Sagget here will handle the filmed coverage of our interview."

Kyle unzipped his bag and placed it on the floor at his

feet, the camera peeking out. "Is this where you want me to set up?"

Before anyone could answer, Skullcap rushed inside the Sufi Shrine. He drew up next to Abu Majid and spoke quietly into his leader's ear, a worried expression on his face.

Max didn't hear much of the conversation, and understood even less, but she did pick out the words *problem* and *Taliban*. Were JEM's rivals stirring up trouble again? Would the drive back to the aid station be a rerun of the jeep attack?

Abu Majid waved off Skullcap, then barked something at his entourage.

The soldiers came out from behind Abu Majid and made a beeline for Kyle. One soldier's foot clipped the duffel bag, and Max heard glass splintering as the camera broke.

She frowned. *What's going—?*

Kyle took a startled step backward, but the soldiers grabbed him too fast, spinning him toward the picnic table and slamming him down on it, face up. The teapot shimmied and a couple of teacups rattled in their saucers.

Kyle spat out an expletive. His arm muscles bulged, but there were too many men holding him for him to get free.

A vein pounded frantically in her temple. "What are you doing?" she asked Abu Majid. "Mr. Sagget and I have come here in good faith."

"Have you?" Abu Majid inquired in a nasty drawl.

She didn't say anything, her mind racing over what JEM could've possibly found out.

If they discover the double-cross, then my head will, quite literally, roll. Yours, too, in all likelihood.

The hairs on the back of her neck stood on end.

"You were instructed not to involve the military," Abu Majid said in an arid tone.

Every nerve and cell in her body went on red alert. Had JEM uncovered Kyle's true identity? *But...how?* Was it because of the Beretta? "And I haven't broken those instructions," she lied. Unless...did several of the Pakistani guard from the aid station take it upon themselves to follow the battered truck?

"The men who ambushed you were shot with military-like precision," Abu Majid returned. "That means that either you are not who you say you are, or this man is not." Abu Majid pointed at Kyle. "I would guess *him.*"

One of the soldiers wearing a *kufiya* produced a knife and jammed the tip under Kyle's chin.

Kyle hissed and tilted his head back, angling away from the sharp point.

For a moment of surreal disconnection, the room drained of color, everything shuttering to black and white except...

Except for the slow, winding drizzle of blood working from the tip of the knife down the arched length of Kyle's throat, inking his beard red.

Max's stomach tried to drop into her feet, and her palms went clammy. From the start of this mission she'd worried about Kyle's life depending on how well she negotiated with JEM, and now here she was—at that exact pressure point.

"Richard Sagget is *ex*-military," she said, speaking in

the kind of deliberate syllables she hoped came across as careful patience and not what it really was: a struggle to keep her voice from giving out. "If you check his biography online, you'll see for yourself." And thank God she'd thought to include it.

Abu Majid said something in Punjabi. Not a stand-down order, unfortunately, or something like, *okay, that makes perfect sense.*

Two of the hard-bitten soldiers came at her.

Her breath shot out of her lungs in a startled cry as they grabbed her and pushed her onto the table next to Kyle.

Abu Majid spoke again in Punjabi.

Two men stretched Max's arms out wide. A third pressed the muzzle of his rifle against her right elbow joint.

Abu Majid said to her in English, "If I don't like what I hear from my man, you lose your arm."

She heard the mechanized *whir* of the laptop by the enclave booting up, and her intestines turned to water.

CHAPTER EIGHTEEN

K YLE FORCED HIS attention away from Max.
He couldn't keep his cool while watching her
eyelashes tremble, and he needed his brain on target right
now. He was officially classifying this mission as FUBAR.
Which meant it was time to go medieval on some terrorist
ass.

Maybe he hadn't been able to speak the words *I'm not
going to let anything happen to you* out loud, but that
didn't mean he was going to roll over and actually allow
anything to happen to Max.

Bad enough these dickwads were frightening her. If
they dared to do anything more, like…like…

His mind wrenched past his control, torqueing
around some pretty unpleasant thoughts.

Max's life would be totally hosed without a right arm.
She'd never be able to race the breaststroke again. She
wouldn't be able to work, or not as well, and…and…so
many other things. Made absolute sense that she was
scared shitless.

Across the room, fingers slowly struck laptop keys.
Click. Pause. *Click.* Pause.

Jesus, had no one ever taught that guy to—

A ferocious clap of thunder shook the building, and
Kyle bit back a curse. It was probably sheer dumb luck

that the man holding the rifle to Max's elbow hadn't startled and accidentally blown her arm off.

And the next time…?

Staring up at the ceiling with a strenuously manufactured expression of calm, Kyle used his periphery to mark where the men in the room were. Four soldiers were on him, two on Max, douchebag driver was the one henpecking the keys of the laptop like a stoned zoo chimpanzee, warlord Majid was by the back wall, and dude with the cloth Dixie cup on his head was just to Kyle's right.

Him. That's who Kyle would go for.

Dude was holding his rifle in a relaxed pose down near his waist. Not paying a whole lot of attention to anything but his own dick-dreams.

Douchebag driver finally stopped typing and spoke to Majid.

Majid blah-blah-blahed back in his own language, then pronounced in English, "You check out, Mr. Sagget."

Kyle was pulled upright.

In the next second, Max was set on her feet too. Her face was white, and her head scarf soaked with sweat.

Kyle ground his teeth. *I check out, do I? So, gee, now I'm just supposed to forgive and forget that you jabbed a knife to my throat and threatened to blow off the arm of a woman who's probably never even hurt a flea.*

Majid gestured at the duffel bag. "We may now begin the filming."

"No, we can't," Kyle snapped back, his lungs pumping heavily. He sucked in a deep breath, trying to calm himself. *You're not in the military today. You're just a cameraman, chasing a hot story.* And another breath. "One of your men broke our camera."

"Then go fetch another one, Mr. Sagget. We shall hold Ms. Dougin with us until your return."

Max swallowed so hard Kyle heard it.

The sound pushed him over the edge of what little restraint he'd managed to muster—which, admittedly, wasn't much. He was now classifying this mission as officially *done*, burnt-to-a-fucking-crisp done, because no way was he leaving Max with these assholes.

He spun right and punched Dixie Cup in the jaw, throwing all his weight into the hit. Dixie Cup staggered off his feet, and while he was sailing down to the floor, Kyle snatched the Kalashnikov rifle out of the guy's hands. Spinning again, he took several large steps toward the warlord, the rifle jacked against his shoulder, and aimed the snout right between Majid's eyes.

To quote a famous military man (Gomer Pyle): *Surprise, surprise, surprise!*

The whole switcheroo had lasted less than two seconds, and not a single bad guy got off a shot. That's what catching the enemy off guard will do for ya.

"The other men all have their rifles pointed at you," Max informed him.

Kyle's move on the warlord had put the rest of the terrorists behind him, still at the picnic table—besides douchebag driver over by the laptop—and Max was being his eyes.

Good ol' Max. She knew to watch his six without being asked.

Kyle drawled Southern style, "Hope no one has a

mind to get an itchy trigger finger, else Grandpappy Warlord here is gonna get his brains splatted all over the walls." For those who didn't speak English, Kyle pressed the snout of his rifle flush against Majid's forehead.

Kind of a universal language, that.

Kyle also gave Majid his most chilling sniper glare. "Tell your men to drop their weapons."

The warlord played stare-down with Kyle, never flinching away. *Not bad.* In scary-guy rankings, this one sat damned high up. Kyle would almost feel sorry for wasting the guy...well, if not for him being an asshole terrorist 'n' all.

Kyle inched a brow up. "No?" It sucked big time that the moment he shot Majid the other terrorists would try to gun him down. Kyle would have to duck and run and shoot like fuck to escape being killed and to save Max. "Alrighty then..." He slipped his right index finger from the trigger guard to the trigger itself.

A staccato burst of foreign language rushed from Majid's mouth.

Behind Kyle, weapons clattered to the floor.

"They've all dropped their rifles," Max confirmed.

Good. No shootout. "Leave the laptop," Kyle ordered douchebag driver, never taking his eyes off Majid, "and join your friends." From his periphery, Kyle saw the man obey. "Max, get my Beretta from that guy."

"Got it."

Be nice if he could also ask her to confiscate the discarded rifles, but there were too many, and not enough time to deal with the pile—he and Max needed to get gone already. A bunch of armed trainees were just outside, and one or some could waltz in here at any minute and start complicating matters.

But that also meant that he and Max couldn't just stroll out of here. The moment they headed outside, the bad guys would just pick up the discarded rifles and follow them out. And that would put him and Max back at square one.

Guess our time with Warlord Dickbrain isn't over yet.

Grabbing Majid by the back of the tunic, Kyle prodded the metal nose of his rifle under the guy's bearded chin. "Let's go." He headed for the door, Max keeping pace.

The other men started jabbering at once.

Kyle couldn't understand a word, but it was a pretty sure bet they weren't happy with their top banana being kidnapped.

Kyle took a cautious step outside, checking across the compound.

For once the U offered up a benny—the trainees were on break from killing gunny-sack people. Or maybe they'd graduated to classroom work...*Homemade Back-pack Nukes* or *DIY Suicide Bomber Belts*.

Thank crap, was all, that he didn't have to deal with more baddies.

They crossed the compound and arrived at the Hilux truck, the piece-of-shit vehicle that had transported them here.

"You drive," Kyle told Max.

Max opened the driver's side door, tossed in Kyle's camera bag and her backpack, then jumped behind the wheel.

Kyle jerked open the passenger side door and shoved Majid into the middle seat.

Men were gathering outside the white building—all re-armed now, of course.

Looked like this day was probably going to end in a shootout after all. He hopped into the truck and banged the door shut. "Do you know where you're going?"

"I hope so." Max started the engine.

Superb. A more confident response would've been preferable.

"If we're in Punjab—which I think we are—we need to head north. But…" Max peered at him across the front of Majid. "E-way on't-day ave-hay uch-may as-gay."

Kyle paused a beat, lowering his eyebrows at her, then—*ah.* She'd spoken to him in Pig Latin so that Majid wouldn't understand.

Kyle rearranged the words in his head and came up with: *We don't have much gas.* Extrapolating further, he figured her real gist was: *We don't have enough gas to get back to the aid station.*

Superb again.

Kyle yanked out the rifle's magazine and checked it. This Kalashnikov was an AKM—a lighter version of the AK-47—with a thirty-load capacity. *But yeah.* Didn't matter how many bullets a firearm could hold if the damned thing wasn't loaded with them.

And this AKM only had three bullets.

And the good times just keep on keepin' on!

Kyle slammed the magazine back in. "My Beretta?"

Max dug the pistol out of her backpack and handed it to him.

The Beretta was carrying a full clip, raising his ammunition total to eighteen rounds. *Eighteen*, against a buttload more terrorist firepower that would be driving up his booty as soon as this truck sputtered to a stop. He was also less than thrilled about a pistol's range of accuracy.

A shame he hadn't thought to grab a few of those discarded rifles.

Max put the truck in gear and drove through the open gate.

Too late now.

CHAPTER NINETEEN

KYLE PROPPED THE AKM between his thighs and thrust the nose of the Beretta into Majid's side. "In case you haven't guessed it by now, dickhead, you've forfeited your right to media coverage. Ms. Dougin and I have nearly been killed twice dealing with you, so we're moving right to the hostage exchange.

"Here's how it's going to go: You'll bring the hostages to the front of the aid station tomorrow at thirteen hundred—to the same bunch of short trees. I don't want to see more than four of your men at the meet. You'll remain back several yards while Ms. Dougin and I thoroughly inspect the hostages. Once we have proof of their well-being, we'll contact the US Government, and you'll be given instructions for how to exchange the hostages for your men in Guantanamo. Is that clear?"

"Yes," Majid ground out.

If looks could kill, Kyle would be pushing up daisies right now. The warlord was clearly more than a mite miffed over—

Thunder boomed, cracking loud enough to wake Australia.

Max startled and gasped.

A jagged fork of lightning sheared open the sky, thunder cracked again, and rain pissed down.

Kyle peered through the windshield at the darkened sky. *Wonder what kind of message the U is trying to send with this.*

Max flicked on the wipers and leaned forward against the steering wheel, squinting at the road ahead. The wipers were swatting ineffectually at the—

A right turn appeared with no warning through the concealing downpour.

"Crap!" Max hit the brakes, skidding through the turn. The left-hand tires threw up sheets of muddy water, and she gasped again "Oh, God!" She'd barely made it. "Sorry, Kyle, but I have to slow down."

He gave her a brusque nod, then checked the road behind them in the side mirror. *Any minute now...*

Max's grip was knuckle-white on the steering wheel. "I'd give my eye teeth for a Denny's to stop at and wait out this rain."

Annnnd here they are. Two trucks appeared on their six o'clock, both packed to the gills with baddies.

Kyle tightened his grip on the Kalashnikov. *Eighteen bullets versus two trucks' worth of assholes.* Wonder what kind of odds he'd get in Vegas for coming out on top of this inevitable confrontation. Ten to one? He scrunched his toes back and forth against the sand in his boots. Twenty...?

A tense, silent hour later, their truck gave several warning chugs.

Majid's head came up.

Kyle kept his focus on the side mirror. "Got any idea how far we are from the aid station right now?"

Max studied the odometer. "Judging by how far I estimate we originally drove to get to the Sufi shrine, I think we've got approximately ten more miles to go."

Majid smiled, his teeth flashing white against that fucking Hermit of the Mountain beard he wore.

"The turnoff to Saaneh is just up ahead," Max added. "If we continue due east on that road, we'll hit home."

"Stop short of the turnoff where the trees are thickest," Kyle instructed, pointing to the spot. "Over there. See?" He wouldn't go so far as to call the forest *thick*, but enough trees were around to offer some degree of concealment. Definitely a helluva lot better than open land. "We'll make the rest of the journey on foot." Unhooking his seatbelt, he passed the strap behind his back, transferring it from his right hand to his left, then used it to tie Majid's wrists together.

Max glanced dubiously at what he was doing.

Yeah, they were leaving behind their assurance of safe passage. "This asshole will just slow us down," Kyle explained.

The truck jerked and coughed.

Max pulled to the side of the road.

The truck was still drifting to a stop when Kyle stepped out, rain drenching him the moment his boots hit the muddy road. He leveled the Kalashnikov at the oncoming trucks.

Both braked to a halt about a hundred yards away.

"Go!" he called out to Max.

She jumped from the truck, leaving the camera duffel behind but shouldering her backpack. She took off into the trees.

A couple of baddies started to get out of the lead

truck.

Kyle fired a warning shot. One headlight on the lead truck exploded.

The baddies got back inside.

Kyle began to walk backwards, keeping his rifle aimed at the baddies. When he reached the tree line, he lowered his weapon, turned, and ran.

Max was already about half a dozen yards ahead, weaving between tree trunks.

He didn't hear any sounds of pursuit, but he didn't slow. He wouldn't find his happy place again until Max was safe inside the aid station.

So, they ran...

He gave Max mondo points for being a tough cookie. She kept up a steady jog for a full hour through the ceaseless rainfall before asking to rest.

"Sorry," she panted. "I'm a swimmer, not a runner." She slung off her backpack. "Although all this rain makes me feel like I'm swimming."

"You're doing great," he told her. "We've been running for a full hour straight."

She collapsed onto her butt in the wet sand.

Kyle stood next to her, rain funneling off his head and rolling down his shoulders. The trees had petered out awhile back, so there wasn't anything to offer even a modicum of shelter. Good thing he hadn't been a door-kicker back in the days of Vietnam. He wasn't sure he could've dealt with the endless monsoons those guys had faced.

Because this blew.

He tried to scrunch his toes, but water had soaked

through his boots and bonded with the sand in them, creating a clay-like substance that glommed onto his feet. He rubbed the stinging spot under his chin where that JEM shit-stick had dug a knife in, then skated his fingers over the old scar running the left side of his jaw.

His jaw must give off a beacon for bad guys to cut.

Only good thing he could say about this tropical storm was that it'd cleansed Pakistan of its normal odor, the stench of arid ground, stale garbage, and decomposing lives, and left behind the scent of nature, spices of the earth, and crisp air.

He checked on Max.

Her forearms were propped on her knees and she was hanging forward between her legs. The points of her shoulder blades thrust up against the blue and white-striped blouse that was plastered to her body. Her head scarf was likewise glued to her skull.

And the rain just kept pelting her.

She started to shiver.

"Do you think you can get going again now?" he asked.

Lightning forked across the sky, followed immediately by a thunder bomb.

Max pressed her palms to her head.

"We're almost there, Max. The aid station is just over this ridge." He recognized it from the day he'd flown in.

She straightened and reached into her backpack. "I need calories first." She pulled out two granola bars and held one up to him.

He took it. Lunch had been hours ago.

She found her thermos and took a couple of deep

draws on it.

Unwrapping the granola bar, Kyle scanned the area through the haze of water in his eyes, his nerves still balled up. The dark clouds were so low they touched the horizon. Electricity zigzagged across the wall of gray.

Dusk was falling, and he'd rather throw his dad a Father of the Year party than be wandering around northern Pakistan after dark.

He ate quickly.

CHAPTER TWENTY

THEY WALKED THE rest of the way and passed through the aid station gate just as the storm-tossed sky turned from purple to charcoal.

Kyle handed the Kalashnikov to the astonished Pakistani sentry. The man peered out from the hood of his dripping slicker at the blood on Kyle's shirt collar with eyes the size of fried eggs.

Kyle led Max down the camp's main footpath, now reduced to a soggy bog. Deep mud sucked at their boots, and water rushed along small trenches on either side of them as if pushed by turbines.

He hopped the gutter in front of his tent, then helped Max over and urged her inside. He flipped on the light.

"You have a *b-bed*? No fair." She hugged her trembling body. "I only have a freaking cot."

"Officers' quarters," he said simply, maneuvering her out of her backpack. He left that and his Beretta on a shelf by the door. Stepping close to her again, he smoothed her headscarf off. "You look soaked as a rabbit I once pulled out of a drainpipe when I was a kid."

She turned her face up to him and met his eyes.

A spot warmed in his chest. He'd bet this was what she looked like after a swim. He could see her now, climbing out of a pool with her lithe body shedding water, her hair slicked back like it was now, highlighting the perfect shape of her small head—her chin suddenly didn't seem so pointy. More like expressive, same as the arc of her eyebrows and the delicate slant of her cheek-bones. A lump wedged into his throat. She was...very pretty, actually.

Another shudder ran through her. "I don't know why I'm shaking s-so much," she chattered. "It's humid out."

"It's also the aftereffects of adrenaline."

She gave him a sickly smile. "Yeah. I didn't much care for almost having my arm blown off."

He gave her his best attempt at a return smile. He hadn't particularly liked that part either.

"Those black hoods also sucked."

He hauled in a deep breath, "The day as a whole blew chunks."

Thunder clapped, reverberating through the canvas walls of the tent.

She jumped. "That's getting old too."

"Let's get you out of these wet clothes."

She stepped back from him and tried to unbutton her blouse, but her fingers were trembling too much.

He tossed her headscarf into a corner of the tent and took over the job.

She peered at him from beneath her lashes. "You're not shaking."

He smiled. "I'm a shake on the inside kind of guy." He pushed her blouse off her shoulders and sent it the way of her headscarf, then crouched down and untied her boots.

She wedged her feet out of them.

He undid her jeans, but she peeled them down her own legs and stepped free.

He stared at her for an arrested moment, nothing but his heartbeat between them. He was very aware that she was only in a bra and panties, but he never let his focus stray below her neck. His periphery picked up the jut of her nipples against her bra, and, oddly, the sight just made him worry about her still being cold.

He moved to the clothesline strung across the foot of Jobs' bed—although Steve had only slept in it once—and yanked a towel off it. He handed it to her.

While she dried off, he stripped down to his skivvies.

She offered the towel back to him, her gaze traveling over his bare chest.

You never take off your shirt, because it covers your heart...

His pulse slowed. He'd never felt quite so naked as he did right now, even with his underwear on. But by his next breath he realized...*it's not so bad.*

Not with her, at least.

"Why don't you hop under the covers?" he suggested. "Warm up."

"In a *real* bed?" She gusted a breath. "You don't have to ask me twice." She scooted into his bed and rolled onto her side, her back to him.

He stared at her for a long moment, just studying the fine contours of each vertebra in her spine, the length of it divided in unequal halves by her bra strap. She was lying in a position of such open trust, the sight humbled him.

Dropping his underwear, he patted his body dry, wiped the glop off his feet, which took a fair amount of effort—fucking sand—then climbed in next to her. Her flesh was chilly as a Budweiser bottle rooted from the bottom of an ice chest.

Naked-on-naked would be the best and quickest way to warm her up—not a tactic, blunt fact—so he unhooked her wet bra and slipped it off. He tucked his fingers into the back waistband of her underwear, paused—no protests? *Okay*—then gently tugged off her panties. He chucked both bra and undies into an unknown area of his tent.

He hauled the blankets up, creating a warm cocoon around them, and pulled her against the curve of his body, wrapping his arms around her. Her petite body was actually a solid weight in his embrace.

Another pleasant surprise.

Her breathing changed rhythm, not by much, but he was attuned to any response.

Was she reacting to his nakedness? Or nearness? Or both?

Was she breathing heavier because of the prod of his hard dick against her?

Yeah, his organ had taken notice of the soft curve of her bare rump.

He felt a low hum of tension in her, like maybe she was wondering what he planned on doing with it.

He murmured against her nape, "Thing has a will of its own."

Because sex was the furthest thing from his mind right now, and not only because she'd put her trust in him, but because just holding her was somehow better than sex. Well, okay, maybe not *better*, but really good.

This was comfort and contentment and—ah, hell, the bright rings of Max's eyes would go extra-shiny over this one...

Connection.

This suck-o day of black hoods and rifles and rain had added more building blocks onto the foundation of connection that Max had somehow slipped in under his radar.

When I was nine years old, I asked my parents for a baby brother for Christmas...

How lonely were you growing up, Max? As lonely as I was?

No one ever *follows through...*

I read you loud and clear on that one, honey.

And now here they were, cozied up...and making him question his belief that the female and male species could never truly connect.

Kyle held Max closer and buried his nose in her hair. She smelled like rain and cherries.

Minutes slid easily by.

The two of them warmed; their bodies relaxed.

His cock settled down, along with the fury of the heavens. Rain fell in only faint patters now.

Max slept in his arms.

She was okay. He'd gotten her back to the aid station in one piece, and... He pressed his eyes closed. And somehow that gave him the right to stand up and say, *I'll be here for you, Max.*

And it would be *real.*

Fuck anyone who doubted it. Screw Sienna, first and foremost, for never giving him a pittance of credit for anything he'd ever done.

Hell, Max *already* believed in him.

It's either all of you or none of you... Like she totally knew there was an *all of him* to give. He wasn't just some scruffy unfortunate to save, but a man worth connecting with.

Thank you for saving me...the day in the ambulance...with ISI. Thank you.

See? You are *that man.*

The Universe spoke to him with such tranquil, golden wisdom, Kyle couldn't figure why he'd never listened before. A distinct full sensation inflated his chest.

Thank you back, Max.

Chapter Twenty-One

KYLE ROLLED OVER on the mattress and slowly lifted his eyelids. Rumpled sheets, empty bed…

Quieting his breathing, he homed in on sounds and got what he knew he would—silence.

No one was in his tent.

Bam! He was back to being a googolplexian-level idiot…not that he'd ever truly graduated from that illustrious status.

He stared at his tent's blank canvas wall. *Fuck me.* He should just stay in bed all day, contemplate how incompetent he was at reading people and situations. At relationships. Problem with that plan was that he was hungry. Last night's dinner had consisted of a single granola bar, and his stomach was complaining about it. *All right.* Eat breakfast first, then crawl back in bed and do a lot of feeling sorry for himself.

Yeah, perfect plan.

Kyle pushed to a sitting position on the edge of his bed and scrubbed a hand over his face, rasping his beard. He'd be able to shave the damned thing off soon. *If* JEM didn't foul anything else up, the mission would be over in the next day or two—and then Max Dougin would be out of his life.

Good riddance. He didn't need any more women

complicating his life.

Standing, Kyle dug into his duffel bag and dressed in whatever his hand grabbed first. All the clothes he'd brought to Pakistan were the same, anyway. He crouched down next to his trashed boot. These suckers were going to need a good cleaning before he could—

And then he saw it.

A note.

Folded neatly in half, it was laying where it'd tumbled off Max's pillow.

He stared at it. Was it real?

He walked over, plucked it off the bed, and unfolded it.

Max had written in clear script:

> *You don't snore.*
> *Your breath smells good, even first thing in the morning.*
> *And you're to-die-for cozy to sleep against.*
> *The rain stopped and I had to pee, but any time you want a bed buddy, I'm in.* ☺
> *Max*

He circled his jaw against a swift surge of emotion.

Max hadn't bailed.

She'd *followed through* and left him a note.

I had to pee... He chuckled, although the noise came out more like a watery hiccup. The note sounded like her. It was a really nice note. He read it three times, and a huge, wide-open space opened inside his chest, unlocking to...possibilities.

Grinning like a lunatic, he leaned over to the small

table by his bed and grabbed his wallet. He refolded the note and tucked it inside. After this mission was over, he and Max would probably go their separate ways, but he was going to secretly keep this note forever. Because something had happened to him with it just now. He didn't know what. But something.

A sudden frown pulled at his brows. *Go their separate ways...* Well, hell. Now the idea of Max soon being out of his life felt like crap.

A knock sounded at his door. "It's me," Max said.

At the sound of her voice, his heart tumbled over itself. Thaaaaat had never happened before. "Come in."

She stepped inside, holding two coffee mugs.

Their gazes caught and held.

Kyle almost started squirming. Max's look of affection was probably the best thing he'd ever seen. Scratch *probably.* It flat-out *was.* "Hey, how are you doing? You get your bathroom issues sorted out?"

Laughing, she handed him one of the mugs. "I made quite a sight this morning, sneaking to the latrine in clothes that were still damp and wrinkled beyond redemption."

He smiled. Damn, he would've loved to have seen her. She probably made a totally cute ragamuffin. "Sorry. I wasn't exactly thinking about laying out your clothes nicely yesterday, just getting you warm."

The brighter blue of her eyes twinkled at him. "You certainly succeeded in that."

He blew on the surface of his coffee. He might be blushing a little.

"You must've woken up this morning feeling like a

pod creature, Kyle. You had a naked woman in your bed last night and you only *slept* with her. Wow."

He lifted one corner of his mouth. "Didn't think I had it in me, did you?"

"Actually, I knew. I wasn't sure you did."

Full-on blush now. *Max already believes in me.*

"Did you get my note?" she asked.

"I did." He cleared his throat. "Thank you."

"So how do you manage that fresh breath thing?" She flared her eyes in mock amazement. "I mean, seriously, it's remarkable."

His chest warmed, and a laugh jostled out of him. "I have no idea." And if this Max was the real flirt, he much preferred her to the woman he'd met at the Jebel Ali Club. Because this Max was being playful and genuine with a man she clearly really liked.

Ha, that's me.

"I have a favor to ask," she said.

"Name it."

"If I get any bright ideas about going on a ten-mile run in the near future, will you put the kibosh on that?" She blew out her cheeks and crossed her eyes. "My legs are killing me."

He chuckled. "Roger that." Skimming his focus down her legs, it hit him then that he could *see* her legs—she was wearing shorts. He snapped his eyes back up. "Why are you dressed in the clothes you wear when you're not leaving the aid station? Don't we have a meet scheduled today at thirteen hundred?"

She sipped her coffee. "My JEM contact called this morning and asked to come tomorrow instead. He said the hostages are too far away to bring them here by this afternoon."

"Too far?" he repeated skeptically. "The JEM compound in northern Punjab was only an hour away."

"Right. And JEM's usual hangout—India's southern Kashmir and Doda region—is even closer. This does seem a bit outside of the box."

"What do you think is really going on?" He took a large gulp of coffee. *Ouch*, it was still too hot. "They spooked?"

"Maybe."

"Shit, I'm sorry, Max. I blew this."

She looked at him over the rim of her mug.

"Yesterday, Majid had just confirmed that Rick Sagget checked out," he said. "Things were chilling, and we could've pressed ahead, but I…" *I threatened to blow Majid's brains out.* He shoved his fingers through his hair. "I just couldn't leave you alone with those assholes."

"You did okay, Kyle. You arranged a proof of well-being inspection, which is what we need to get in close enough to hand off the GPS tracker to one of the hostages." She gave him a small smile.

"Yeah, but fat lotta good that does if JEM doesn't even bring the hostages to us."

"My sense is that they'll bring them," she said. "The thing to consider is that JEM might be buying time to put another plan in motion. A double-cross to counter ours? A betrayal of some sort? We won't know until they drop it on our heads."

"Great."

She shrugged. "We don't have any other choice but to

press ahead. No matter what JEM throws at us, passing the GPS tracker to a hostage is still key to the mission."

"Yeah. Roger that." He exhaled. "So...again, we wait."

"Again, we wait."

He drank more coffee. "Have any ideas how we might fill the time?" He smirked at her, but the expression felt more teasing this time than out-'n'-out dickified male.

She twinkled at him again. "Actually, I do."

Oh, this oughta be good. "Yeeees?"

"I want to ask you out."

"Out where?"

She rolled her eyes. "On a date. To dinner."

"Share a table with you in the mess tent?" *Hehehe.*

"Hmmm, no. I want to cook for you."

"Yeah?" He dropped the cocky expression as eagerness took over. The saying *the way to a man's heart is through his stomach* had been invented for a guy like him.

"I've arranged with the mess cooks to borrow a corner of the kitchen to make some fried chicken. I figure no self-respecting Southern boy could refuse a good home-cooked meal."

He laughed. *Fried chicken!* Wasn't it cute how she thought she had to convince him? Still...it might be fun to play a little hard-to-get. "How good is the fried chicken we're talking about?"

Her lips twitched. "Extremely."

"Count me in, then."

She cupped her mug in one hand and smiled. "My tent. Eighteen hundred. Kitty will be in the post-op ward tending to patients till nine."

"I'll be there." His taste buds were practically dancing already.

"See you then." She turned and left.

He stood still for a second, just staring at the back of his door, then—*hot damn!* Setting down his coffee mug, he rushed over and grabbed his boots. He was going to have to get these bad boys cleaned up, and, crap, he wished he had other clothes to wear besides desert rat garb. Maybe his flight suit? No. That would be weird. And a gift of some sort... He needed something nice to bring to Max.

Stepping outside his tent door, he upended his boots and clacked them together to knock all the muck out. He *whatever'd* the sand this time, though.

He was back to grinning like a lunatic.

CHAPTER TWENTY-TWO

KITTY SHIVERED AS Steve's lips found her throat, his warm breath caressing her flesh. His kisses graced a path to the ticklish shell of her ear, and her nipples puckered up so tight she almost moaned. That would've been a bad thing.

Just outside the supply tent, all manner of activity was going on, folks bustling hither and yon with the day's chores. Anyone could mosey in here and catch her and Steve at any moment…though a part of her couldn't give a fiddle.

It felt so darned nice to be wanted and liked, especially by a man of such high quality. And there was no doubt he liked her—aside from the obvious part of him kissing her.

Eight days had passed since Steve was injured, long enough for him to have healed and then returned to the tent he shared with Lieutenant Hammond.

But he hadn't left the post-op ward.

He'd stayed, living in a pair of scrubs, and she didn't see any reason for him doing that other than to stay close to her. Which was real sweet, and, admittedly, she'd taken full advantage, spending time with Steve every chance she got.

They played cards together and did crosswords, and

no matter what, talked and talked. He was the easiest man to just sit and jaw with, none better. One of her favorite things to do was watch him fix stuff, and so after he'd finished repairing the autoclave, she took him here to the supply tent to see if any other mechanical thingamajigs might be tucked away in need of mending.

As she opened a large wooden cupboard, Steve had moved up behind her, turned her around, and just planted his lips on hers, close-mouthed and awestruck. Awkward by a bit, too, which he must've cottoned on to because he almost immediately moved on to kiss her neck. Which felt mighty fine, and she sort of wished she didn't have to stop him, but...

Her always hungering after love was one of the things that got her into the most trouble. Sam Faulk, Brady Collins, Ron Divins, Clete Randall...they'd all wanted her, and look how they'd turned out.

"Steve," she whispered.

He lifted his head and gazed down at her with a look she'd seen plenty of times on men—the look of a fella wanting a woman.

Her belly twisted. "This thing you're trying to start between us has nowhere to go."

His face tightened. "Don't keep saying that."

"Well, our situation hasn't changed none."

He exhaled and stepped back. "First off, I'm not in a position of power over you, so your officer-versus-enlisted argument doesn't apply."

Well, that was just plumb silly. "Last I checked, I still have to salute you."

A muscle jumped in his lean cheek. "I don't write

your evaluations, and I don't hold any sway over your advancement in rate. So I have an idea, Kitty—why don't we just not tell anyone about us? Believe me, we wouldn't be the first officer and enlisted couple ever to get together."

True enough, but... "If we get caught, things will go worse for you than me." They'd both be sent to Captain's Mast, but people in positions of leadership tended to get punished harder for misconduct. "If you go to Mast, it could ruin your career."

"You let me worry about that."

She sighed. He was being so doggone determined and heartfelt that she didn't know how she was going to keep telling him *no.* Maybe she should try out a relationship for a day or two...? *Ugh. Listen to you go on.* "Right now, I got all kinds of excuses sounding in my head, trying to talk me into saying yes."

"Good."

"No, Steve, not good. I... Look, I'm also sort of on shaky ground here. I don't have the best decision-making abilities when it comes to men, and this here's a perfect instance, with me trying to cover my eyes to a wrong situation because I like you so danged much."

Sam Faulk, Brady Collins, Ron Divins, Clete Randall...the hurt those boys had caused her was *nothing* compared to the pain her one long-term relationship with Shane Madden had brought her. She'd been *so sure* that the Navy SEAL was heaven-sent, only to have him pert near give her frost bite with how cold he was.

"Not Larson Holmes," Steve said.

"What?"

"You knew the weasel was a bad choice for you, and so you got yourself out of it."

She opened her mouth, closed it. "But...that's different. I didn't actually date Larson."

"It's not different," Steve countered. "It's an example of you using sound judgment and good decision-making skills."

She pulled her eyebrows together. That'd felt like pure survival instinct, not—

"Why can't you believe that, Kitty?" he pressed. "Why are you so determined to see yourself in a bad light?"

"I..." Her lips trembled, cutting off the rest of her sentence.

She's a dimwitted child. Always has been...

She looked down at the floor with stinging eyes, memories of mocking laughter ringing hollowly in her ears. Had anyone *ever* thought well of her? When she finally managed to summon her voice, it was a mere whisper. "I just don't know how many more mistakes I have left in me, Steve."

"I'm not a mistake," Steve came back. "I *won't* be. I'll make you a great boyfriend."

Boyfriend? She looked up. He didn't merely want a quickie affair, but a...relationship?

"I know those other jerks you dated didn't take good care of you, but I'm not like that. Please, Kitty, just give me a chance to show you."

She swallowed, her throat muscles doing a shaky job of it. An urge niggled at the back of her mind: *trust him!* But a contrary voice arrived right on its heels, warning her that once again she was wanting too danged much for a fella to love her.

Steve licked his lips. "I've never been a boyfriend before, so I don't know what to do or say to make you believe me. I just know I'll be a good one."

She gazed into his earnest eyes. Gads, she was as confused as a cow on Astroturf, he was being so—"Wait." She blinked. *Never?* "You've never been with a girl *at all*, like in, uh…"

Steve blushed such a deep shade of red his freckles disappeared.

Oh, my. Kitty bit into her bottom lip. *Butter my butt and call me a biscuit.* Lieutenant Steve Whitmore was a virgin.

CHAPTER TWENTY-THREE

FIVE MINUTES TO six o'clock…
Max was ready.

She'd borrowed a small card table and two folding chairs from supply and erected them in the middle of her tent, then put a white bedsheet on as a tablecloth. That looked more clinical than romantic, though, so she'd laid one of her blue hijabs over the top of the sheet. Two place settings from the kitchen and a votive candle from Kitty rounded out the scene.

Three large bowls sat center table, covered with napkins to keep everything warm until Kyle—

A knock.

Max smiled. *He's early.*

She opened the door, and—lifted her brows high. Wow, he looked spiffy. His beard was trimmed, his hair neatly combed, and he smelled really good. "This date warranted you taking a shower, did it?" She smiled playfully. "Impressive."

"Only the best for fried chicken."

Not for *her*, but for *fried chicken*. She laughed—he was only playing back. "Nice to know where your priorities lie."

He winked. "Here, I brought you these." Deadpan, he held out a bouquet of—

Another laugh launched itself out of Max. He'd made a bouquet of flowers out of cotton balls glued to the ends of tongue depressors. "That is the coolest thing ever!" She took the bouquet and pretended to sniff it.

Tiny lines speared out from the corners of his eyes. "Since there isn't a flower for a hundred square miles, I had to get inventive."

Some of the flowers were the white of the cotton, but others were orange. "Where did you get the orange dye?"

"It's iodine."

"Oh, God, I love it! Well, come on in." She angled out of the doorway so he could enter. "You've definitely earned your home-cooked meal with these."

Chuckling, he came inside and sat in the folding chair closest to Kitty's cot.

She stuck the bouquet in a coffee mug and placed it in the center of the table.

He watched her, a pleased expression on his face, then he looked up, catching and holding her gaze.

Her heart danced a strange sidestep. There was something deep and meaningful in the way he was looking at her, same as this morning when she'd come to his tent bearing mugs of coffee.

She drew in a deep breath. That *something more* she sensed he wanted from her seemed stronger than ever.

In her too. Yesterday, Kyle had taken such tender care of her, spending the whole night holding her—only sleeping with her, not *sleeping* with her—she couldn't help but feel moved by it.

He smiled. "And here's a more practical gift." He offered her a small bottle of lotion.

"What? More?" She took the lotion. The label was written in both English and a language that looked like Arabic. It'd been made in Iran and was scented with lavender and rosemary.

"I got it off Doctor Barr," he said.

"So many gifts!" She unscrewed the bottle and held it to her nose, inhaling a satisfying whiff. "This is wonderful. Thank you." Secretly, she preferred his handmade bouquet. It'd obviously taken a great deal of effort to make, and he'd done it for *her*. She set the lotion on the shelf next to her cot. "Damn, Kyle, now the pressure's really on for my fried chicken to be good."

The lines near his eyes lengthened. "Hey, you're a Virginia gal. I'm sure you know what you're doing." His focus latched onto the napkin-covered bowls. "It sure as hell smells great. Let's eat."

She chuckled. Maybe it was silly of her to be so tickled over his eagerness for her cooking, but she was. "Alrighty, here goes." She whisked the napkin off the biggest bowl, releasing more great smells. "Golden fried chicken."

Kyle's eyes lit up. "Ho-leee shit."

"Next—" She ceremoniously removed another napkin. "Homemade biscuits."

He whistled low on his breath. "Would you take a look at those."

She smiled so widely the expression hurt her cheeks. "I made a dozen, but the mess cooks took half as payment for my kitchen time."

"Fuckers," Kyle growled, but good-naturedly.

"Finally, fruit salad." The last napkin came off. "Del

Monte Fruit Cocktail from a can, so less spectacular than the rest, but there wasn't any fresh fruit. Sorry."

"Are you kidding me? This is great, Max. *All* of it." He smiled at her, and it was probably the most genuinely affectionate smile he'd ever given her.

And wasn't that an even better gift than his cotton-ball bouquet—which was really saying something. She sat down across from him and unfolded her napkin in her lap. "Dig in."

She watched in delighted amusement as he took a breast, a drumstick, a wing, and three biscuits. She gave him a sardonic look. "How long has it been since you've eaten?"

Kyle took a large bite of the breast and—"Oh, sweet Jesus." His eyes rolled back into his head. "This is mind-blowing."

She plucked a drumstick off the top of the chicken pile and bit into it, halfway hiding the biggest smile ever to cross her face.

They ate and chatted—no interviews, no power brokering, just two people easily sharing their lives. She told him about other assignments she'd been on as a reporter—the heads of state she'd met, the secrets and lies she was privy to—and he told her about past deployments—the perfect cruises and the perfectly awful ones, his greatest battles and proudest achievements.

With him busy eating and talking, she was able to indulge in openly observing him. Again and again, her focus meandered to the front of his T-shirt. Last night he'd stripped naked in front of her, and even though her back had been to him the whole time, the impact of him fully undressing was as powerful as if she saw him in all his naked glory.

He'd taken his *shirt* off.

And, no, she was under no delusions that him baring this part of his body automatically meant he was also baring his heart—despite the point A to point B line she'd drawn between the two—but she still had to believe it meant *something*.

It certainly *felt* like something. Sleeping in the refuge of warmth he'd created for her, emotions had been jarred loose inside her. Low down... Deep within...

Attraction... Sexual wanting... *God, yes.* And those went beyond the magnetism she was initially drawn to in Kyle on the *Bunker Hill.* She was now fascinated by the little things about him—the creases along his knuckles, the neat construction of his earlobes, the strong muscles in his jaw working as he ate.

A drop of sweet, golden butter was glistening along the edge of his bottom lip...and she could totally picture herself licking it off.

She ripped meat off her drumstick bone and chewed with vigor, struggling with an insane urge to leap across the table and tackle him to the floor. *Focus on what he's saying, Max, not on how badly you want him to get naked again, but this time—*

Oh... He was telling the story about how he'd earned the scars on his leg and the underside of his chin—several drug dealers had tried to kill him in a Colombian jungle.

"How scary," she said.

He snorted. "It wasn't an optimal situation."

This was the same thing he'd said after JEM made

them wear the black hoods. "Which was worse?" she asked. "The knife-fight in Colombia or everything going pear-shaped with JEM yesterday?"

Kyle sat back, probably thinking about everything that *had* gone pear-shaped: beyond the black hoods, JEM threatened his life by sticking a knife to his throat and then put her right arm in jeopardy with a rifle.

It'd been quite a day.

"The knife fight was harder on me physically, but both times I was worried about letting people down." Kyle carefully parted a biscuit, releasing a small puff of steam from the two halves. "In Colombia, my friend, Eric, was depending on me. Yesterday, you were."

I was? His words made her take a mental step back. *Had* she been depending on him? She searched her memory but could only remember worrying over Majid discovering Kyle's true identity or finding out the real goal of their mission. She'd also been especially anxious about her negotiations with JEM—because *Kyle's* well-being depended on *her.*

Weird. Any sane person would've been glad not to face down such trauma alone. But she hadn't allowed herself any other option but to deal with it herself. She'd pushed aside her feelings as best she could and focused on getting out of the mess.

You're so fucking removed from it all...

She fingered her drumstick bone. Maybe she was worse about that than she'd realized. Although when the nose of a rifle had been pressed to her right arm, she was pretty damned afraid, and when they returned to the aid station—and she was drenched and shaking—she definitely let Kyle take over.

Those things were something, weren't they? Signs of improvement.

Here's an idea. Maybe instead of spinning your wheels figuring out everything yourself—taking care of everyone else—you could let someone else carry the load for a change.

She frowned internally. Had she done the right thing and *let* Kyle take over or did he just take control on his own? Well, either way, everything worked out so much better because of his help, so...

She needed to remember that.

She smiled at him. "I owe you thanks again, Kyle. I needed a good bed buddy last night, and you were the perfect man for the job."

He seemed to startle over that—he actually stopped eating—then he slowly set down the chicken wing he was about to finish and lifted his eyes to hers.

Her breath caught, and she blushed clear to the roots of her hair over the intense way he was looking at her. *Bed buddy.* Oh, he wanted way more than that...

As their gazes clung, the world disappeared—this tent, the aid station beyond, all of Pakistan and its terrorists—and only their little romantic bubble re-mained—the scatter of mostly-eaten food on the table, the orange pekoe scent of the lit votive, the *burble* of leftover rainwater along the gutter outside.

Kyle finally broke eye contact to gaze at her mouth.

She returned the favor and stared at his lips.

He set his napkin on the table beside—

She jumped up.

A millisecond later he was on his feet.

They surged around the table and threw themselves into each other's arms, mouths meeting in a hungry kiss, lips fused and already parted. Their tongues reached out, seeking contact. The softness of his tongue touched hers, and a streak of such hot pleasure shot through her loins that it pushed her to within inches of a climax. *That* fast. She groaned. *He's so—*

Kyle leapt back, nearly stumbling, and stared round-eyed at her. "Jesus Christ." He briefly pressed the back of his fist to his lips. "What was that?"

What was that? Only the most powerful blast of passion she'd ever felt in her life.

"Did you feel it?"

Her next breath hitched out of her. "Yes."

"Have you ever felt anything like that before?"

"No."

"Not even with that Brian Mulligan dildo?"

She choked on a laugh. "No. How about you?"

"Never."

Never. He said *never.*

"Uh...what does it mean?"

"I'm not sure." She was treading on uncharted territory here too. "Do you think it means we're falling for each other?"

His throat moved.

Uh-oh. "Would that be, um, bad?"

He inhaled audibly, then moved forward a step and put two strong hands on her waist.

She gazed deep into his silver-blue eyes, checking for signs of terror.

Her chest swelled when she didn't find any.

His thumbs brushed over the sides of her ribcage, sending tingles skipping along her flesh. "I think," he said softly, "it'd be the best thing that ever happened to me." His arms slid around her waist and he pulled her against his chest.

She didn't think her heart could swell with any more emotions, but it filled to bursting when he ducked his head and added whisper-soft against her ear, "…Samantha."

CHAPTER TWENTY-FOUR

A TREMOR SHOT through Kyle, and his eyelids fell shut. Pulling Max into his arms was like flying out of a storm, when the air suddenly smoothed out and everything felt fine after a shitload of turbulence. Better than *fine*, because mist would still be in the air, but creating rainbows, and maybe beams of light would be piercing through the dark clouds. Everything suddenly perfect—like Max.

The seamless way she fit against his body made her feel like she'd been built to exact military specs, just for him—something he never would've guessed, her being so small. But here she was, an armful of heaven.

With a low groan, he planted his lips on hers again, his heart nearly exploding when she welcomed him without hesitation into his mouth. The feminine softness of her tongue rocked him, her taste shooting straight to his groin, just like it had before.

Breathlessly, he backed off a bit and gazed down at her.

Her eyes were a lazy shade of blue on blue.

The thought drifted through his head again, how a guy could fall in love with Max Dougin based on her eyes alone.

And this time he was pretty sure he meant that *he* was that guy. Sure as hell was starting to feel like it anyway.

He swept her bangs off her brow, the blond of her hair catching the light. Her hair was all different shades of blonde, and it was stunning. "You're so beautiful."

She grinned and twinkled at him.

A weird pleasure-pain wrenched his belly. Why had he let himself live without looks like this for so long?

"You ready for dessert?" she teased, tugging the back of his shirt out of his waistband.

"I thought the fruit salad was dessert." But he smiled and lifted his arms, letting her pull his shirt off.

They were back against each other, bodies melding, lips slanting against lips. His blood raced and his cock throbbed, and his arms tightened around her without him thinking about it. He just never wanted her to go away.

Maybe she read his mind, because her fingers threaded through his hair, holding him in place while she captured his tongue again and again.

Damn, she felt so good.

He thought he knew women, how soft they were, how amazing they smelled, but it was as if he was a young man all over again, discovering for the first time the wonders of the female body. Or maybe it was because this was *Max*, like being crazy about her had already padlocked him onto her pheromones, heightening everything about her to extremes—as if he'd never been with her before, even though he had.

But this wasn't the woman he'd hiked up against a wall behind the Jebel Ali Club.

Kissing Max now, Kyle felt an added warmth throughout his body and a fullness in his chest that had everything to do with wanting to use sex to get closer to Max.

Not just forget everything else in his life.

Oh, this must be a proud moment for the U.

Truthfully, he probably didn't know what the hell he was talking about. The sensations ran too deep and went too far outside his wheelhouse for him to completely understand or explain. All he could say was that love stories got it right—kissing a woman you were crazy about set off all kinds of fireworks in a guy's heart.

It was also a cold-water-in-the-face reminder of how empty his life had always been...and of how much he needed Max to fill it.

Between kisses he managed to strip her of her T-shirt. He removed her bra and gazed at her breasts, round and pale, topped with incredible nipples. Her aureoles were larger than he would've guessed on a small-breasted woman, and a deep magenta color. He would've expected something pinker on a blonde, but this darker shade was luscious and ripe. There was no way he couldn't devour her nipples.

Wrapping an arm around the small of her back, Kyle picked Max off her feet and brought one of her breasts to his mouth. He closed his lips around the pert bud and suckled her with a whole lot of *delicious* going on in his brain.

She was better than all his favorite foods combined.

She groaned and arched as he relentlessly tugged on her with his lips, adding tongue-action here and there, lapping or flicking at her erect nipple. He let her slide back down his body, then used his free hand to take a good grip on her other breast, squeezing and molding it, feeling her flesh plump into his palm. She was an amazing mix of fine textures and freshness.

Atom-level awareness of her swept through him like a slow fire.

She squirmed against him, clearly eager for more.

He lowered a hand to knead her butt, releasing her nipple to glance up at her.

Her head had fallen back on her neck in a look of un-inhibited passion, and the vision of her like that—abandoned so completely to him—brought such a surge of blood into his engorged shaft, he clamped his teeth in pain.

He quickly undid the button and zipper on her shorts and jammed his hands down the back. Clasping her naked butt, he squeezed and pulled her hard against his erect length, hissing air as he backed her toward her cot. "If this is at all uncomfortable," he said in a guttural tone, "tell me."

"It won't be." She nibbled at his throat. "I'm already really wet."

He froze. The combo of her admission and the havoc she was wreaking on his neck with her little teeth was off this planet. "Not sure I believe you. Need to investigate." He shoved her shorts down and—froze again. She didn't have a pubic hair in sight.

Today's woman seemed to have embraced a denuding fad he wasn't sure what to make of. He generally liked his women to look like *women*. But as he stared at Max's sweet private area, the unencumbered view he was receiving of her graceful folds and the little button of her clitoris got her a *yes* vote from him for being pube-free.

He kicked off his boots. "I wouldn't have taken you for the porn star type," he teased, anyway.

She slanted a look at him. "It's because I'm a swimmer." She crawled onto her cot and lay down on her back, knees bent.

He tore himself out of his pants and skivvies, then climbed onto her cot, too, but low down, with his shoulders near her knees. He took another peek at her privates and—his cock bucked violently. *Fuck.* The sight of her was...*fuck!* She was so wet, moisture was glistening on both sides of her outer lips, and if that wasn't the hottest thing he'd ever seen, he would change his call sign to Bunny.

Primal hunger drove him forward. His shoulders bonked her shins. He growled.

"What are you doing?"

"Open," he ordered, "and you'll find out."

A breathy laugh came out of her. "There's no room on this cot."

He took her by the ankle and placed the arch of her foot on one of parallel wooden slats that made up the frame of her cot, then repeated the process with the other foot.

"Ah," she said.

He shouldered between her legs and her thighs fell open.

Oh, yeah. He moved in closer, took hold of her hips, and tended to a little housekeeping first, licking up the moisture from the smooth side of one lip, then the other.

Max huffed something unintelligible, and he heard wood *creak* as her toes clenched on the slats.

He dipped down to her opening, coated his tongue with more of her lubrication, then dragged upward to her clit and started with his usual A, B, C, D...

It might sound funky, but a sure-fire way to bring a

woman to climax was to lick the alphabet on her. It'd always been an interesting diversion to see how far he could get before she came—furthest he'd ever reached was Q—but this time the alphabet song fell out of his head after a few strokes.

Technique went out the window.

It was just him, here and now, in the moment with Max, enjoying the simple, unthinking act of exploring every inch of her sex. He tongued her clit with unhurried care and lapped at her wet folds, occasionally using a gentle finger to caress her opening while—

She came suddenly in his face, hard and fast, her opening squeezing rhythmically against his chin. Her gasping moans drifted through his ears, and the sound was so full of real ecstasy that he couldn't believe he'd let the fake noises she'd made at the Jebel Ali Club sucker him.

She writhed all the way through the throes of her orgasm, the silky flesh of her hips gliding back and forth in his hands, her hipbones gently nudging his palms on each twist.

When her body finally sagged into the cot in limp satiation, he reared above her. And then he was on her, coming down between her thighs, his naked body sliding against hers, his cock nudging her core.

It was the oddest emotional hiccup in his life when he found that he didn't know how to proceed.

Max's small hands clasped his buttocks, her touch everything—caring and soft, eager and strong. She pulled his hips into hers.

He pressed his eyelids together. All rational thought left him as he pushed inside the haven of her body and put his whole heart into thrusting inside her.

CHAPTER TWENTY-FIVE

B REATHING HEAVILY, MAX hugged Kyle to her as hard as she could, holding him so close and tight there wasn't a single nerve left untouched between them. Her nipples peaked firmer with each of his thrusts, rubbing against the soft whorls of his chest hair, and her sex was practically vibrating.

Naked Kyle was even better than she'd thought, a beautiful construction of power and strength.

In the past, she'd mostly dated liberal hippie types who didn't bicep-curl anything heftier than a laptop. And, boy, had she been missing out by not having a significant amount of man to hold onto. Kyle was *solid*, a magnificent bulk of muscles extending across his broad shoulders, the wide, hard slabs of his pectorals sprinkled with light-colored hair, his dog tags nestled in the crevice between. He didn't have six-pack abs but was thick around the middle. Not fat. Rather like a man who was built big-boned and compact...a man who liked to eat, especially *her* food. Smiling, she closed her legs harder around his waist.

"Christ," Kyle rasped, rocking his pelvis faster against her.

The hinges on her cot screamed a high-pitched *eee-aaah, eee-aaah*. She dug her fingertips into his flesh. She never would've guessed how erotic and masculine muscles were until Kyle weighted her down.

And then there was the well-endowed part of him. Kyle's size had been a bit of a negative the night at the Jebel Ali Club when she wasn't well-prepared. This time she was wet and slick and ready for his intrusion, but also stretched so tight around him that the friction of his thick shaft was rapidly pushing her toward a second orgasm.

Exhilaration dizzied her, and her jaw slackened around heavier pants.

Do you think we're falling for each other?

Oh, no doubt about it. She was.

Would that be bad?

I think it'd be the best thing that ever happened to me, Samantha.

Her heart took off to the races.

Kyle shoved his face into her neck, the gentle chafing of his beard keeping the memory alive of other areas where his whiskers had worked their tender lightning: her breasts and inner thighs. She was a mere step away from another pinnacle.

"Lift up," she gasped, and gave Kyle's shoulder a nudge.

He immediately rose onto braced arms—such compliance.

She reached between their bodies and stroked her clitoris, her feet linked tightly over Kyle's butt. His hands gripped the wooden slats of her cot, and she could feel the hard labor of his muscles.

She shivered and bucked. She was closer than she'd— *oh!* She cried out as liquid pulsations came swiftly over her. "Oh, God!"

Kyle increased his speed, his dog tags tapping her chin on each forward surge of his hips.

She almost laughed at that. Heavens, between her orgasmic crooning and all the noise her cot was making, she wouldn't be surprised if an audience had gathered outside her tent. She would die of embarrassment if one had. But there was nothing she could do to quiet herself. Being sent into climatic orbit Kyle-Hammond-style was just too much of a good thing.

As her pulsations faded, she wrapped her hands around Kyle's nape and pulled him back down to her.

With a low rumble, he latched onto the upper part of her breast with his mouth and sucked hard on her flesh as he thundered toward his own finish line.

She caught her breath at the sharp pleasure-pain. Was he...giving her a hickie? She hadn't had one since high school, although something about what he was doing seemed like more than just adolescent fooling around. More like—

Kyle began to jerk and strain. She felt the pulsation of his shaft inside her, and in the moment of his climax, his face turned into a beautiful mask of carnal ecstasy. He let out a guttural bellow of release, then collapsed on top of her, his hips still rocking slightly as he bit into her shoulder.

She jumped. The bite was so unexpectedly animalistic, another orgasm ambushed her. She yelped and shuddered. *Wow.* She hadn't needed her usual extra clitoral stimulation. Gulping for air, she lay like a lump beneath him, just gazing at the ceiling through halfway closed lids. Her bones had melted inside her skin, and—

A loud siren went off.

Kyle's head bolted up.

Max popped her eyes open wide. *What the heck is*—?

The door to the tent flew open.

"Incoming wounded!" Kitty called out. "All hands are needed to—oh, my dear Lord!" Kitty whirled around, putting her back to the room.

Kyle sprang off Max and fumbled for his clothes.

"I'm so sorry," Kitty apologized. "But your help is needed in triage."

Max scrambled off her cot, too. "It's okay." She found her underwear and bra. "We'll be right there."

KITTY SHUFFLED OUT of the medical tent and spotted Max sitting on the bench beside the door. She plopped down next to her, and the moment her rear hit the wood, the nine hours straight she'd spent on her feet handing medical instruments to Dr. Barr in surgery caught up to her. The last of her energy trickled away.

"I don't smoke," Kitty said, wearily tugging her surgical cap off. "But times like this, I feel like I could use a cigarette."

"Or a very bracing gin and tonic."

Kitty glanced at Max. Sweat had formed twin rings under her armpits and a huge oval down from her collar like a bib. Her T-shirt was also smudged all over with blood, so unless Max liked gruesome tie-dye, her shirt was ruined.

Not that Kitty's scrubs were in any better shape. She reached up to pat her bun. As suspected, it was in tatters. She probably looked like ten miles of bad road. Smelled it, too.

Max released a long-drawn-out breath.

If Kitty was plumb tuckered, then Max had to be feeling wrung out as a dishrag. Kitty was used to running all over Hell's half acre with this kind of work. Max was probably more used to sitting at a desk and plonking away at computer keys.

"You okay?" Kitty asked. Max had managed triage during the night, bandaging up those men wounded by crossfire and stabilizing them as best she could. It was grisly work for anybody, but especially a greenhorn. "Seeing people wounded in battle can be hard the first time." *Or all the time.* It never ceased to amaze Kitty what all damage a bullet could do to the human body.

Max knuckled her right eye. "I'm mostly tired."

That was probably true. Max did seem to handle most matters with a quiet confidence Kitty admired...and ached a little with longing over. If only Shirleen had been a calmer person—instead of always het up about one thing or another—maybe Kitty would've turned out more like Max, calm and confident.

"Whhhhat"—Max yawned out—"time is it, anyway?"

"Zero-five-hundred."

Max propped the back of her head against the tent wall, her throat arched, her eyes half-closed. "We've been up all night."

Kitty gazed at the first weak streaks of sunrise seeping up from the horizon.

"How many wounded came through?" Max asked.

"A good fifteen or so. Over half the beds are full now. So Lieutenant Whitmore left the ward to go roommate with Lieutenant Hammond again."

Max nodded vaguely, her head still pressed back against the tent wall.

Speaking of Lieutenant Hammond… Kitty bit into her bottom lip. "Sorry again about earlier, busting in on you." It'd been quite the mortification barging in on two naked people engaged in the act of love—and also a rush to see.

Kitty's cheeks tinged with heat. Been a long time since she'd slept with a fella, going on a good two months ago now. She'd been in Plainview, home on leave before deploying on the *Mercy*.

She went back to Texas once a year, and even though the purpose of those trips was to visit her parents, she never stayed with Shirleen and Howard.

They'd once kicked her out of their house, so that was that.

She bunked with her old high school friend, Mary Beth, from the Dairy Queen, and on this last trip, Kitty and Mary Beth's brother had shared a six pack of Lone Stars one night in the kitchen. Later Kitty gave him a poke on the living room sofa. A couch spring jabbed her in the butt the whole time, and she heard Mary Beth snoring softly in the next room. No surprise Kitty didn't have an orgasm, but it was still good to have a man inside her, and Billy smelled nicely of wood chips.

"It's okay." Max turned her head to look at Kitty, her eyes still partially closed.

Kitty smiled tentatively. "I guess we should've come

up with a signal—a sock tied to the door handle or something."

A gusty sigh came out of Max. "I wouldn't have remembered to put it out, anyway. Kyle and I fell into each other's arms too suddenly and too passionately to stop for a signal."

"Sudden, huh?" Kitty raised her eyebrows high. "Should I be asking you if you know what you're doing?"

Max laughed unevenly. "I appreciate it, but no. What Kyle and I did wasn't a mistake."

"How do you know that...I mean, like, for sure?" Kitty could stand a lesson or two on the subject.

Max straightened a bit. "I don't know. I guess I just feel it."

Kitty sighed. That wasn't helpful. "You're lucky then. I can't ever trust my own feelings. My yearnings are always leading me astray."

Max came more awake but didn't say anything.

Some people were like that—they merely waited patiently for a soul to make her confessions, no pushing or pulling about it.

Kitty ran her surgical cap through her fingers. "Seems like I always believe fellas like me, then turns out they don't. I suppose there's a part of me that's always yearning to feel like I belong somewhere and with someone." She smiled weakly. "My friend Mary Beth says it's because I didn't get none of that as a child."

Max's eyebrows started to edge together, but then her mouth twisted. "I know what you mean, actually. My mom and dad didn't pay much attention to me. They weren't bad parents, per se. They were good at the job of parenting when they did it. They just...rarely did." Max gazed at the lightening horizon. "They were always so busy."

"It's horrible," Kitty said, "feeling so unnoticed. Unfortunately, *I'm* always making stupid decisions because of it, forever picking the wrong guy." Lord, if brains were leather, she wouldn't have enough to saddle a June bug.

Max looked at her again. "You seem really big-hearted, Kitty. It's understandable that you might fall in love too easily."

Max was trying to put a positive spin on it, and Kitty appreciated it, but her friend was a bit off. "It's not so much that I fall for fellas too much—it's that I want fellas to fall for me and think I'm pretty." Kitty peered down at her cap. "Fact is, I've only been in love once—with Shane."

"Shane?" Max asked. "Who's that?"

CHAPTER TWENTY-SIX

K ITTY DUMPED THE cooked spaghetti into a colander, then opened a fresh jar of Ragu sauce. "I don't have parmesan," she called out to Shane.

He was in the living room watching football.

She transferred the noodles to a bowl and mixed the tomato-and-meat sauce in with a large spoon. "I hope it's all right."

"Yeah," Shane called back. "Long as you got bread."

Uh-oh, shoot. Kitty grimaced at the can of Pillsbury French Bread she'd forgotten to pop in the oven. Well, darn it, why did Shane need to eat pasta *and* bread for dinner? She blew a strand of hair off her forehead. Because he was a SEAL, that's why, and he carbo-loaded like nobody's business.

What such massive amounts of carbs would do to her body, she didn't even want to consider.

On Shane, every single calorie he put into his mouth became rock-hard muscle.

She sprinkled some dressing on the salad, then rummaged in the cupboard for bread—best not to upset Shane any more than he already was. He'd returned today from a month-long training in a foul state. What might've put him in such a mood, she didn't know—he hadn't told her. No big surprise, there. Shane only shared things about himself in tiny bits of piecemeal.

In the last few months, though, he'd gotten even worse about it. She kept trying to urge him to talk, tell her what was wrong, but he never would. She understood that he was a SEAL and so had to keep his feelings under tight wraps, but...she had a queer sense that it was more than just his job that kept him so distant.

This time around, she was just about at her wit's end about it. On especially weepy nights, she even considered throwing in the towel on their whole dang-nabbed relationship and walking out, but...this was *Shane*.

No man had ever turned her head like Shane Madden. No man could be more charming and fun—when he wanted to be—and the sex was incredible.

Not that they were doing it anymore.

Pushing aside the loaf of wheat bread that she preferred—but Shane hated—she luckily found a couple of slices of sourdough. She stuck those in the toaster, then brought the pasta out to the dining room.

She and Shane lived together in a two-story, two-bedroom, two-and-a-half bath apartment in Imperial Beach Gardens, a neatly landscaped complex of beige buildings with a communal pool.

Imperial Beach was located at the southern tip of a narrow length of Coronado Island known as "the strand," and was one of the southernmost towns in San Diego County—IB was a mere eight miles from the Mexican border. But it was also only a little over seven miles from the Naval Amphibious Base on Coronado where SEAL

Teams One, Three, Five, and Seven were stationed, so a lot of commandos lived in IB—Coronado proper was through-the-roof expensive.

Shane was a member of the Team Three "Punishers."

When Shane's old roommate left on an extended deployment, Shane asked him if it was okay if Kitty moved in to take his place. The fella said yes, and so here Kitty had been for the last year, playing house...although for the life of her she couldn't remember Shane asking *her* if she wanted to set up housekeeping with him.

He'd just made space for her, and that was that.

Their apartment was still decorated the way it'd originally been, with the kind of square-shaped furniture that boys liked and posters on the walls instead of artwork. Even today, the place smelled vaguely of man stuff, like a logging compound, maybe—chainsaws and sawdust and thick-soled boots—although she'd never been able to figure out why.

Returning to the kitchen, Kitty buttered the sourdough toast, then brought it out to the table along with a tossed salad, which mostly she'd eat.

Dusting her hands off, she stepped into the doorway leading to the living room.

Shane was sprawled on the couch, a bottle of Schlitz beer propped between his open thighs. He was wearing a pair of black nylon basketball shorts and a navy-blue T-shirt with the SEAL insignia—a US Navy anchor, a flintlock-style pistol, and an eagle clutching a trident—over the left pocket. He wore his dark brown hair longer than standard navy regulation permitted and kept a rugged five o'clock shadow on his jaw. This was so he could travel anywhere in the world at the drop of a hat and not be recognizable as military.

"I've set up supper in the dining room," she told him.

His attention never left the TV screen. "I want to watch the game." He took a draw on his beer. When Shane was on standby, he was allowed two beers.

"Shane, c'mon, honey. I haven't seen hide nor hair of you for a month. I'd like to spend some time with you."

He drank more beer, his focus still on football. "Go get your plate, sit on the couch, and eat suppah here next to me."

Her chest clenched. Shane's South Boston accent only peeked out when he was annoyed. *What* in tarnation had put such a big burr in the man's blanket?

"Then we'll be spending time together," he added.

"I thought we could"—she swallowed—"talk a bit over supper."

He turned to level a look at her. Head on, she could see the nasty scar that marred the entire left side of his face. It slashed down from temple to chin, narrowly missing his left eye and the corner of his mouth. Brown eyes the color of an ancient oak stared at her, icy and flat.

If anyone else were to see him right now, they might worry Shane was on the verge of hitting her. He wasn't, but...what in thunderation brought on these dark spells? What kind of man lurked inside Shane? Not for the first time Kitty wanted to shake him to rattle loose whoever it was.

"Just watch the game with me, for fuck's sake. I—" His phone cut him off.

Shane had set his message notifications to a soft *bong*,

and Kitty had come to think of it as the most hated noise in the world. Her throat spasmed in automatic response to it.

Shane dug his cell out of his shorts pocket, already hopping to his feet as he glanced at the screen. "Gotta go." He took off into their bedroom.

Kitty quickly followed. She stopped in the doorway and watched him slap open the closet door. "What is it?"

"Work." He stripped out of his shorts and T-shirt.

Like every other SEAL Kitty had ever met, Shane was built tough. He was massively bulked across the shoulders and biceps, but the rest of him was rangy and lean. It was a body type built for stamina and speed as much as for managing the incredible amount of gear he regularly carried—his body also just so happened to be perfectly constructed for sex. His agility made itself known with skilled hip movements in bed, and all those muscles were a complete turn-on. No two ways about it, Shane Madden was the most exciting man she'd ever slept with...at least back when they used to have sex.

"You just returned from a month of training, Shane."

"It's how it is. You know that." He was dressing in his military gear.

"But... Where are you going?"

"Don't know. Hand me my socks from the draw'."

She didn't move. A dull ache throbbed in her chest.

He shot her a glance—more annoyance—then stalked over to the dresser and snatched a pair out of the drawer himself.

"Is this another training op or the real thing?" she asked.

"Dammit, Kitty, *I don't know.*" He sat on the edge of the bed and hauled on his socks and boots. "They don't say fuck-all to me in a *text*, and even if they did, I couldn't tell you." He tied off a boot with a hard yank on the laces. "Quit acting like you're stupid about shit like this."

Her mouth went dry. "Please don't call me stupid."

"I didn't," he snapped. "I said you're *acting* stupid."

She didn't see a whole lotta difference between the two. Either way made her feel small as a bug. She swallowed painfully. "It's not fair, Shane. You constantly leave me at all hours, and I never know where you're going or when you'll be back. It's just…it's not *fair.*"

He made a *tsk* noise in the back of his throat. "Lodge a complaint with the CNO. There's nothing I can do about it." He thrust to his feet and started for the door.

Wherever he was going, he didn't seem to give two figs about leaving her again. She exhaled a sharp breath as something snapped her on the inside—she felt it almost like a bee sting against her heart muscle.

What woman went into a relationship to be *alone*? None that she knew. Not her. Yet that's what she was *all the time.* "No, Shane." She braced her hands on either side of the jamb, barring his way. "You're not leaving."

Shane halted in front of her, his hands on his hips, his dark brows low.

"I'll call your CO," she said, "and tell him you're barfing your guts out with the stomach flu, so you can't—"

"You've *got* to be fucking kidding me."

"I'm not."

"Move." It was a hard command.

The hairs on Kitty's nape prickled. Shane would never hit her, she trusted him on that, but there was…so much violence living within him. Again she had a queer sense that it came from more than the requirements of his job, but she didn't have a notion from where. She didn't know *anything*!

"There *is* something you could do about this, Shane, for damn sure there is. You can stop being more committed to those SEAL boys than you are to your own girlfriend."

Shane's jaw tightened. "You sound like a broken record with this jealousy bullshit you keep pullin', Kitty. Why don't you try changin' it up and blame me fah cheatin' on you with another woman?"

Shane would never step out on her—she trusted him on that, too. A strict moral code guided his… Lord, how awful was it that he wouldn't have an affair because of *behavior rules* rather than over undying love for her?

Her chin trembled. "You…" She choked on a ball of tears in her throat. "You…you have to… I need you to…" She trailed off.

"What, Kitty," he bit out, impatient and frustrated. "What do you want from me?"

Tears rolled down her cheeks. "I want you t-to talk to me."

"You couldn't pick a bettah time to pull this." Shane glanced rigidly at his watch. "I'm on a one-hour recall."

"I'm not asking you to get all sappy on me," she came back tremulously. "But you don't talk to me *at all*. I've lived with you a year and I barely know you. Can't you just tell me about your day? Or…or sometimes talk about when you were a kid? Did you used to—"

"Fuck this." Snarling, he shouldered past one of her raised arms, forcing her to drop it.

She chased after him, yelling at his back, "We don't even sleep together anymore!"

Knots ran up and down his jaw. "That sure as shit ain't my fault."

She darted past him and pressed her spine to the front door, blocking him again. "It *is* your fault!" she kept yelling. "How can you expect me to make love to you when you give me nothing of yourself?"

"Didn't seem to stop you with all those other guys you fucked."

His words hit her with the force of a body blow. Her lungs shrank down, cutting into her oxygen supply. She'd been *used* by those other boys. How could Shane not see that? "Why, thank you ever so much for calling me a whore."

He offered her a bland shrug. "If the shoe fits."

More tears fell. What was *wrong* with him? He never talked to her mean-like. "Shane Madden, you're lower than a snake's belly in a wagon rut."

His eyes darkened. "Get out of my way, or I *will* move you myself."

"If you leave now, with things like this, I…I won't be here when you get back."

"Christ." He blasted air from both nostrils. "Another thing you're a broken record about. All right, Kitty, you win. I'll call my chief and say, 'Excuse me, Aloha, I can't report for duty because my girlfriend needs me *to talk about my childhood.*'" Shane's lip curled. "Would you like me to give you a mani-pedi too?"

Humiliation washed the feeling out of her cheeks. "You don't have to be so…so…" She dragged the back of her hand over her dripping nose. "I just want to know you care about me. Why can't you give me that?!"

"I will *always* protect you." Shane lifted a clenched fist in front of her, showing her his massive power. "I will always provide for you. *That's* how you know I care. You want talk," he grated, "get it from your girlfriends. I can only give what I can give, and if it's not enough, then you do need to fuckin' bail."

He grabbed her by the waist, spun her off the front door, and stalked outside.

CHAPTER TWENTY-SEVEN

KITTY PICKED A piece of lint off her surgical cap. Dawn had broken fully across the horizon now, tinging the sky with orange and gold. One of the orderlies came out of the medical tent for a smoke break, flicking a lighter as strolled toward flag circle.

When he was out of earshot, Max said, "Wow, that...that sounds rough, Kitty. I'm so sorry."

Kitty nodded. She'd gone through some pretty sad days in her life but that one had been a big'un.

"What happened after Shane left?" Max asked.

"I stomped around the apartment, crying and losing my nerve to leave, then..." She glanced up from her cap. "I tore open a letter that'd come in earlier and saw I'd been accepted into a nursing program I applied for. It gave me courage." For the first time in a long time, she hadn't felt so stupid and incapable when she read, *we are pleased to inform you...* The confidence hadn't lasted—she never ended up going to nursing school—but for that night she was able to do what needed doing. "So I packed my belongings and left."

Max paused before asking, "Any regrets?"

"Oh, 'bout a million. But any time I think about running back to Shane, I make myself remember that he never *once* contacted me after I moved out—not a call, not a text. Nothing. Like all the time we were together ceased to exist, or he erased it from his mind like *that*." She snapped her fingers. "I don't need a man in my life that cares so little for me." She met Max's gaze. "Right?"

"Absolutely."

Kitty nodded firmly, but then made a face. "Still hurts, though."

"I know, but here's something else you can remember—from everything you described about Shane, it sounds like he wasn't ready for a relationship. Nothing *you* did or didn't do could've changed him."

"Yeah." But a bitter taste of bile rose onto the back of Kitty's tongue anyway. It was hard not to blame herself. Women were supposed to be in charge of the emotions in a relationship—men just weren't raised with that kind of knowing—so it seemed like she should've figured out some way to reach Shane.

"Maybe some time in the future Shane will be ready," Max said hopefully, "and you can try again."

"Maybe." Kitty inspected her cap for more lint. "But, see...there's another fella in my life right now...a good fella...who likes me, and..."

Max did that thing again where she didn't probe, just waited for Kitty to go on.

"And this time I like him back," Kitty admitted. "But I don't know if I can trust my feelings about it, considering how much I've messed up with other men in the past. Although, truth be told, he's not like any fella I ever dated. He's...he's high quality." Which just made her doubt herself even more.

Steve was smart and mannerly and sweet and treated

her well, and maybe she wanted him too much because of all his positives, making her ignore the likelihood that he'd turn out to be like most other fellas—just bent on using her for sex. What virgin didn't want to get some experience under his belt after all?

"I can understand why you're gun-shy about men," Max said, "but you left Shane because you knew you deserved better. If you truly believe that about yourself, then…shouldn't you give this high-quality man a chance?"

MAX SLOUCHED OVER a half-eaten meal of scrambled eggs and toast, and blearily sipped her coffee. She'd changed out of her bloody T-shirt into a short-sleeved button-up, but that was doing little to refresh her. Probably nothing could perk her up—she'd only gotten a couple hours of sleep last night.

It was the height of the breakfast hour, and the mess tent was packed with busy eaters, utensils clattering against trays, a dozen different conversations going on, the *siss* of coffee dripping onto a burner every time the pot was pulled out to—

A tray slapped down on the table and Kyle planted his butt on the bench across from her, *hard*. Probably hard enough to squash a pea through a stack of twenty mattresses.

She might be exhausted, but it didn't take fully awake brain power for her to detect that Kyle was in a bad mood. Besides all the noise he was making, his silver-blue eyes were steely shards of ice.

"Jeez, what's up?" she asked. "You look like someone urinated in your boots."

"Last night," he said through closed teeth. "That's what's up."

She squinted at him, trying to compute his words. She couldn't manage it. Her deductive skills were evidently running on empty along with the rest of her, because as far as she could remember, there wasn't anything they'd done last night that would cause so much grumpiness this morning. "You're suffering from a case of the morning-afters, Kyle? Really?"

His jaw jutted at her. "We didn't use a condom last night."

So that's what's bothering him. "True." She rubbed the heel of one hand into her temple. She smothered a yawn in her palm. "Is that all?"

He gave her an astounded look for the space of two heartbeats. "*Is that all?*" he hissed. "You're damned well not going to say anything else about it?"

"Correct. That's all I have. Maybe I can come up with more after a second cup of coffee." *Unless...* "Unless you're here to tell me that you gave me a disease."

"No," he grated. "I didn't. And do you know why?"

Since a vein in his forehead appeared to be on the verge of explosion, she was going to treat the question as rhetorical.

"Because I *always* use a condom."

"Nice. Okay, good. I'm glad to hear you're Kyle the Careful." She dragged a finger through a drip of coffee on the side of her mug, then licked it off her fingertip. She glanced back up at him—he was scowling. "Are you waiting for applause?"

His scowl sharpened to a glare.

"Or are you afraid *I* gave *you* a disease? Because I didn't, either."

"Motherfuck," he growled. "Are you on birth control?"

Ah, so now they were at the real crux of it. "Nope."

Kyle grabbed his fork in a tight fist.

If he planned to stab her with it, she was too weary to talk him out of it. "Can we discuss this later? I'm still on my first cup of coffee." She peered into her mug. "Not even one whole cup, actually."

"You need to start fucking paying attention here, Max." He clipped every word. "What if I got you pregnant?"

She waved his concern aside. "You didn't. I can tell when I'm ovulating, and I'm not."

He tossed down his fork. "Just like that, you're *sure*?"

"Yes, Kyle, I'm sure. I know my body, and it functions like clockwork."

"Well, me myself?" he bit out. "I'm not sure. Far from it. And if you are pregnant—"

"I'm not."

"*If. You. Are.*" His eyes narrowed. "You're not having it. You got that? No. Fucking. Way."

She stiffened in her seat, coming fully awake on a blast of indignation. She ground her molars together. *Correction.* This feeling was full-on, very un-Max-like rage. How *dare* he fling the option of an abortion at her so cavalierly. More than that, he was *insisting* on it.

She rocketed to her feet and curled her hands into fists.

Kyle leaned forward, his eyes locked on her expectantly, the look on his face turning—

Wait...*expectantly?*

She exhaled a long breath, her anger disappearing as her deductive skills came back online and understanding washed over her. Kyle wasn't really pushing the idea of an abortion on her—he'd only said all that to provoke a fight.

He *wanted* her to rip him a new one.

The question was: why?

Whatever you do to connect, do it, so we can get on with it.

Last I checked, Max, orgasms feel good. If you could stop analyzing the ethology of male-female bonding behavior long enough to shut up, maybe you could make the same discovery.

She blinked a slow blink.

It's horrible, feeling so unnoticed...

And then she knew.

Chapter Twenty-Eight

MAX TOOK A step back from the table and gestured for Kyle to get up. "Let's talk about this in the privacy of your tent."

Kyle narrowed his eyes, staring at her through the slits of his lids for a stubborn moment, but then rose to his feet and walked with her to tent number eight.

Steve Whitmore was inside.

"Do you mind if I have a moment alone with Kyle?" Max said.

Steve took one look at Kyle's expression, grabbed his shoes, and bolted.

She gestured at Kyle's bed. "Please, sit."

Kyle sat on the edge of his bed, spine straight, nostrils white. He was braced for battle.

Too bad he wasn't getting one. "I know what you're doing, Kyle, and it isn't going to work. I've figured you out."

"How nice for you," he drawled in a nasty tone. "Do *you* want some applause?"

"Okay, here's the deal: you're going to be quiet for a bit now"—she smiled indulgently—"and just let me talk."

His lips flexed tight over set teeth.

"This is your Kyle the Shithead act," she informed him. "I've seen it before. You use it when you want to pare down sex to just sex, no feelings attached, because that's where you feel most comfortable. None of your heart involved, right? But last night wasn't *just sex*. We talked about falling for each other, and we had wonderful, meaningful sex. And it's shaken you. Do you know why it has? Don't try to answer. I'm going to tell you. You think I'm going to abandon you after you've fallen for me, so to test me, you're being a complete shithead."

His mouth screwed tighter at the corners.

"Don't try to deny it. I recognized the look on your face earlier in the mess tent." She exhaled a short breath. "I've seen it enough times in the mirror on my own face. The kid who's always being let down...? That's you and me. Because you were right when you said my mom and dad spent more time at their jobs than with me. So I *know* what it feels like. In fact, after you said that, I wondered if you knew what it was like to be a loner too. And you do." She held his gaze for a wordless moment, then asked, "Who checked out on you? Mom, Dad, both?"

Kyle broke eye contact. He looked at his boots, his fingers, the door, the wall—anywhere but at her. Finally, he said through stiff lips, "Dad." A tic twitched in his upper lip. "He was a deadbeat, waste of skin. Any little trouble sent him running for the hills, often for months at a time."

Max's throat wrenched. *How awful.* A boy needed his father. "I'm sorry."

"Yeah," he returned. "Whatever."

More pieces of the puzzle showered over her in a landslide. "Do you see how deeply it affected us that we weren't worth our parents' time? Like, I deal with being let down by not depending on anyone, and you deal by sabotaging anything good in your life…probably to prove that you're as worthless as your dad made you feel."

Kyle's eyes snapped to hers. "Get off it, Max."

"You don't see it? I mean…look at the way you earned the call sign Mikey."

Kyle's eyebrows angled into a fierce vee. "How the hell do you know about—" He broke off. "That asshat Tarzan." He growled at her. "Would you quit interviewing my AW about me."

"I can't help it—I'm a reporter."

"You're a pain in the ass."

She ignored that and returned to the story. "On a port call during your first long cruise, a group of you pilots and AWs were at a sleazy bar. Several of the guys were in the back, screwing a prostitute on a table. You were dared to go down on her after they were done, so you stuck your face in her crotch…until someone named LZ pulled you off. From then on, you were known as Mikey, after the Life Cereal kid who would eat anything."

Kyle reddened. "I was extremely fucking drunk that night, okay?"

"What you were," she countered, "was the squadron's new, hotshot young pilot—your whole career ahead of you, your reputation yours for the making." She flung a hand out. "And you did *that* to yourself?" She pointed a finger at him. "Sabotage. And what about Sienna?"

His expression blackened. "Don't—"

"You keep your ex in your life because her regular shaming and ridiculing reminds you, again and again, of who you really are: Kyle the Worthless Shithead."

The sides of Kyle's jaw bulged. "Would you shut up, already."

"No. Because here's the thing—you're trying to sabotage us. But I'm not going to let you. Do you hear me? Give it your best shot, Kyle, blast me with both barrels, but *nothing* you do will work. I'm not leaving you."

His throat jerked a couple of times.

"To come full circle back to the original point—" She dropped down into a crouch in front of him and softened her tone. "I'm not pregnant, Kyle." She set her hands on his knees. "But if I were, we'd make a decision about what to do from the position of two people who care about each other." She squeezed his knees. "However, I'm telling you right now that nothing in this world could make me give up your baby."

He looked pole-axed for the two beats it took for that to sink in, then he shoved his face into his hands. "Max, you don't fucking understand. I…" Muscles were jumping all along his jawline.

She watched him struggle, waiting quietly for him to compose himself.

When he dropped his hands, his eyes were shiny. "There was one other time I didn't wear a condom. I got Sienna pregnant. It was years ago. She never told me. I was never supposed to know we had a son. But the kid's sick with cancer now, so the adoptive parents needed me to give some of my bone marrow."

Max could do no more than swallow thickly. *How terrible.*

"Ever since I found out, I've wanted to get genetic

testing done. Because the thought of having another sick kid scares me cross-eyed, so…so, uh, if you're pregnant…" He looked down, a few muscles in his jaw still spasming. "I don't know if I could forgive myself if I gave you a sick kid."

"Kyle," she whispered, her heart in her throat. Seeing him torn up like this was worse than watching terrorists hold him down over a table. "Honey, sometimes kids just get sick, okay, and it has nothing to do with a gene either parent passed on. You didn't do anything wrong."

"Maybe." His cheeks were stark white.

She stroked her thumbs over the tops of his knees. "How's he doing now?"

"My son?" Kyle looked up. "Better."

"I'm glad."

He blinked slowly.

She smiled into his eyes.

"It doesn't bother you that I have a son? Although"—he snorted—"I guess I don't really. It's not like I'm raising him." He pressed a knuckle into the corner of his eye. "Good thing. I'd suck at it."

"Are you kidding me? You're going to be an awesome father someday."

His lips slanted. "I appreciate the attempt to boost my morale, Max, but there's no way you could know something like that about me."

"Sure, I can. I've seen the way you deal with your men—firm, fair, fun, all when appropriate. It's a good indicator about how great you'll be as a father."

He gazed into her eyes for long seconds, the whole time shaking his head and exhaling. "You're really something, you know that?"

She smiled, then gave him a goofy, cockeyed look. "This conversation didn't go the way you thought it would, did it?"

He chuckled. "No, it did not." He brushed her bangs off her forehead with his fingertips. "And since you're not letting me offload you with my consummate sabotage skills, I think that means we need to take things to the next level."

"Which is?"

"You being my girlfriend."

"Oh?" Jumping up and down would be a completely weird to do, right? "Are you talking about commitment? Monogamy?"

His lips slanted. "That's the offer on the table, yeah."

She fluttered her lashes. "You do those things?"

He chuckled. "Amazingly, yes." He brushed her shirt collar aside and pointed at the hickie on her upper breast. "*Mine.*"

"Oh, my God," she exclaimed. "Is that what you were doing? Marking me?"

His eyes danced. "Have I ever led you to believe that I'm not a caveman?"

"No." She laughed. "I suppose not. Okay. I accept your offer. Gotta appreciate such honesty in a man."

"Cool." His smile widened. "All right. Logistics time. Where do you live?"

"My parents have a vacation home in Lake Arrowhead where I mostly hole up. It's about halfway between Los Angeles and Camp Pendleton, where my brother is stationed. So it's convenient for when I need to go into the newsroom or visit Kevin."

"But basically, you can work from anywhere on your computer?"

"Yes."

"Meaning you could work from San Diego, where I live?"

She held back a smile. "Yes."

He pursed his lips at her. "And?"

"All right. When I get back to the States after this mission, I'll look for a place in San Diego."

"Near Pacific Beach," he added.

"Okay."

He came to his feet, helping her up with him, then pulled her into a hug. He pressed his nose to her hair. "You always smell like cherries."

She said, "Hmm." She had no idea why that would be the case.

His arms were strong around her waist. "I'll be faithful to you, Max, you don't need to worry about that."

Good to know. Because cheating on her would be an effective sabotage technique. "I believe you," she said, snuggling her face into the area where his neck met his shoulder. "I relied on you to help me get safely home from the JEM fiasco yesterday, and you didn't let me down. You've proved that you *are* my follow-through person, Kyle. I can depend on you."

She felt a shudder run through him. "How do you always know the exact right thing to say?"

"It's one of my superpowers."

A laugh rumbled in his chest. "Do I have a superpower?"

"Absolutely. Being a good bed buddy." She leaned back in his arms. "Which gives me an idea."

One of his eyebrows edged up.

"Take a nap with me—I only got a few hours of sleep last night." She stepped out of his arms and crawled onto his comfy bed. The scent of him permeated the blanket. *Sheer heaven.* She curled into a cuddly ball and sighed in anticipation of Kyle's warm, heavy body spooning hers.

He climbed into bed and scooted next to her. Setting a hand on her shoulder, he rolled her onto her back. "Let's make this a combat nap."

She peered at him through half-closed lids. "What's that?"

He canted his hips forward, and his erection prodded her thigh.

Her eyes came open. "Oh."

CHAPTER TWENTY-NINE

*T*HEY'RE HEEERE.

Carol Anne's creepy little voice from the *Polter-geist* movie chimed in Kyle's head as a couple of dust clouds appeared down the road.

He was standing beside Max next to the same bunch of short trees as yesterday, but this time he'd brought backup—he was flanked by Tarzan and Jobs.

Both were armed with AKs commandeered from the aid station's guard shack. Kyle's Beretta was a hard, comforting presence against the small of his back.

All three men were dressed in civilian clothes. Scruffy whiskers and longish hair added to their cover as nonmilitary, despite the firepower.

As far as facial hair went, Tarzan would win a beard-growing contest—a favorite long-cruise pastime—between the three of them, hands down. The AW must have some Wookiee in his DNA, because within a week, Tarzan had grown the kind of bushy beard that would've done Allah proud. Tarzan's military barber back home was probably sending a son or daughter through college on the AW's business alone.

Within the same seven-day period, Jobs hadn't managed to sprout much more than a few sapling stragglers of hair on his chin. Kyle had been tempted to make the kid shave—looking at that shit was just *wrong*.

Max sipped coffee from her thermos. "My relationship with dust clouds will never be the same after this assignment."

Kyle snorted.

"Are you seeing what I'm seeing?" she asked. "*Two* vehicles."

"Affirmative."

"Didn't you tell Abu Majid not to bring any more than four men?"

"I guess he decided to thumb his nose at that order." *Go figure.*

"Hmm," Max said, probably trying to decide if she should be bothered by that or not.

"At least the sky is clear today." No storm clouds were preparing to take a massive whiz on Kyle's head, so the Universe must approve of Kyle's recent life choices. He cut a glance at Max. Yeah, that was a no-brainer. What wasn't to like?

The piece-of-shit blue Hilux truck Kyle and Max had stolen yesterday—re-claimed and gassed up—pulled to a halt first, stopping three hundred yards away.

The rear door flopped down and around a dozen armed baddies hopped out of the flatbed.

Tarzan stiffened. "That's a helluva lot more than four men, sir."

Yeah, Kyle wasn't a fan of the numbers either. "You think JEM is paranoid about further ISI interference?" he asked Max. "Or worried about us?"

"Well, we *are* standing here with two AKs, aren't we?"

Kyle made a noise in his throat. "Not the worst of all

decisions, considering what I'm seeing."

"The aid station also isn't very far off," Max pointed out. "JEM might be taking precautions against the Pakistani guard rushing out to overwhelm them and just snatch the hostages back."

"So this is about protecting their investment?"

Max stuffed her thermos into her backpack. "Hopefully."

The second vehicle was a dusty Chrysler LeBaron painted to look like a station wagon. It pulled up next to the Hilux truck, and Dixie Cup hopped out of the driver's side. He took a moment to give Kyle an eat-my-ass look—clearly having a flashback moment to yesterday, when Kyle had punched him in the jaw and helped himself to the guy's Kalashnikov rifle.

Kyle didn't give the dude the satisfaction of a reaction. Also, he needed to play nice until the four American engineers were back in US hands.

Time stretched as their side and the enemy side did an OK-Corral-style stare down back and forth for a while.

Finally, Dixie Cup made a chopping gesture.

All the remaining doors of the LeBaron flew open and four people stepped out—three men and one woman.

Another gesture from Dixie Cup sent them walking slowly toward Kyle's group.

As the hostages drew closer, Kyle scanned the men for Sienna's cousin, Todd. Maybe recognition bells would ring, after all. But they didn't—Kyle couldn't pick Todd out. None of the men showed signs of recognizing Kyle, either, so it looked like Todd remembered Kyle about as well as the other way around.

"Come to a stop in a line," Kyle instructed them, "four abreast, shoulder to shoulder." The position would help hide the shenanigans he and Max were planning to pull.

The four did as they were told, and Kyle and Max moved forward.

Tarzan and Jobs stayed back, keeping an eye on the baddies against the possibility that JEM wasn't just protecting their investment but planned their own brand of shenanigans.

Kyle stepped up close to the first guy in line and—whoa! If the dude did a sniff-check of his armpits, he'd probably keel. But then life had no doubt been minus a lot of basic comforts for these four recently.

"We have to act like we're checking you for injuries," Kyle said, kneading the first guy's shoulders, then tipping his chin up to check underneath.

"Y-you're getting us away from these jerks, right?" the guy stammered.

"Yes," Kyle answered. "But not now."

"W-why not?"

If this was Todd, then Sienna's cousin liked to ask idiotic questions. *There's four of us and over a dozen of them, all armed. You do the math, bro.*

Max answered. "A SEAL unit is going to come get you." She shifted to stand directly in front of the one female hostage. "We have a GPS tracking device we need to plant on you in order to engineer your rescue," Max told her.

Chin down, the woman observed Max through a tangled curtain of hair.

As stink went, this woman had patented a new degree of rank.

The woman shook her head. "They'll search us after being so close to you."

"We figured on that," Max agreed. "So...uh...I put the tracker in a small plastic tube the size and shape of a tampon. Which means you'll have to hide it in...um..."

Kyle moved on to the next man and kneaded his shoulders.

The woman's lips trembled. "What makes you think it'll be safe from discovery there?"

Max paused, here brows flickering, then her eyelids sank closed.

Anger burned through Kyle's chest. Time to go back to that OK-Corral moment, but this time shoot every one of the terrorist fuckers. "Maybe we should—"

"We need to stick to the plan," Max cut him off.

The woman leveled a look at Max, her chin coming up. The movement of her head revealed a striking face underneath her mess of hair.

Kyle's jaw knotted convulsively. No, this woman hadn't been having a hoedown at the Grand Ole Opry while in captivity, had she?

The woman exhaled sharply. "All right, give me the tracker."

Max discreetly eased the small tube out of her front pocket.

The woman took it and quickly jammed her hand down the front of her pants.

Kyle looked away.

"Just please hurry," the woman said tautly.

"We will," Max came back, her tone heavy with sympathy. "The rescue team is on standby, ready to go."

"Thank you," the woman whispered.

Kyle sent the hostages back and watched them climb into the LeBaron with eyes that felt hot. Sweeping his focus over the terrorists, he found Dixie Cup again. "We'll contact you in two hours with details of the exchange," he yelled across to the man, lying his ass off, of course.

Dixie Cup nodded once, then turned abruptly and got back into the LeBaron. The car and the Hilux truck drove off.

Dust clouds roiled on the road, and Kyle hard-stared them. "I feel like a complete shit."

Max sighed. "I'm sorry, but saving the hostages wasn't our part of the mission." She turned toward him. "But we'll make sure the rest of the job gets done."

An hour later they got the call from their CIA contact. The hostages' GPS tracker had stopped moving.

The rescue team now had a strike zone.

CHAPTER THIRTY

T HE CIA SENT satellite pictures of the target location via an encrypted message. Max brought up the images on her laptop, and Kyle bent over her shoulder to study them. On the map, he saw a small town called Chhajja situated a few thousand feet west of the Mangla Dam. He counted a grouping of nine buildings surrounding a courtyard. A red dot was on the southernmost building—the GPS tracker signal pinpointing the hostages' exact location.

Kyle did some quick calculations. "That town is only a little over twenty miles from our current location. Granted, that's as the crow flies, so add on another thirty miles when you have to drive around the dam to get there, but still...seems to me that JEM didn't need an extra day to transport the hostages to us for a proof of life check."

"I agree," Max said.

He turned his head to look at her. "Any ideas about the reason behind the delay? You still think JEM's up to a double-cross?"

"Impossible to tell," she admitted. "At the very least I'd say JEM used the time to call in extra protection for the hostages."

But the images the CIA provided were of normal terrain, not infrared. Kyle straightened. "With no human-shaped heat signatures visible, it's also impossible to tell how many extra tangoes we might be talking about."

She looked up at him. "We can wait to gather more intel, but who knows how long the hostages will be at this exact location. If they're moved, we'll have to start all over again. And, obviously, every day the hostages are with JEM is a day they're in danger."

They held each other's gazes, both of them thinking the same thing—they'd told that poor female hostage they would act fast to save her.

Kyle seamed his lips. "I'll put in a call to Admiral Kelleman, see what his orders are."

He went in search of Dr. Barr. The only encrypted satellite phone on site was kept under lock and key in her tent.

After the doctor set Kyle up with the phone, it took about a five-minute runaround before he finally got Admiral Kelleman on the line. "Sir, Dougin and I were able to conduct a proof of life inspection of the hostages approximately ninety minutes ago. All the hostages are accounted for and healthy, and we successfully planted the GPS tracking device."

"Very good, Lieutenant."

"Yes, sir," he said. "But, sir, there might be a glitch."

"Speak, Lieutenant."

Kyle laid out the issues with JEM's delay—his suspicions that the rescue mission was now more complicated and dangerous, but that he didn't have eyes-on to confirm or deny the presence of more tangoes.

Kelleman's unhappy grunt came through the phone

line. "I don't want to scrub this op."

"No, sir. Neither do I."

"I can order a drone to pass over the target and take some infrared imaging," the admiral mused, "but that would create an unacceptable delay. We need to act now."

"Yes, sir."

"I want you to fly in ahead of the strike team and recon the target, Hammond—obtain the additional intel the rescue team needs."

Kyle nearly dropped the phone. "Excuse me?" he blurted out.

"You can radio back information to the team, and then they'll know what they're up against."

Kyle didn't say anything. All speech had been flabbergasted out of him. Kelleman wanted *Kyle* to be a part of a SPECOPS rescue mission?

"You can do that, can't you?" Kelleman asked testily.

Kyle finally managed to produce something intelligible. "Yes, sir. My Seahawk has FLIR." Although the admiral no doubt knew that.

"Very good. I'll order the strike team to rendezvous at your location. You can brief them about these new parameters at the aid station."

"Yes, sir. I won't—" *let you down.*

But Kelleman had already hung up.

Kyle left to go hunt down his guys, finding both Tarzan and Jobs in the mess tent. He told them about the change in plans. "Turn 'n' burn, gentleman."

With no time to waste, the three of them got hopping, changing into their flight suits and gear, then taking down the tent of desert camouflage netting from over the helo. While Jobs and Tarzan started the final pre-flight checks of the bird, Kyle headed to Max's tent to fill her in.

She was stretched out on her cot, reading, but when he ducked inside, she lurched to her feet, the book dangling from her fingertips.

"A *flight suit*?" She gaped. "What's going on?"

He told her.

"But…" She blinked a couple of times. "If you're flying in ahead of everyone else, isn't that kind of like being first man through the door?"

"Yes. But also, no—I'll be at a decent altitude."

She still paled.

He wedged the book out of her hand and tossed it on her cot, then pulled her into a hug. "I'll be okay, Max."

"You'd better be." She laid her cheek on his chest and wrapped her arms around his waist. "So, this is it, huh? After tonight, it's over."

"The missions will be over," he said against her sweet-smelling hair. "*We're* not done."

"But I won't get to see you every day anymore." She curled her fingers against his spine. "How much longer is your deployment anyway?"

He closed his eyes and rubbed his cheek against her hair. "Five months."

"Oh." She deflated. "Bummer."

"Yeah, it's a long time. Sorry." His gut knotted. Damn, this was new, leaving behind someone who really mattered.

"Well, whenever I get lonely, I'll just imagine you in your flight suit." She tightened her hug. "I'd forgotten how hot you look in it."

He couldn't help himself—he leaned back and smirked at her. "Care to share what you'll be doing while you're imagining me in all my hotness?"

She laughed. "Better not. It might shock you."

He *hah'd*. "A man could make it through long cruise on those words alone."

She laughed again and gazed up at him with her twinkly blue-on-blue eyes.

He lightly touched her bangs. Her eyes, he swore to himself, would be the last thing he thought about when he went to sleep at night and the first thing he thought about when he woke up in the morning.

"You make me feel like I can conquer the world," he told her softly.

She smiled, but it was closed-lipped this time. "Don't do anything crazy with that idea."

"No, I won't. I'm going to try and knock off the sabotaging for a while."

"I like the sound of that." She reached up and ran the backs of her slim fingers along his bearded cheek. "You'll be clean-shaven when you return from deployment." A stitch appeared between her brows. "I probably won't even recognize you."

He took her hand in his and squeezed it. "We'll figure each other out."

She exhaled a slow breath.

"If, uh...if it turns out you're pregnant, please let me know while I'm floating, okay? Don't wait for me to get back."

"I will. But—"

"You're not pregnant. Right. I remember."

"Just don't worry about anything but getting home safe."

"Yes, ma'am."

She touched the tip of his chin with her forefinger. "I'm going to miss you so much."

He hid a swallow. "Back atcha, sugah."

Her mouth slanted. "Such a romantic."

Both of their cell phones *beeped* incoming messages.

They stepped apart.

He dug into the right leg pocket of his flight suit for his phone while Max went for hers in her backpack.

"It's my brother, Kevin," Max told him, reading off her screen. "Just telling me that he's going to be gone all next month on maneuvers."

Kyle glanced at his screen, and—*shit*. He looked at Max and grimaced. "Sienna," he said the name with all the sourness he felt for the person.

"What does she want?"

"I don't know, and I don't want to know. Watch this—" He hovered his thumb over the delete button. "This is me deleting the message."

"You're not even going to read it?"

"Nope." He jammed his thumb down on the button.

Max tilted her head to one side.

Maybe she knew how momentous it was that he'd just done that.

"When I return to the States," he said, "I'll buy a new phone chip, then my ex won't even have my number anymore. Meanwhile—" He slipped Max's phone out of her hand. "Here's my number." He inputted it, then handed her cell back. "We can FaceTime while I'm gone, too."

"Okay."

He shoved his own phone away. "I better go. I gotta make sure my bird's squared away. But let's plan on meeting later at my tent, spend our last night together being bed buddies."

Max smiled. "I like the sound of that, too."

He kissed her, then left, detouring to his tent on his way to the motor pool.

If you're flying in ahead of everyone else, isn't that kind of like being first man through the door?

He wrote the final letter he'd never written.

He addressed it to Max, then headed to the medical tent and gave it to Dr. Barr for safekeeping. He was still standing in the post-op ward when he heard it—distant but steadily approaching.

The thunder of helicopters.

CHAPTER THIRTY-ONE

THE DOOR TO the post-op ward opened, and Kitty stepped aside to allow Lieutenant Hammond to pass.

Her heart flopped over and fell down when she saw that he was dressed in a flight suit. So it was true—the Wolfpack crew *was* going on the rescue op. The hostages would soon be saved, the mission concluded, and then the whole gang would fly back to the *Bunker Hill*.

Kitty would lose a great roommate in Max…and also her chance to see if things could've ever turned out good between her and Steve.

If you left Shane because you truly believe you deserve better, then shouldn't you give this high-quality man a chance?

She should—she *wanted* too—but her heart clenched up like a tight fist whenever she got too close to saying yes. She was always so back-and-forth about it, so dad-burned wishy-washy, it was as if God hadn't given her a lick of horse sense when it came to matters of the heart.

Lieutenant Hammond smiled at her. "If I don't see you when I get back, make sure you don't go breaking too many hearts. You hear, corpsman?"

Her return smile was a second late in coming. Did Lieutenant Hammond know about her and Steve? *But no.* He was merely being nice. "Yes, sir. I'll do my best." She tossed off a quick salute, even though she wasn't supposed to do that to anyone while at the aid station. "Go give those terrorists what for, sir."

"Roger that." The lieutenant jogged off.

Kitty continued inside, finding Dr. Barr seated at a large desk positioned just inside the door. The desk was massive, probably six or seven feet long with side panels that dropped all the way to the floor. It was too big and heavy for a *mobile* aid station, but it was probably an unwanted castoff, like so much of their equipment was.

"Ma'am? You sent for me?" Out of habit, Kitty took a quick peek into the ward to check on her patients—everyone appeared to be resting comfortably—before moving to the edge of the desk.

"Yes, Kitty. I have something to tell you."

Kitty didn't tense up or set to worrying. Farrin's expression was pleasant, so the doctor wasn't fixing to dole out bad news.

Farrin sifted through a stack of papers on her desk. "Here we go." She picked out an official-looking letter. "You've been promoted to E5." She grinned. "Congratulations! By next month you'll be a Hospital Corpsman, second class."

HM2, really? A smile burst across Kitty's face. She'd taken the advancement exam, but hadn't expected to pass, especially not the first time. "Ma'am, thank you, ma'am."

"You're an exemplary corpsman." Farrin handed her the promotion letter. "Have you ever considered going to OCS?"

Officer Candidate School? "I...yes. I once thought about becoming a nurse." She folded the letter into a neat square and tucked it into the breast pocket on her scrubs. "I wasn't sure if I could handle it, though."

Farrin *tsked*. "Of course you can handle it. If you ever need a letter of recommendation for anything, just let me know. I'll write you a glowing one."

"Yes, ma'am." A blush heated Kitty's face. "Thank you, ma'am."

Farrin check her wristwatch. "We'd better get to rounds before—"

The *thump-thump* of rotor blades cut her off.

Farrin glanced at the ceiling. "Incoming."

Kitty's stomach seized. The rescue team was arriving.

Steve would be gone soon, robbing her life of all its sweetness.

I know those other jerks you dated didn't take good care of you, but I'm not like that. Please, Kitty, just give me a chance to show you.

Here she was back to *giving chances*…

If you were my girl, I would never leave you.

If you were my girl, I would've done anything to help you.

Steve certainly said stuff that made it sound like he was different from all the other fellas she'd dated. But words were just words, not deeds.

Except…

The only way to see if Steve's deeds matched his words—to see if he really would be as great of a boyfriend as he promised—was to take the perilous steps into a relationship with him. She had to trust her gut—the gut that'd always let her down.

Her heart started to sink, but she forced herself to

gather her wits. She had to stop living her life afraid. Even if she was having a hard time believing in herself right now, maybe she could take heart from those who thought well of her and let that buoy her.

You're an exemplary corpsman…

She drew in a deep breath.

Of course you can handle it. If you ever need a letter of recommendation for anything, just let me know. I'll write you a glowing one.

Not Larson Holmes. You knew the weasel was a bad choice for you, and so you got yourself out of it.

See? She did have some good sense here and there, on those occasions when she stopped listening to those folks bent on making her feel stupid and instead listened to those who knew her best—and when she truly listened to herself.

The sound of the approaching helicopters grew louder.

Shoot, she didn't have much time.

"Ma'am, do you mind if I dash off for a moment before we start rounds? There's something I need to tell our Navy boys."

"Go ahead."

"Might I have one of those Post-it notes?"

Farrin peeled one off the stack on her desk and gave it to Kitty.

She jotted down her email address. "Thank you." She hurried outside and ran to the area by the motor pool that was a helicopter landing pad.

A man wearing a flight suit and a flight helmet was crouched down in front of the Wolfpack bird, peering at something under the aircraft. Kitty couldn't see his face, but the moment he straightened, she knew it was Steve. The way he moved was burned into a special part of her memory.

Kitty stood rooted to the spot. Sweating. Twisting her fingers together. *Don't be a yaller dog!* Even if she didn't fully believe in herself yet that didn't mean she couldn't at least act in ways that made it seem like she believed until she really did. Which was a little confusing, but she was pretty sure she understood herself.

She cupped her hands around her mouth and shouted, "Lieutenant Whitmore!"

Steve turned around.

Her heart pattering, she waved him over.

Steve said something to Tarzan—who was examining the mounted machine gun—then trotted over to her. He wrenched off his helmet.

She grabbed his injured arm and started probing it.

"Hey." He frowned. "C'mon, I'm fine. People need to quit babying me."

"I know," she said. "I'm just using this as an excuse to talk to you."

He went still, his eyes latching onto hers.

Her insides shook under the heat of his gaze. Her tongue balled in her mouth, but she lifted her chin. *Don't start chickening out again! Aren't you the girl who lived in a shed for a month to escape a life you didn't want?* "When's your next port call?" she asked him.

"Um…in a couple of weeks, in Bahrain"

"Do you know exactly when?"

"No."

"When's your birthday?"

He gave her a strange look. "November twenty-seventh."

"Here's my email address." She quickly stuffed the Post-it note inside the zippered pocket below Steve's name tag. "I know you can't put your ship's movements in an email, so when you find out the exact date you'll be in Bahrain, tell me how many days it is from your birthday, then I'll get leave during the same time and meet you there."

He blinked. "Wait. What?"

Over Steve's shoulder, she saw two steel-colored helicopters cut across a strip of milky clouds. She gave him a quick smile. "For a romantic getaway."

A floodtide of red slowly crept into his cheeks. "Holy moly." The two words were spoken on an astounded breath. "You mean it?"

"Yes." Her next smile felt oddly shy.

A long *hooooo* escaped his lips, then his face cracked into a gigantic grin.

It was the best smile she'd ever seen. But—"Don't smile at me like that, Steve, or you'll give us away." Especially because his expression was pushing her to the brink of throwing her arms around his neck and raining kisses all over his face.

"I really wish I could hug you right now." He was still gazing at her with besotted Basset Hound eyes.

"There will be plenty of time for that later." She paused. "And more."

Steve had meant his hug in the sweetest way imaginable, so when she added this insinuation to their exchange, he blushed again, even darker than before, if possible.

"H-how about tonight?" he stammered.

"Tonight?"

"Yeah, um, after my mission...you and I could meet...somewhere...I mean to talk and-and..."

Steve's face was officially a cherry.

The rescue helos were now practically right on top of them—Kitty had to shout to be heard over the noise. "Find me in the post-op ward when you get back, okay! Just peek in at me, and that will be our signal to meet at the supply tent!"

His eyes lit up like a kid's in a candy store. "Okay!"

Catching back all but the smallest giggle, she stepped back. "I'll see you then!"

CHAPTER THIRTY-TWO

EAR PROTECTORS ON and a clipboard full of the strike zone's satellite photos clutched in one hand, Kyle watched the Navy H-60 Sierra helicopters touch down on the aid station's landing pad. Two sets of massive, whirling rotors stirred up a huge backdraft of sand.

The commotion roused some of the camp to come and rubberneck, including Max.

While the blades were still turning, the lead pilots and head SEALs of both birds hopped out and jogged over to where Kyle stood next to the mini-bus ambulance.

The first pilot was—

Well, whaddya know. Kyle knew the guy. "As I live and breathe," he drawled, "if it ain't Casanova."

Lieutenant Commander Jason "Casanova" Vanderby was Danny "Beans" Vanderby's older brother—Beans was a Wolfpack squadron mate of Kyle's.

Casanova had earned his call sign because he was good-looking enough to have the ladies dripping off him, but the joke was, he never did anything about it. Kyle had always thought the man was sort of a dink for that, but now Max was in Kyle's life, he understood the value of selectivity.

Quality was so much better than quantity.

"Hey, Mikey." Casanova jerked his chin at Kyle. "We

were told you have some extra intel for us."

"Affirmative." The rescue team had only been given the LAT LONG coordinates of the strike zone and information about the terrain so they could plan their ingress.

Kyle would brief them about the potential for extra terrorists, but before he started, Casanova introduced the other men.

Lead pilot of the second bird was LCDR Vic "VD" Davidson, and his accompanying SEAL was Chief Isaac "Aloha" Gagailoa. The chief had dark eyes and tan skin, his features veering toward Pacific Islander.

Casanova's SEAL had a stern face, a prominent scar on his left cheek that humbled Kyle about his own—his jaw scar, while nasty, was way less visible—and the kind of aggressive-bordering-on-insane look in his dark brown eyes that only serious operators mastered. Kyle was taller, but that was pretty much a *so what?* all other things considered.

Kyle waited for Casanova to introduce his SEAL, but he didn't. In fact, the men seemed uncomfortable and tense around each other, like two people who'd watched each other do kinky shit on a port call, and now couldn't meet each other's eyes.

Kyle waved over Max. "This is Samantha Dougin with the *LA Times*, the Pakistan expert who spearheaded the ground mission."

She nodded to the men. "Call me Max."

Kyle rolled into the brief. "Max and I have reason to believe that JEM recently amassed more troops to protect their hostage stronghold. Satellite imagery is limited, so we have no idea how many extra men have been added."

Kyle handed Casanova the clipboard of pictures, and VD looked on from Casanova's right. "Due to this potential, unknown buildup of force, Admiral Kelleman has ordered me to be the team's ISR."

Casanova's brows shot up.

"I'll fly in ahead of you and Davidson, maintaining a higher altitude than the rescue team can, and after I recon the field with my FLIR, I'll report back."

"And then what?" Casanova said. "Change our operational plan in flight on our way to the strike zone?" Shaking his head, he lowered the clipboard. "We usually mensurate a target for hours before an attack—often days."

"Understood," Kyle said. "But the overall consensus is that we need to act now. If we delay, we run the risk of the hostages being moved."

Tension pulled the skin around Casanova's eyes tight. He clearly wasn't hoorah about this idea. "Rushing an op can lead to mistakes."

Kyle spread his hands. "These are Admiral Kelleman's orders." He dropped his arms back to his sides. "One of the hostages is his nephew."

Casanova's brows rose again.

"*And*," Max inserted, "the female hostage is not having a good time of it."

Casanova cast a quick glance at her, then returned to Kyle.

"She looked pretty bad," he confirmed.

Casanova lifted the clipboard and studied the satellite images again. "Eight buildings sit next to or near to our target building," he observed.

"Affirmative," Kyle said.

Casanova glanced up. "Thing is, Mikey, FLIR doesn't give you X-ray vision through walls, so you won't be able see inside those buildings. The total number of terrorists will remain an unknown."

"True, but we'll have a much better idea of the situation than we do now."

VD crossed his arms. "Look, Vanderby, if Mikey reports back a fuckload of bad guys, we can do a strafing run first—clear out some tangoes before we fast-rope our commandos in." The Sierras had plenty of firepower for that, with two gunners, one on either side of the aircraft, each manning an M240. "Or we can abort altogether, if anything starts to feel too hinky."

Casanova exhaled a hard breath. "All right, we're here now, so let's at least fly in and see if the op is doable." He handed the clipboard back to Kyle. "Work as a team and everyone be tight on your game, prepared to pivot rapidly if—"

Pop, pop, pop...

Kyle startled. That sounded like—

The rubberneckers knew the sound well—*yes, gunfire!*—and they screamed and scattered.

*Ping, ding, ding...*the next bullets struck the ambulance.

Shit! Kyle dove for Max, but she'd already hit the dirt. He landed heavily on top of her, crushing an *oomph* out of her.

Belly-down on the ground, VD gave Kyle a peeved look. "What the *hell*, Mikey?" Davidson had partially face-planted on the way down, and now the end of his chin was sand-dipped like a sugar-coated ice cream cone.

"Is this JEM?" Casanova asked Kyle from his position

next to Davidson.

Kyle did Cobra Posture, lifting his head partially up to search beyond the aid station site. He spotted a small group of Pakistani regulars being chased and fired upon by a larger band of Indian soldiers. Several of the aid station's Pakistani guardsmen were running along the fence line, shouting at the fighters in their own language and gesturing.

Kyle also checked on his men. Tarzan had taken cover under the Wolfpack bird; Jobs was on the ground next to the ambulance.

The two SEALs were standing with their backs pressed to the medical tent, rifles raised. Leave it to the operators to move into an offensive position at the first sound of gunfire.

"Not JEM," Kyle answered Casanova, lowering back down. "It's a Pakistani-Indian skirmish. We're catching stray bullets through the baling wire perimeter."

Pop, pop—crash!

Glass exploded out of the copilot's window on Casanova's bird.

"Dammit," Casanova growled. "The helos are taking on fire. We need to get the hell off the deck."

He got up and ran, crouched over, to his helo.

Davidson sprinted in the same manner for his.

The scar-faced SEAL from Casanova's aircraft peered around the edge of the medical tent, a Heckler and Koch rifle nestled against his right shoulder. He sighted.

"Hold your fire!" Kyle bellowed at him.

Beneath him, he felt Max angle her head sideways to see what was going on.

The SEAL glanced over.

"Those men aren't shooting at us," Kyle shouted. "We're just catching their crossfire."

The SEAL narrowed his eyes.

Jesus. Had no one briefed this guy about Rules of Engagement—*you may not fire unless fired upon*—or was he just a hothead? "You are *not* cleared hot," Kyle yelled.

Pop, pop, pop...

More screams. More running.

"Mikey!" Casanova raced back over and lay down next to Kyle. "When that bullet took out my copilot's window, he caught a face full of glass. Some of it went in his eyes, so he's out."

Pop, pop, pop...

Casanova ducked lower. "I need someone to fly the left seat."

"I'll do it!" Jobs volunteered as he belly-crawled over to their position.

The fuck if you will. "Negative," Kyle barked. "You don't know the Sierra."

"Actually, I did a flight exchange with a Sierra squadron," Jobs said. "I have over forty hours of flight time in that bird."

"You're in." Casanova got to his knees. "Let's—"

"No," Kyle bit out. Truth was, he was more concerned about Jobs' well-being than the kid's skillset. The Wolfpack's part of this mission was dangerous, yeah, but not as dangerous as hovering over a hot zone to fast-rope SEALs into known enemy territory.

"I need a co-pilot who knows the Sierra's weapon systems," Casanova argued. "I'm taking your man." He waved Jobs to follow as he crouch-ran back to the aircraft.

Jobs grinned at Kyle. "I'll be okay." He took off.

Kyle scowled after him. *Annoying twerp.*

"Our boy's growing up," Max said.

Kyle glanced down at her and exhaled a large breath, the rush of air ruffling her bangs. Having bullets fly while she was around equaled: *not fun.* He looked back up in time to see Casanova helping his copilot out of the aircraft.

Jobs climbed into the left seat, while Casanova handed his guy over to the care of a scared-looking orderly.

Eyes streaming tears, the injured pilot let the orderly lead him inside the medical tent.

The two SEALs raced over to their respective helos and jumped into the back. Side doors were slammed closed.

The mission was spooling up.

Kyle shouted to Tarzan, "Get in the aircraft!"

Tarzan crawled out from underneath the Wolfpack bird and leapt into the gunner's seat.

Kyle shoved to his feet, pulling Max up with him, and hustled her to the medical tent, shielding her with his body the whole way.

Dr. Barr was standing just inside the door next to a massive desk, her satellite phone pressed to her ear, her brows down.

Kyle took Max by the arms. "You going to be okay?" It was more of a command than a question.

"Yes, I'll—"

"Change in plans," Dr. Barr interrupted, setting her phone on the desk. "I've been ordered to evacuate the aid station. You need to take Ms. Dougin with you, Lieutenant Hammond."

Into combat? He inhaled a short breath. Was the doctor out of her mind? "I can't do that, ma'am."

Dr. Barr gestured at her satellite phone. "I just received word that there's a real threat to this aid station being overtaken. That means all but essential personnel must go. In other words, everyone but *me*."

"It's okay" Max assured Kyle. "I've flown into hairy situations in news helicopters before."

Not exactly the same thing as flying into battle. But then…Kyle's job on this mission wasn't the fighting part. He was only doing recon. And the alternative to taking Max into potential danger with him was to leave her behind at the aid station in danger. *Talk about a suck-o Catch-22.*

"All right," Kyle said to Max. "You're with me."

"Stay safe," Max called back to Dr. Barr.

Outside the medical tent, Kyle didn't hear active fire anymore, but he still rushed getting Max into the back of his bird. He helped her into the left-hand passenger seat and worked at strapping her in.

"Oh, wait," she said. "My luggage is still in my tent."

"We'll send for it."

She snorted. "I just realized how stupid that sounded."

"Not at all." He flashed her a smile. "And no worries about this op. Piece of cake."

"Right. I'll probably take a nap back here."

He laughed, then took a precious moment to gaze into her eyes. She gave him one of those looks that made him feel like he could overcome any obstacle.

So that's what he was going to do—*succeed.*

He tugged on her five-point restraint to check it, planted a kiss on her, then mounted up.

CHAPTER THIRTY-THREE

K YLE'S BELLY UNCLENCHED somewhat when he ascended to three thousand feet, putting his helo—and everyone in it—at a relatively safe altitude away from attack. "Bandit One," he said into his helmet mic, checking in with Casanova. "Bandit Three, arriving on target."

"Copy that," Casanova's voice crackled in response. "Talk to me."

Kyle studied his helo's FLIR screen. The nine buildings surrounding a courtyard were represented in green, while human heat signatures were white. "I mark movers to the north and to the east." Only about seven or eight bodies were wandering about, while a few more remained still, like sentries manning their posts. "Under a dozen."

"Solid copy," Casanova said. "So what's you call?"

Kyle made a face. Christ, but it sucked that he was the man in charge of making this call. A sound decision was impossible with only half the picture in front of him. "Based on what I'm seeing *outside*, we're a go. But as you pointed out, I don't have complete intel. Recommend you—" He caught movement on the roof of the north-west building. "Stand by. There's—"

He squinted. Someone was… Hold up. Why would anyone be on a *roof?* Sentries appeared to be posted only at ground level, so it shouldn't be a guard. No, nobody would be up on a roof unless…

"Bandit Three," Casanova crackled. "Repeat last."

Kyle's blood ran cold. Unless the terrorists were lying in wait for this air strike.

Almost as if they *knew* the Americans were coming.

Yeah, Kyle had suspected JEM was planning their own double-cross, but he thought they'd pull their shenanigans *during* the hostage exchange. Not now. Because JEM shouldn't know about this secret rescue operation.

The only person outside the aid station who was aware of it was Kelleman—and Kyle and the admiral had discussed the op over an encrypted line. The rest who knew about it were inside the aid station—Dr. Barr, of course, and so by association probably HM3 Hart, Jobs and Tarzan and Max.

Everyone else at the aid station had seen the Wolfpack crew dressed in flight suits and preparing the bird for flight, but as far as anyone knew, Kyle and his guys were merely prepping to return to the *Bunker Hill*.

No one would—

Kyle's thoughts jerked to a halt.

He'd told Jobs and Tarzan about the op while those two were in the chow hall—*turn 'n' burn, gentleman*—then later filled in Max in her tent.

Someone could've overheard either of those conversations.

But who would care enough to listen?

Anyone else American military besides the corpsman?

Two Seamen orderlies have been lent to me off the

USNS Mercy. *Other IHMR employees are civilians, including a secretary, a supply administrator, an anesthesiologist, and two cooks. The two men who do the laundry are Pakistani locals, and the guards are all Pakistani military.*

"We're five minutes out. Bandit Three…?"

Kyle's heart turned to lead. *Oh, sweet Jesus.*

His own words rang back to him: *Are you telling me Pakistani Intelligence just tried to take us out?*

Then Max saying, *how was ISI able to attack us exactly on this road at this time, if not for a spy inside JEM?*

Holy fucking shit, there *was* a spy.

But not from inside JEM…

The two men who do the laundry are Pakistani locals…

The spies were inside the damned aid station!

The realization hit him like a cement brick: JEM *had* delayed the proof of life inspection because they were amassing more men, but not a few piddling extras from their own brethren.

They'd joined forces with the massive ISI-backed Taliban.

"Bandit One," Kyle snapped out. "Be advised—"

His FLIR screen lit up as the buildings surrounding the courtyard disgorged hundreds of human heat signatures.

Hundreds!

"Abort, abort, abort!" Kyle called into his mic.

The two bodies on the roof hopped to their feet, both of them propping long tubes on their shoulders.

Shoulder launch missiles!

"Ambush! Wave off!" Kyle banked hard right, checking his altitude as he leaned steeply into the turn. His stomach clenched again—he was at twenty-five hundred feet. Without Jobs to help fly the aircraft while Kyle monitored the FLIR screen, he'd drifted into striking range.

A white light flared supernova on the FLIR screen.

Jerking his eyes away, Kyle leveled out and hauled up on the collective, adding power.

Weeeeeeeeeeeee!

So that's what a missile-lock-on alarm sounded like...

Kyle's flesh went damp against a rapid onrush of adrenaline. "Bandit One, did you copy my last?" He jammed the stick full-forward, pouring on the speed. "Abort the mission. Ambush underway! Repeat. Abort!"

The lock-on alarm took on a warbled sound.

The missile was tracking him.

His helo's countermeasure system automatically released chaff and flaff. But...

It didn't work.

Kyle's hands went icy. Those terrorist assholes hadn't fired a mere RPG at him—which was a matter of point, shoot, and pray—but an SA7 or SA14 heat-seeking motherfucker.

The missile was following him across the sky— *hunting* him.

Fuck, this is bad.

Kyle aimed east toward the Mangla Dam, trying to fly the hell out of range. When he got over the water, he dumped power, rapidly descending.

Tarzan was used to dealing with this kind of evasive maneuvering from the back, but Max's stomach was probably bouncing up and down in her throat.

Kyle leaned forward. *Come on, baby.* He hissed. *Go, go, go.* He had no more power to give. He was flying as fast as he—

WHAM!

Another alarm wailed as Kyle was thrown violently sideways in his seat. The straps of his restraints burned his flesh through his flight suit and survival vest and his brain knocked around inside his skull. He was probably doing a perfect Bobblehead impression.

The controls went mushy in his hands, and his mind seemed to process the information outside of conscious thought.

The missile blew off my tail. I no longer have a rear rotor.

The data rolled by inside his brain like a stock ticker in the New York Exchange—very matter-of-factly, very calmly, even though this was very bad.

Long years of training kicked in and orchestrated his movements. He automatically slammed down the collective, reducing power and torque on the rotors to prepare for a crash landing, then he chopped off the throttles.

In his rearview mirror, he saw another explosion. Someone else on his team just got hit.

Kyle's stomach squeezed down to a tiny ball.

Casanova or Davidson?

The aircraft shuddered around him. Not a little shudder, but a whole-body catastrophic, doomsday shudder. Jaw clamped, Kyle horsed the stick around, fighting to maintain control.

The Mangla Dam was coming up to meet him at

screaming velocity.

He pulled back on the stick, yanking the nose up to bleed off more speed, but his helmeted head just banged back against the headrest.

He'd lost more of his tail than he'd realized. He had no fucking control whatsoever. No way would he be able to pull off a clean autorotation.

They were going to crash.

Sweat poured down his face, and for the first time in his life, he felt real fear in the cockpit.

Max!

THE HELICOPTER DROPPED like a stone tossed down a well.

Max grabbed the bottom edge of her seat with a knuckle-aching grip and locked her teeth together. This couldn't be normal…

"Mayday! Mayday! Mayday!" Kyle's voice blasted into her earpiece. "Ditch! Ditch! Ditch!"

Max choked on her next breath as the world jerked wildly before her eyes. She was in a Steven Spielberg WWII movie battle sequence…or a basketball being dribbled down court. The aircraft suddenly swung brutally to the right, the incredible force of the motion hurling Tarzan out the open side door.

The sight of the AW disappearing into the dark unknown jolted a scream out of her—a bursting, stuttering, hiccupping noise full of terror, like someone was repeatedly punching her in the chest while she was yelling.

She broke off the noise when the helicopter reared into a nose-up position, going *completely vertical*—if the pretty picture of the starry sky whirling by the cockpit windshield was to be believed. From there, the helo dropped straight down, sending her stomach into her diaphragm to become one. The tail of the bird drilled into the surface of the water, and then several tons of steel heaved over onto its side, like a whale breaching the sea.

Max sling-shotted against her restraints, her head slamming forward into an exaggerated bow, then whamming back against the headrest, her vertebrae Lego'ing together.

The helicopter rolled violently, once, twice—

Ratatatatatatata!

The rotor blades detonated into shrapnel and the cockpit windshield exploded.

Good God—Kyle! All that flying glass had hit him.

The helicopter splashed to a stop onto its right side, the final impact sucking all the air out of her lungs. Her peripheral vision snapped off. Blood poured down her cheeks and forehead, creating a network of wet webbing along her nose and into her eye sockets.

Suddenly, surrealistically, everything went quiet.

There was only the gentle *shush* of water from the Mangla Dam rushing into the cockpit.

Dazed, Max blinked dumbly from her awkward position—she was dangling from her restraints like a human meal caught in a jungle cannibal's net. She blinked and blinked…until reality took hold.

Water was rapidly filling the aircraft.

Oh, no, Kyle…

She struggled to see him.

His pilot's seat was on the right side of the aircraft, closest to the water, so it would only take a moment for it to—God, no!

His seat just sank completely underwater!

His name rose like a bloodletting scream inside her mind.

Kyle!

With shaking, half-numb fingers, she clawed at the five-point restraint belting her in. How did this frigging thing work?! She couldn't unhook herself.

The water level rose.

Shush, shush, shush.

"Kyle." It was a whispered croak. *Don't die.*

Cold water touched her right elbow, oily with gasoline.

Her heartbeat leapt into the back of her mouth and boomed in her ears. She could hear her own breathing, harsh and rapid.

No.

The water kept coming.

Higher and higher…

She kicked her legs wildly while she renewed her efforts to free herself from the complicated seatbelt. These freaking straps were trapping her! "Help!" she called out. "Somebody—!"

Bam! Bam! Bam!

She jumped. Someone was pounding on her passenger window. She cranked her head around to see, the twisting movement sending a concerning dart of pain down the length of her spinal cord, and—

She gaped.

It was Kyle.

He was kneeling on the outside of the aircraft.

How in the world did he get outside?

He jabbed a finger at her windshield. "Pull the black-and-yellow handle!"

What? The what...?

Water sloshed against her belly and covered her right breast.

No.

Her teeth chattered. Blood throbbed painfully in her temples.

No.

Water slithered up to her collarbone, a cold, consuming Leviathan.

No.

She angled her chin up as high as it would go. Her eyeballs swelled against their sockets.

"Sam!" Kyle yelled.

Of all the things to call her... Her cheeks worked like bellows. She hauled in a last, hysterical breath as water, always her friend, slipped over her head and became her enemy.

CHAPTER THIRTY-FOUR

THE WORLD WAS wavy…dreamlike…

Max sank deeper and deeper into the cold isolation of darkness, her fear an oddly distant pressure, like her mind wasn't clear enough to process emotions. Her skull was caving in, her eardrums about to implode.

She instinctively squeezed her nose and blew out, equalizing the pressure in her ears.

Out the passenger window, she saw the light gliding away, shrinking into a smaller and smaller circle on the surface…a cymbal…a dartboard…

Her fingers still worried at her restraints. A new light blazed into the dwindling circle above her. *Pink* light? Ah, a flare. Someone had shot a flare into the sky…

A dinner plate…a tortilla…

So cold…so empty…so lonely…

But she wasn't alone.

There was a human shape in the passenger window, the bent-over form silhouetted by the red-pink glare of the flare. A man.

Kyle.

He was kneeling on the aircraft and working at prying open her passenger window.

Pull the black-and-yellow handle!

The words *clonged* through her mind as a dead

weight. But then…

She saw her own hand moving through the water in slow motion. It reached toward a metal rod. Her fingers wrapped around it.

She pulled.

The window disengaged from its frame. *Lift off!* She watched the flat plane of glass soar away.

Kyle swam forward.

She felt a tug near her lap, and then her body was buoyant, floating free. Kyle had unhooked her. She was no longer trapped!

He towed her out of the aircraft and shoved her helmet off her head.

It rolled away, slowly spinning through the water like a lost probe in outer space.

Kyle started to swim for the surface, urging her along. *Swim, yes…*

She kicked her legs and moved her arms, the familiarity of her favorite sport focusing her mind.

She saw Kyle yank a cord on the floatation device around his neck. Nothing happened.

Water blurred her vision, but she could still make out the alarm on his face.

He turned his chin toward the surface.

A hockey puck…an Oreo…

Then he looked back at her, his alarm deepening to fear.

They'd sunk too deep.

She processed her own fear now. It ballooned in her belly, squeezing acid up the pipe of her throat. She eye-locked Kyle and swam harder.

Come on! Go!

They faced each other while they swam, fighting to make it to the top.

The Oreo grew back into a hockey puck, but their upward movement just wasn't fast enough.

An expression of abject terror leapt into Kyle's eyes—he'd run out of air!

Grabbing onto her arms, he kept his eyes on hers. The terror faded, and there was only *I love you…*

And *goodbye.*

Max sobbed inside her chest.

No!

His eyes bugged. His gritted teeth shone dimly through the water the moment before his mouth opened in an instinctive search for air. But there was only water. He sucked in a lung full of it. He thrashed once, horribly, then went still, his eyes glazing over.

NO! She screamed the word; water filled her open mouth. *NO!*

Fisting one hand in the front of Kyle's survival vest, she swam harder. As hard as she ever had. She pinned her focus on the surface—her finish line. *Swim to win! Take this race!*

She concentrated on her form, nothing else: swift, hard kicks with her legs, an efficient, sweeping stroke with her one available arm.

Push your emotions away. Don't think. Don't feel.
Just swim.

Her lungs burned and compressed. How many minutes had she been holding her breath? Four minutes? Five? Impossible.

A dartboard…a cymbal…

The light above was growing larger, but she saw it through dimming vision. Unconsciousness was closing in on her. *I'm not going to make it.*

Panic edged in.

Don't give up. Win this!

The circle of light on the surface miraculously widened to the circumference of an ice-skating rink. *Almost there.* It took every ounce of concentration she owned not to flail those last few feet. Swift, hard kicks…sweeping strokes…

She broke the surface with an in-rushing *haaaaaaaaaa* of air, pulling Kyle up with her. She cried between more gulps of oxygen.

His face was blue!

Struggling to keep Kyle from sinking, she tried the cord on his floatation device again, yanking hard. It inflated this time. He floated onto his back, and she began mouth-to-mouth resuscitation.

Debris from the crash bumped into her while she worked to revive him: a notebook, a canvas bag, a seat cushion.

Come on, Kyle. Come on!

She became aware of a helicopter circling above. A spotlight beamed down from the nose of the bird, searching the crash site. The beam swept past her and Kyle, jolted back, and latched on.

Max frantically pounded on Kyle's chest and blew harder into his mouth.

Finally he vomited up a bucket of water. It smelled like gasoline. Thank God, he was breathing—although only weakly.

The helicopter descended to hover directly over them, the spinning rotors churning up a swirling mist of spray and rousing small waves to the surface of the dam.

A man wearing a wetsuit and swim fins moved to sit on the edge of the helo's open door.

An Aviation Warfare Specialist is also a certified search and rescue swimmer. Pretty much a jack of all trades...

The man jumped out of the helicopter and splashed in.

Treading water, he waited for a horse collar to be lowered from the aircraft, then he swam over to them, the collar looped through his arm.

He made for her, probably because she was a woman.

"Take him!" she shouted, pushing Kyle's body toward the guy. "He's worse!"

The rescue swimmer hesitated.

"He just drowned!" she cried. "Please!"

Nodding, the rescue swimmer slipped the horse collar onto Kyle, catching him around the armpits, then he aimed a thumbs-up at the pilots above.

Kyle slowly started to rise, water raining off his inert legs, the toes of his flight boots lightly tapping together.

The horse collar was lowered again, and the rescue swimmer got her settled into it, but two feet off the water a line of excruciating fire burned up the length of her spine.

She started screaming.

The rescue swimmer signaled the pilots above, and she was immediately lowered back into the water.

The horse collar was sent back up and a stretcher

made out of a metal basketweave was started down in its place.

She waited for what seemed like an eternity of teeth chattering. The Mangla Dam wasn't even all that cold—she didn't know why she couldn't stop her stupid teeth from playing the castanets.

It's the aftereffects of adrenaline...

And also all the damned pain.

The stretched finally splashed down beside her, and the rescue swimmer got her strapped into it.

A thumbs-up, and she began to rise.

Her heart pounded at the idea of being in a helicopter again, but she was too weak and too hurt to do anything about it.

The sound of the rotors grew louder, and the next thing she knew, she was being hauled into the back of the helo by a man dressed in camouflage—a corpsman. She was laid next to Kyle.

Beyond Kyle, there was another man lying on his back, who—

Tarzan!

He was wearing a neck brace and an ankle splint.

"Is he okay?" she croaked out.

"Broke his ankle and has whiplash," the corpsman answered. "But otherwise, yeah." He fit her into her own neck brace. "You probably have whiplash too, ma'am, so I need you to stay as still as possible."

Considering that every time she moved, her spine pulsed with electrical points of fire, she would try her best to follow those orders.

Max closed her eyes.

She woke to the feel of being hefted off the helicopter.

A couple of corpsmen bent low under the rotor wash and hustled her along, her back zinging with every one of their footsteps.

Kitty Hart's face appeared above her, bobbing against the night sky as she jogged alongside the stretcher. "Heavens above." Her brow pleated. "You're bruised from top to bottom."

"That's dye marker, actually." Dr. Barr's voice said that. "It must've auto-activated from Lieutenant Hammond's survival vest when he hit the water, and now Ms. Dougin's skin is stained with it."

Great. She probably looked like Oscar the Grouch's inbred cousin.

The ceiling of the medical tent appeared above her.

"Your head is bleeding profusely." Dr. Barr lightly prodded Max's skull. "Possible fracture of the cranium," she reported.

"How's Kyle?" Max asked hoarsely.

"I was told that the military injured are being flown to the trauma hospital at the Bagram base in Afghanistan."

"Is he going to be okay?" It tasted like the Indy 500 had raced all two hundred laps in her mouth.

"I'm sorry, Ms. Dougin, but I don't know anything more."

Kitty worked at hooking up Max to an IV.

Dr. Barr set a hand gently on Max's forearm. "Where does it hurt?"

"My back."

Dr. Barr told the corpsmen, "Bring her directly to x-ray."

"The pain, it's...it's severe."

"I'll take care of that as soon as I know if you're concussed or not."

Thank God it didn't take long for Dr. Barr to deter-
mine that Max's forehead had been lacerated by a sharp
edge of her helmet, but she was not, in fact, concussed.

Kitty plunged a syringe of meds into Max's IV line,
and...

One beat. Two.

Max gratefully checked out of all the pain and worry.

CHAPTER THIRTY-FIVE

"**L**IEUTENANT…? LIEUTENANT?! CAN you hear me?!"
Yes, I can hear you. Wheeze. Gasp. *Stop touching me.*

"He's barely conscious, Doctor."

"He's inhaled jet fuel into his lungs along with water. Let's roll him onto his side."

I said don't bother—head spins, temples throb.

"Lieutenant, if you can hear me, I'm going to pound your back rather hard now. I need to break loose the contaminants in your lungs so that I can suction them out."

Please, stop—body jerks. Ribs squeak and grind. *Stop!*

"All right, put him on his back again.

"Yes, Doctor."

"Suction."

No, get that fucking tube out of my throat. Choking. Scraping. Strangling.

"This is bad. Increase the power by two degrees."

Fire and stars. Cactus spines.

"Dammit…"

"Doctor?"

"Check the Lieutenant's dog tags and find out who his next of kin is."

"Yes, Doctor."

Blank.

The next morning
Naval Air Station, North Island, San Diego

AT ZERO-SIX-HUNDRED ON the dot, Lieutenant Eric "LZ" O'Dwyer switched on the coffeemaker that was set up on the sideboard running the length of his office.

Although *office* was probably too generous of a term for the small, utilitarian space where his desk sat just outside the door to the large, plush office of his boss, Admiral Stanfield, Commander Air Forces Pacific—otherwise known as AIRPAC.

Eric was Stanfield's aide, but even though being an admiral's aide was a great job when it came to career advancement, it sounded fancier than it was. *Because, seriously, look around*—his office was a closet.

Damn, but he missed flying with his Wolfpack buddies. Not that he missed the deployments that went along with being a part of the fleet—those would've taken him away from his new girlfriend, Nicole, for far too long. Being able to crawl into bed with her at the end of every day was sheer bliss, and it made the long work hours as an aide—and the tedious bullshit he sometimes had to deal with as a glorified gofer—worth it.

While Mr. Coffee got its groove on with a lot of hissing and grumbling, Eric sat at his desk and opened his emails. Stanfield traditionally came in at zero-seven-hundred on the dot, and Eric needed to get the jump on message traffic so he could brief his boss about the day's hot items.

Eric skimmed down the subject lines and—*shit*.

There was a *mishap notification* message from Admiral Kelleman, Commander Strike Group One.

Eric opened the email and started reading.

...official mishap notification will be out soon, but I wanted to give you the word that two helicopters were shot down by terrorists last night in Pakistan, a Sierra bird and a Romeo ...a PINNACLE OPREP THREE report has been sent to the White House. Recommend pushing information up the chain of command to CNO. One of the aircraft went down with a newspaper reporter, and we anticipate high press interest...

Eric shoved a hand through his hair. *Damn. Two* helicopters had been lost. That was always a hard blow to the aviation community.

He scanned down the email, jumping to the Killed/Injured/MIA list Kelleman had included. Most of the names appeared to be enlisted SEALs: *Petty Officer Samuel Jacob Tyson, United States Navy, Petty Officer Bradley Hugh Emerson, United States Navy, Lieutenant Kyle Jonathan Hammond, United States—*

Eric froze. *What...Kyle?* "Holy fuck," he hissed, his abdominals jerking tight. His best friend had been in the accident...?

No. It can't be true.

Although it was true that Mikey tended to be a magnet for bad luck. In fact, Kyle's bad luck brigade included some real biggies: during Kyle's inaugural helicopter hop in flight school, he and Eric hit a flock of birds and almost crashed; on their first cruise together with the BattleCats squadron, Kyle made a complete drunken idiot of himself with a prostitute on liberty; on their second cruise together with the Wolfpack doing counterdrug ops, Mikey slipped off a cliff and fell into the hands of some Columbian bad guys, again almost dying.

And then there was Kyle's relationship with his ex-girlfriend, Sienna, which was pure disaster from start to finish—not that it was even finished—including a secret, seriously ill kid who'd recently popped up into Mikey's life.

But even with all this back-blow, Mikey didn't do a lot of pissing and moaning. He had strong opinions about certain things, yeah, but mostly he was a fun guy to hang out with. A great friend. Eric couldn't even begin to wrap his brain around the idea of Mikey not being around anymore.

You must never jump to conclusions, Eric. If you do, you might stop fighting.

Right. Kyle was listed as *critically injured*, not KIA, so there was still a chance his friend could—

Admiral Stanfield strode inside, his posture erect, and... He frowned at Eric on the way toward his large office.

Oh, crap. Eric was still sitting on his duff, having failed to come respectfully to his feet the moment his boss entered the room—*early*, which the prick did to him some mornings.

"Sir." Eric leapt up just as the admiral disappeared into his office. *Well, this morning already officially bites.*

Eric jabbed his index finger down on the *print* button, and while he waited for the printer to print, he grabbed a mug and filled it with coffee. Heading for Stanfield's office, he snatched up the printout on the way by and read the rest of the list as he walked inside.

His stomach sank when he spotted another familiar name.

"Sir." Eric set the mug of coffee on the admiral's desk in front of him. "Two birds were shot down in a terrorist attack in Pakistan," he said without preamble, handing Stanfield the printout of Kelleman's email message. "A Sierra and a Romeo."

Stanfield took the paper, his frown deepening as he read. "Any fatalities?"

"Yes, sir. Just about an entire chalk of SEALs didn't survive. And also a pilot was killed. One of our own out of North Island."

Stanfield's focus snapped up. "Who?"

MAX PEELED HER eyelids open. A blurry image of empty, neatly made beds was to her right and a standing curtain-screen to her left, everything gradually changing from fuzzy to clear.

She was in the aid station's post-op ward.

She didn't try to move, just lay in a near-comatose heap, smelling clammy, her overtaxed muscles totally spent. Her whole body was so limp she doubted she could've moved, even if she wanted to.

She didn't want to.

Her back was still a fire of pain, although not as bad as before.

She glanced up at the full IV bag hanging on a metal pole next to her.

God love painkillers.

Kitty bustled around the standing screen and stopped short. "Oh! You're awake." She leaned back around the screen and called down the aisle, "Ma'am."

Dr. Barr appeared a moment later. "Ms. Dougin, how are you feeling this morning?"

"Like I was in a helicopter crash yesterday."

Dr. Barr smiled, the movement of her lips slight but pleasant. "I can imagine. How's the pain in your back?"

"Tolerable. Although I have a feeling it wouldn't be without that." She flipped her eyes toward the IV bag.

Dr. Barr made a sound of agreement in her throat. "You're going to be in a good deal of pain for a while, I'm afraid. I've examined your x-rays, and you have a hairline fracture in the lumbar region of your spine. The L5 vertebra to be exact."

"I..." Max felt her lips parting. "Dear God, I broke my back?"

"Let's say you *cracked* it. The fracture is small enough that it doesn't require surgery to repair. That's very good news, especially considering you were in a helicopter crash yesterday." The small smile flickered across Dr. Barr's mouth again. "The injury can be treated with rest and pain medication. You also show signs of whiplash, but mostly that's a muscular issue—your cervical vertebrae looked fine. I've put you on anti-inflammatory medication for that."

"Okay."

"But here's the bad news."

Max's heart stopped. "Oh, my God, is Kyle okay?"

Dr. Barr blinked. "Oh, I'm sorry, I didn't mean to

frighten you. I still don't have any information on the military injured. However, early this morning I did receive another phone call warning of imminent danger to this aid station. So as uncomfortable as it will be to move you right now, I'm going to have to evacuate you along with HM3 Hart." Dr. Barr nodded at Kitty. "She'll oversee your care on the flight to St. George's Hospital trauma center in London. You'll make a stopover there to receive any treatment necessary to prepare you for the trip back stateside." She looked at Kitty. "From St. George's you'll fly out to the *USNS Mercy*, where you'll be temporarily assigned until I receive the all-clear to bring you back here."

"Yes, ma'am."

Dr. Barr tucked her hands into the pockets of her white lab coat. "I need to make a few more phone calls, finish smoothing out the details for your air transport. I'll also try to find out the status of the Wolfpack crew. Once I have all the information, I'll let you two know."

Chapter Thirty-Six

"**I** HAVE SOMETHING to tell you."

Kitty *did* tense up when Farrin said those words this time, because *this time* the doctor wasn't grinning like a possum eating a sweet tater. In fact, her face was about as somber as a gravedigger's, which meant that the news Farrin was about to dole out was bad.

Kitty probably should've suspected as much when she'd been summoned to Farrin's personal tent, instead of just going to the post-op ward.

As the head of the aid station, Dr. Barr was the only person who lived in a private tent. It was a spacious living quarter with a double-sized bed on the right, colorful pictures on all the walls, and on the left—where another bed normally would've been—was a small desk.

Farrin was seated at it now.

Kitty was tempted to take the coward's way out of this discussion and hide her head under it. "Is this about Lieutenant Hammond, ma'am?" Max had told Kitty about how bad off the lieutenant was, so if terrible news was coming, it was probably about him.

"Why don't you sit down." Farrin gestured at her bed.

Kitty's legs suddenly felt like twin saplings off a rubber tree plant. So, setting was probably a good idea. "Yes, ma'am." She propped her bottom on the edge of Farrin's mattress.

"This is about the other helicopter that was shot down." Farrin picked up a pen from her desk. "The Pakistani government is in an uproar about their sovereign airspace being violated, so they won't allow the Americans a salvage operation. But the MEDEVAC helicopter that dropped off Ms. Dougin here last night was able to land briefly at the crash site to look for survivors." Farrin slid the pen to the tops of her fingers, clicked it open, clicked it closed, slid it back down.

Kitty's stomach was in more knots than her Aunt Clara's hair after a weekend bender. "Yes, ma'am."

Farrin set down the pen and folded her hands in her lap. "The corpsman who checked inside the helicopter ascertained that two men are missing in action, a SEAL and a pilot. The rest were confirmed killed on impact, including..." Farrin stopped to swallow.

Kitty watched Farrin's throat move, and goosebumps rose along her flesh, just like when static electricity pricked the fine hairs on her arms to warn of an oncoming lightning storm. A storm was brewing, a storm of a different sort, but its destructive force was fixing to flatten her all the same. "Yes, ma'am," she whispered.

"One of those killed was Lieutenant Whitmore."

"Who?" she gulped out the word.

"Kitty—"

"No." Kitty shook her head. "Ma'am, I'm sorry, but you have it wrong. Steve can't be dead. He wasn't flying in the second bird, so he's at Bagram Hospital with the other military injured."

Farrin looked at Kitty with deeply saddened eyes. "Apparently a last-minute switch was made. Lieutenant Whitmore took the place of the pilot whose eye was injured by glass."

Kitty dragged her tongue across her lips. If there was any moisture left in her mouth and throat, it was hiding. "No, ma'am. See, I took a chance on him. I was brave this time. I...I finally chose the right man. So...so... Don't you see?"

Farrin just watched her, her throat still moving.

Kitty blinked rapidly and the tip of her nose stung. "Steve said that if I was his girl, he would never leave me, so...so you're wrong. He-he can't... He said..."

I really wish I could hug you right now.

Kitty tented her hands over her mouth. "I told him that I'd see him later, so I *have* to see him later." Tears fell down her face. "I *told* him."

"I'm so sorry." Farrin's eyes looked like they'd grown extra lines around them in the last half hour. "But..." Farrin's eyelashes lowered slowly. "There's more, I'm afraid."

Kitty dropped her hands. They landed in her lap with a *thump.*

"The two men who are MIA from the helicopter wreckage have been identified as the head pilot, Lieutenant Commander Jason Vanderby, and the lead SEAL."

Creepers of ice inched along Kitty spine. *A SEAL...*

"Kitty, the missing SEAL is your ex-boyfriend, Shane. He and Commander Vanderby have been listed as presumed dead or captured."

Kitty's innards filled with a soupy swill of panic.

Shane...dead...

The image of the doctor slipped out of her field of vision—actually, it was Kitty herself who was slipping, her rump sliding off the edge of the bed.

Those stories folks tell 'bout falling unconscious when pain gets too fierce? Doesn't happen. A body feels all the suffering...

Except this time a fainting spell blessedly released Kitty from the agony of losing two men she loved.

Her back hit the mattress once and bounced, then she flopped onto Farrin's floor into blackness.

One week later
Lake Arrowhead, California

IF MAX NEVER saw the inside of another hospital for as long as she lived, it would be too soon.

She'd just made it back to the States after a week at St. George's, the doctors there having been appalled to learn that Max flew for nine hours straight with a broken back—although she'd spent most of the flight from Pakistan to England lying flat on a special cot in a cargo plane.

And, yes, the doctors at St. George's said *broken.*

So the hospital kept her in London, and even though they probably managed her pain better than if Max had been at home, they also prescribed *total* rest and relaxation as a part of her recovery. Which meant no upsetting internet access—*upsetting* because that's what the hospital staff saw in Max every time she hit a brick wall trying to track down Kyle. The staff had let her contact her parents and boss to let them know of her whereabouts, then that was it.

She was left with no way to get in touch with Kyle.

She had his phone number from when he gave it to her at the aid station, but her cell had been in her back pocket when she went into the Mangla dam, so it was ruined from the drenching it took, and she wouldn't be able to buy a new chip for a new phone till she got back to the States. Without the internet, she had no other way to find Kyle, which was *more* upsetting than all the brick walls, but none of the nurses seemed to want to put two-and-two together on that.

Now, thank God, she had a new chip and a new phone in hand. Two and a half hours ago, she'd landed in LAX—she had to splurge for business class for the trip from London to Los Angeles to guarantee a comfortable seat—and as soon as she got off the plane, she made right for a Verizon kiosk.

"Is this the place?" the driver asked her—the *LA Times* had sent a van to take her on the hour and a half trip from the airport to her parents' vacation home in Lake Arrowhead.

She peered out the side window at the wooden cabin tucked into a circle of pines. "Yes, thank you."

The shutters were closed; the house was empty. No Mom and Dad waited inside to greet their world-weary daughter. Although in her parents' defense, Max hadn't told them exactly when she'd be coming home. Because she'd rather have *lack of information* be the reason they weren't here, rather than their busy careers once again keeping them away…and she supposed that part was not defensible.

The van pulled to a stop at the front door, and the driver glanced at Max in the rearview, then quickly looked away.

She was still a weird shade of vomity yellow from left-over dye-marker stains.

She got out, mindful of how she lifted her duffel bag and backpack. Her lower spine twinged with a hot dart, but not too badly. She'd downgraded from Percocet to Vicodin for pain relief, and she had a bottle of the latter in her backpack, enough pills to see her through until she could visit her regular doctor.

She clomped inside the cabin and went directly into her bedroom, dropping her duffel and backpack on the bed. She hadn't opened her duffel since leaving the aid station. Kitty had packed her belongings for her, seeing as Max had been laid up in the post-op ward, and Max left St. George's in the clothes she'd arrived in.

Unzipping the bag now was like sending a sledge-hammer smashing through her chest.

Right on top of her clothing was Kyle's cotton ball bouquet.

Max pressed a hand over her mouth and just stared at it for several long seconds. *Kyle, where are you? Please, be okay.* With tears stinging her nose, she carefully picked up the bouquet and hugged it to her breasts. That's when she saw an envelope had been left under the bouquet, with a handwritten not from Dr. Barr paperclipped to it.

Ms. Dougin,

Lieutenant Hammond gave me this letter to give to you. It's a final letter to be opened in the event of his death. I truly hope you don't have to open it, but I thought you should have it nonetheless.

I wish you a speedy recovery.

Please let me know if there's anything I can do for you.

Farrin

Max gazed at the envelope with hollow-feeling eyes. A swallow worked its way, inch by choking inch, down her throat, and an incredible weight landed dead-center on her lungs. Her next breath was nearly impossible to draw in—grief was taking up too much space in her chest.

Are *you dead, Kyle*?

Max fumbled her new cell out of her backpack, then tugged the chip programmed with her old phone number out of its plastic wrap and snapped it inside.

The Apple icon appeared on the screen, and a few seconds later several texts popped up.

Robyn from the LA Times' editorial desk wanted to know if Max could sub in for Craig's column next month because he was having his gallbladder removed, and LA Fitness was reminding her that her gym membership expired this month. The last text was from Kitty, asking how she was doing.

The real question was how Kitty was doing. During the whole flight from Pakistan to England, the stricken young woman looked like someone had beaten her with a stick.

Steve Whitmore got killed, and Shane's lost or captured by terrorists, maybe dead too...

Talk of grief.

Tears scalded Max's eyes as memories of Steve Whitmore flooded over her, his freckle-faced eagerness the day of the ambulance crash, how so much of life still lay ahead of him that now would never be lived.

It was so unfair.

What about you, Kyle? Did you make it?

Max scrolled through her contacts and found "Kyle Hammond."

She smiled briefly over him imputing his last name. Like she wouldn't know who *Kyle* was.

She pushed the call button.

Nothing happened.

A spasm of anguish gripped her heart. Pressing a palm over her eyes, she sat down heavily on her bed and sobbed.

The line was as dead as Kyle probably was.

Chapter Thirty-Seven

One week later
Balboa Naval Hospital, Pulmonary Clinic, San Diego

KYLE WAS PUTTING on the last of his civilian clothes when a nurse poked her head inside the door to his hospital room.

"Your friends are here to take you home, Lieutenant," she told him.

"Okay, thanks." And thank crap he was finally getting the hell out of here. He'd made very little progress in hunting down Max over the past two weeks.

Partly because finding her would require a shit-ton of calls, and patients weren't allowed to use hospital phones for more than a few basic calls. He'd managed to sneak in only two.

The first was to the rescue swimmer who'd pulled him out of the drink—under the guise of wanting to thank the guy, Kyle got hold of the AW's contact number.

Hey, man, do you know where the LA Times reporter was taken to?

"...one helluva woman," the guy had gone on about Max, "...dragged you up from the wreck, gave you mouth-to-mouth..."

Most of those words had gone in one of Kyle's ears

and out the other. Because he was too focused on what the guy said about Max being hurt so badly in the crash, she hadn't been able to bear a horse collar—she'd required a stretcher.

Exactly how bad was that?

The second person he'd tracked down was Max's editor, Edward Aubrey, who was only able to tell him that Max had been out on sick leave ever since departing Pakistan, but last he heard she was stuck in a trauma center in London.

Trauma center and *stuck* were very much things Kyle didn't want to hear either. What kind of heinous aftereffects from the crash was she dealing with? Had she been maimed in some way...?

If only he had a damned cell phone. But his old one was no doubt worming its way through a fish's digestive tract in Mangla Dam at this very moment, and he'd been out of the real world—away from cell phone stores—for too long as a patient, first in Bagram, where he spent two days being stabilized—which later he learned was touch-and-go—then in Landstuhl Army Hospital in Germany, where he spent a week relearning how to breathe. Today, he'd just finished another week at Balboa Naval Hospital's Pulmonary Clinic, going through rehab—basically making sure he *really* knew how to breathe.

Kyle walked fast as he left his hospital room and cut into the hallway. The place was standard-issue medical clinic, lots of uninviting antiseptic smells coupled with equally unappealing white linoleum floors and white walls, every few feet a poster or a flyer warning everyone to *Wash Your Hands!*

Kyle exited into the waiting room and saw his best friend, Eric "LZ" O'Dwyer.

Eric had been to Balboa a couple times over the past week to visit Kyle, but this time Eric was with his girl-friend, Nicole.

Nicole walked up to Kyle and engulfed him in a hug. "Sorry, I couldn't come sooner to see you. I was on assignment."

Nicole Gamboa was a half-Hawaiian, half-Colombian knockout DEA Agent who'd worked with Kyle and Eric on a counterdrug operation in Colombia almost a year ago. Kyle and Nicole had started out as pissy adversaries—mostly due to Kyle being a dick to her—while Eric ended up landing Nicole as his squeeze. They looked good together—Nicole's toffee-colored skin and hair matched well with Eric's black Irish looks.

"Why do you smell like gasoline?" Nicole asked, stepping back.

Oh, merely one of the many lingering perks of taking in a gallon's worth of JP5 jet fuel into his lungs. "Let's just say it's a good thing I don't smoke. Light a match near my mouth right now and my whole head is likely to go boom."

Nicole frowned, then sighed. "*Dios mío*, Kyle. You've really had a hard time of it, haven't you?"

"You could say that."

Nicole held Kyle's gaze, sorrow weighting her eyes. "I was sorry to hear about Steve Whitmore."

Nicole knew Jobs from the counterdrug mission. Steve and Eric had flown Nicole and her DEA partner on a fast-rope op down to a hidden drug sub—a mission Kyle normally would've flown, but he'd been too much of a nutjob at the time from just finding out he'd fathered a sick son.

"Yeah." Kyle pushed a hand through his hair. "It's gonna be tough getting over Jobs' death." Just hearing the kid's name backed up saliva into Kyle's mouth, heightening the petroleum flavor basting his tongue with every swallow. "Steve was my responsibility."

"He didn't die on your bird, Mikey," Eric pointed out.

Didn't matter, not to him.

"From every report I've read," Eric went on, "you were waylaid by those terrorists. There was nothing anyone on the op did wrong based on the intel you had."

Kyle nodded. He didn't mean the nod. Because in his mind he'd suspected a double-cross, and yet he still let the team get ensnared in a trap—although granted, JEM by themselves wouldn't have had heat-seeking missiles. It was the Taliban who brought the high-tech weaponry that was able to take out the rescue team, and their interference had been left out of the intel equation.

"Let's just get out of here, okay?" Kyle said. "I'm sick of this place."

The three of them went outside, exiting onto the third-floor open air balcony running the entire outer circumference of the building. Balboa Hospital was a massive installation of three beige high rises surrounding a courtyard where patients and visitors could find Dunkin' Donuts, Subway Sandwiches, and benches to sit on. Building Three, where they were, mostly housed outpatient clinics.

Kyle aimed for the bay of elevators. "Do you mind if we stop at an AT&T on the way back to my place?" he asked Eric. "I have to make some calls that can't wait."

"Everything okay?" Eric asked, obviously picking up on Kyle's tension.

"Not really. I need to get in touch with the *LA Times* again about the woman who worked with me in Pakistan."

"A reporter?"

"Yeah."

"Mikey, you know you're supposed to let the Navy PR people handle everything with the *Times* about the crash, right? Otherwise—"

"This is about *her*, LZ, not the fucking newspaper." Kyle skidded to a stop in front of the elevators. "I need to make sure she's okay. I need to…I need to ask her to marry me."

Kyle blinked. Whoa, he hadn't realized he was going to say that. The words just came blasting out of his mouth—but instantly he felt the rightness of them. As much time as he'd spent in Landstuhl relearning how to make his lungs work, fact was he'd never breathe right again without Max in his life.

Eric stood unmoving with an *oh-shit* expression on his face.

Nicole darted a quick glance at her boyfriend.

"Mikey…" Eric started hesitantly.

"I know I sound insane," Kyle admitted. "But I'm not." *Not this time. Not with Max.*

"Mikey…" Eric began again. "C'mon, man, your track record with women has always been…" A brief grimace touched his mouth. "Look, your decision-making has never been particularly good in this area, and right now, can you maybe admit that you might not be thinking clearly? You almost died. That's got to be coloring the situation."

"I'll admit that I've always been bugfuck crazy when it comes to women, LZ. But in all the time you've known me, with all the women you've seen me go through, have I ever once said I was in love with one of them?"

Eric's mouth twisted, like pushing the name out was painful. "Sienna."

Kyle curled his own lips, but he did make himself think about Sienna, the only woman who'd ever been in his life longer than a week. And, okay, LZ might have a point—Kyle had always believed she was the one. As dysfunctional as their relationship was, he still imagined what was between them was love just trying to get better. But now that he felt what he did for Max, the wrongness of Sienna was like a fist choking off the blood supply to his heart.

"Have I ever said I wanted to marry anyone before?" Kyle countered.

"No." Eric blew out a long breath. "And I don't mean to be an asshole about it, but... How long have you known this woman?"

"About a week. And, yeah, that sounds even more insane, even to my own ears, but it's not. I don't know how to explain it to you." The best he could come up with was that the Universe wasn't pissing and moaning in his ear, and if that wasn't his gut telling him Max was the absolute right choice for him, he didn't know what was.

Calm assurance clicked into place, and Kyle gave his friend a slight smile. "And you're not being an asshole, LZ. You're looking out for me, like you always have, and I appreciate it. I needed it before." *Like the fuckup little brother of the family.* "But I don't need it this time."

Eric glanced at Nicole, who didn't seem bunched up about Kyle's decision, then looked back at Kyle. "All right." Eric nodded slowly. "I'm sure I'll get on board with your plan once I meet her."

Max would totally win Eric over in a second. "I'd *love* for you to meet her, but I can't fucking find her."

"No?" Nicole tugged her cell phone out of the back pocket of her jeans shorts. "What's her name? I'll find her for you."

Kyle stared at Nicole.

"I'm in law enforcement, remember?" Nicole bobbed her eyebrows and grinned. "I have access to all kinds of cool databases."

For the first time in a long time, the congested feeling in Kyle's chest completely cleared. "Her name is Samantha Dougin," he breathed out, "and I'm so having your babies, Gamboa."

Nicole started typing on her phone. "Don't you still owe me babies for the Vicodin I gave you in Colombia?"

Kyle glanced sharply at LZ. "You told her I said that?"

Eric's smile broadened and he offered up an unrepentant shrug.

CHAPTER THIRTY-EIGHT

M AX COULDN'T FIND *anyone* who had information about her boyfriend.

Kyle's Wolfpack CO was deployed, Kyle's *Bunker Hill* skipper was likewise still floating, and Kyle's AW, Tarzan, was on leave somewhere nursing a broken ankle. Dr. Barr had been able to chase down Kyle as far as his move from Bagram trauma hospital in Afghanistan to Landstuhl Army Hospital in Germany, but then lost him from there—whoever had overseen Kyle's transfer out of Landstuhl had since left that post.

No one at the Army hospital would talk directly to Max due to confidentiality restrictions.

So she knew that Kyle had lived long enough to spend a week at Landstuhl, but she didn't know if he was still alive.

What a wonderful thing not to know.

She sank down into a dining room chair and propped an elbow on the table, resting her forehead in one palm while she pressed her thumb to the camera icon on her cell phone.

Up popped the picture of Kyle she'd taken the day she created his false Rick Sagget biography. The crooked smile he'd tossed at the camera was such quintessential *Kyle*, a little bit of the smirky bad boy mixed with the man who was a connoisseur of life's ironies, a seer of truths, and a bigger hero than he would ever know.

Max sniffed and rubbed her nose.

Ever since watching Kyle's boots tap together while he was being hoisted into the MEDEVAC helicopter, she'd been a house on stilts in a hurricane. Now, as she gazed down at the face she loved so deeply, those stilts turned into toothpicks and down she came, foundations plummeting off snapping supports.

She couldn't find Kyle, and she couldn't think of any other avenues to search for him. She was utterly depleted.

Her next breath was a ragged, tear-filled gasp.

You just keep to your own lane, so fucking removed from it all…

"Yeah, well, do you see me now, Kyle? *Do you see me now?*" She closed her eyes, her heart alternately squeezing down to a spare lump, then ballooning to twice its normal size: a feeling of love, but when it was also agony.

"Pl-please come back to me." She clasped her cell phone in a tighter fist. And in her other fist…she held the envelope.

Kyle's letter to her—his *final* letter.

Do you see *why* I keep to my own lane, Kyle? Tears streamed down her face and dripped off her chin. BECAUSE THIS IS UNBEARABLE!

But also…

She pressed the envelope over her eyes. But also, she'd never felt love so powerfully as she did when she looked at Kyle's photo. Opening herself up to him had, yes, bared her to pain. But she never would've experienced the profound joy of a deep and true love if she hadn't swum out of her lonely lane and joined all the other splashing.

Kyle had pushed her to do that, and whether he ended up back in her life or not, she needed to try her hardest not to live on the outside looking in anymore.

She needed to make this new skin she wore to be Kyle's lasting gift to her.

Someone knocked.

She set down her phone and the letter and grabbed a tissue off the kitchen counter on her way to the front door. Wiping her eyes and nose, she opened the door on a clean-shaven man with short hair. He was casually dressed in jeans and a T-shirt with the words Pacific Beach arching over a setting sun.

Max frowned. She'd been expecting her middle-aged neighbor.

Gladys was the only one who generally dropped by, usually when she was baking up a batch of—Max snapped her eyes down to the front of the man's T-shirt again. *Pacific Beach...*

Meaning you could work from San Diego, where I live near Pacific Beach?

She whipped her eyes back up, then rolled backward off her heels, heading in a collision course toward the floor. Her convalescing back wouldn't have liked that kind of impact, and so thank God Kyle was quick enough to grab her before she hit.

Kyle! Dear God, it was him.

"Where the hell have you been?!" she cried out and threw her arms around his neck. Pushing her face against his ear, she wet his throat with a renewed rush of tears. "I've been looking everywhere for you."

"You have?" He hugged her closer.

"Yes, dammit, and I couldn't find you."

He brushed his nose across the top of her hair. "I couldn't find you either."

She leaned back in his arms and cocked her head at him. "Well, here you are."

A smile touched his lips. "Only because a Fed friend of mine looked up your parents' Lake Arrowhead address in one of her databases. Before that, all I knew was that you'd ended up at a trauma hospital in London." His expression sobered.

"Yes," she sighed. "I broke my back."

"Jesus, what?" He took a quick step back and frantically looked her over. "Are you okay?"

"I'm doing better."

"Do you mean it?" His eyebrows started to gather together. "You're not playing anything down, like when you jammed your wrist after the ambulance crash?"

"I still have to be careful how I move—and thank you for stopping me from falling—but yes. I'm okay. How are you?"

"Good."

"Are *you* sure? You, um, smell kind of funny."

He snorted. "Yeah, sorry. When I took in that big breath underwater, I sucked jet fuel into my lungs along with a lot of Mangla Dam. Trust me, I used to smell much worse."

She shook her head. She couldn't believe he was apologizing. "You're here and you're okay—nothing else matters beyond that." She lifted a hand and stroked her palm over his smooth cheek. "Although I can hardly believe it's really you. Just as I'd feared, you don't look like you anymore. You're so clean-cut." A total, all-American Navy man.

His gaze danced as he searched her face. "The saying *sight for sore eyes*—that's what you look like."

Her heart warming, she kept caressing his face. "Who knew you had such a chiseled jaw?" she murmured.

His laugh was a pleased rumble. Leaning forward, he kissed her.

The feel of his lips on hers immediately set her heart to skittering like hail on a skylight. Looping her arms around his neck again, she threw all of herself into kissing him back, pressing her lips to his like he was an indispensable life source she never wanted to do without. Which he was. And she really didn't.

His kiss never broke from being breathtakingly gentle, the touch of his lips sweet, the soft tip of his tongue making only a brief foray into her mouth. Her lips melted and warmed—her whole body did. He tugged her lower lip between his teeth and gave her an affectionate nibble before easing back. He gazed into her eyes, his head still bent to her.

Desire pooled in pure chemical response to his stare—to the heat in it. To the love. Her breath caught.

I think falling for you would be the best thing that ever happened to me...

And now everything he felt for her was right there in his eyes for her to see—no holding back.

How was this the same Kyle as the one she'd started out the mission with? "Maybe we should get out of the doorway," she suggested, "and enjoy a proper homecoming."

"In your parents' home?" He glanced over her shoulder to the inside of the house and made a face. "There's a bit of a gack-factor for me with that."

"You're kidding?" She tilted her head. "Isn't that a little old-fashioned?"

His eyes met hers again.

"Look out," she teased, "you might need to catch me from falling over again."

His cheeks creased with a smile. "I just want you to come home with me, smart ass. It's where you belong."

CHAPTER THIRTY-NINE

T HE AIR WAS redolent with the briny scents of the sea in the town of Pacific Beach, one of San Diego's lovely seaside communities. The quaint streets were lined with unique cafés, small pubs, tourist shops, and boutique clothing stores specializing in coastal wear. The town gave off a mixed vibe of laid-back beach bum combined with a youthful movers-and-shakers feel.

Max could see why a young bachelor would want to live here.

Kyle carried her duffel and backpack into his second-floor apartment, leading her from a small foyer into a living room that was a total guy space, complete with a Naugahyde couch and two chairs of the same brown color—one a recliner—a chunky glass coffee table, a monstrous stereo system, and a mammoth flat screen television.

The carpet was shag in multicolored brown shades—beige, tan, and coffee all twisted together. Luckily, there were two huge windows letting in a lot of sunlight, or the place would've come off as dreary rather than earthy. A shelf under the TV was stacked with CDs and Blu-rays, and the walls displayed a helter-skelter collection of framed photographs instead of paintings or posters—candid shots showing Kyle in all aspects of his life: in a flight suit with other Navy buddies, in a white military uniform, having an award medal pinned on his chest, out with friends at parties or on vacation, snow skiing and hiking.

"You thirsty?" he asked, dropping her bags by the couch next to another suitcase—his, undoubtedly.

"I'm fine."

"Hungry?"

"Nope."

"You sure? There's nothing I can get you?"

She observed him for a quiet moment. "You seem nervous all of a sudden."

"Do I? Nah. I'm not nervous." He paused, a smile creeping over his mouth. "Okay, maybe I'm a little nervous."

"Over our impending homecoming celebration?" She laughed in a burst. "Isn't that taking the Old-Fashioned-Kyle role a tad far?"

He smirked. "Sex is not the issue here, sugah. I'm just not sure what you're going to say to *this*." He swung his suitcase onto the couch and snapped it open.

"To what?" She watched him shove his hand into the top inside pocket of his suitcase.

"I made two stops on the way home. One at an AT&T to buy a new cell phone. The other at a jewelry store." He pulled a ring box from the suitcase pocket. "For this." He held it out to her.

Her mouth dropped open. "Whaaaaaat?"

Smiling, Kyle opened the box on an engagement ring.

It was like getting hit in the face with the flat head of a shovel—totally unexpected and surprising.

Kyle's smile widened, although his eyes remained serious. "I know we haven't known each other for long, Max, but you're the one for me. *The absolute one.* I don't have the slightest doubt in my mind. I'm crazy in love with you."

She forgot about breathing. Chillbumps cascaded down her arms. She continued to gape at the ring nestled in dark velvet. Mounted on a gold band was a setting of a single round diamond surrounded by tiny round sapphires. It was... ridiculously stunning.

"I wanted there to be blue stones, for...you know, to represent water." He reached out and traced his fingers along a couple of strands of her bangs. "Because you're my champion swimmer." His voice thickened. "You saved my life, Max."

She pressed a hand to her chest. Her heart was beating like a jazz musician gone wild on a snare drum. She should probably sit down before she almost fell down again.

"All right, so...your eyelashes are moving so much they're, like, twerking. And in this case, I can't tell if that's good or bad." He stared down at her intently, as if searching her for answers. "Honey, if you need a long engagement to be sure about me, I don't mind. Just say yes. Okay? Please say yes."

She finally got her vocal cords to produce sound. "K-Kyle." *Okay, barely.* "Yes...a million times *yes!*"

His face split into a broad grin.

Tears clouded her vision. "And how does next month sound for a wedding?"

He tossed his head back and laughed. "Sounds absolutely perfect. Oh, wait…hell. I forgot to kneel." He dropped down on one knee, plucked the engagement ring from its box, and took her left hand in his. He gazed up at her with loving eyes as he gently pushed the diamond on her ring finger. "I promise to love you faithfully forever, Samantha Dougin, and with all my heart."

More tears fell. Her lips trembled around her response. "You're the best thing that's ever happened to me, Kyle Hammond—I'm crazy in love with you too." What would she have done if he'd died? Even being apart from him for two weeks had felt like an eternity of—"Oh! I forgot. I have something for you as well."

He pushed back to his feet. "Yeah?"

She dug into her backpack and pulled out the envelope she'd recently crushed in her hand. "It's your letter," she said, holding it out to him. "Um, your final letter."

He gave her a startled look.

"Dr. Barr passed it on to me," she explained softly. "Just in case."

He stared down at the envelope for a long moment, then slowly raised his eyes to hers. "You didn't open it?"

"No. Dr. Barr said only to open it if you died, and I couldn't lose hope that you were okay—somewhere out there."

His throat moved. "It was a hard letter to write, but…" He held her gaze. "It was also pretty damned nice to have someone in my life I wanted to leave it to."

She smiled, her heart filling her chest. That was probably the best thing anyone had ever said to her.

"You really didn't sneak a peek?" he asked, then his lips twisted. "You're a woman and a reporter—doesn't that make you the most curious creature on the planet?"

"I *am* curious, true. I mean…now that you're officially okay and all, maybe I can just…" She flipped the letter over to the side where the flap was sealed.

"Oh, hells no." He whooshed the letter out of her hand. "There's some seriously mushy stuff in here. I've got my rep to consider."

She arched her brows. "Really? How mushy are we talking about?"

He folded the letter in half and jammed it into his back pocket. "How about I put some of it in my wedding vows?"

"Oooh, I can't wait."

He smirked. "Get set, baby. I'm going to rock your world."

She laughed. "I'm thinking a man should be rewarded for such sentiment." She took his hand and led him toward the one hallway, continuing along until she found his bedroom. She brought him inside and urged him to sit on the edge of his mattress.

His eyes gleamed up at her.

She lowered herself into a crouch and pushed his legs wide, scooting between the splayed vee of his thighs.

The gleam in his eyes snapped into a sharper glint. "You got a hankering for finishing what we started in Pakistan, do ya?"

"Very much." She slashed a look at him from beneath her lashes. "Unless you're planning on walking out on me again."

He busted out laughing. "Not a chance."

"Then take off your shirt," she tossed at him. "I want

to see your body."

He chuckled low in his throat.

She was copying the scene they'd played in her tent the day of the cell phone exchange—or almost played.

This time Kyle said, "Gladly," and yanked off his shirt.

Her breath grew tight. His skin was blotchy with yellow spots—dye marker stains that had faded over the last two weeks, same as hers.

She reached out and traced one with her fingers.

"I look like the victim of a gang-bang golden shower gone wrong, don't I?"

"You look alive," she whispered. She couldn't speak offhandedly about his injuries. Not yet. Maybe never. "You look incredible." Pushing up on her knees, she ran her hands over his muscular shoulders to the solid, warm planes of his pecs, and slowly down to his abs. She tickled her fingertips along the waistband of his pants.

A deep moan spilled out of him. "I'm probably going to embarrass myself and come in two seconds."

"Probably," she agreed, bobbing her eyebrows at him while she undid his belt and unzipped his pants. "Because I *do* have great gag-reflex control."

His responding laugh was cut short when she encircled his hard cock with her hand. *Hmm.* Her fingers didn't meet around the circumference of it—maybe great gag-reflex control wasn't going to be enough to manage such an imposing organ.

She needed to get creative.

With her other hand, she nudged the middle of Kyle's chest till he got the hint and lay down flat on his back, his legs still hanging off the edge of his bed.

She climbed onto the mattress, settling beside his hips, her hand still grasping his erection. She examined it from every angle. Probably best to work her way up to the big gulp. She licked her tongue across the wide, smooth top of it.

The muscles in Kyle's thighs flexed and he released another deep moan.

Come to think on it, she could probably do no wrong here, even if she couldn't deep throat him. He'd probably be happy enough for her mouth to be anywhere in the near vicinity of his organ.

She went back to teasing him, swirling and swirling her tongue around the rim of his sex and all over the plump crest.

His breathing sped up.

She switched to the lollypop treatment, dragging her tongue down the length of him, then back up, then back down. She spied his hands twitching. He grabbed up fistfuls of the sheets. A ribbon of desire twisted through her belly. She was really starting to undo him. *Ha! I am woman.* Back up, back down...*all* the way down, this time to his balls.

Slipping one hand underneath his sac, she gently lifted his balls to her mouth. She kissed and licked and nibbled, and Kyle's next couple of breaths rushed out of his open mouth.

She smiled against the warm, supple flesh of his scrotum, then glided her tongue back up the long stretch of him, pressing his cock into the flat of her palm as she did. This time when she reached his head, he tasted salty—the drop of virile flavor on her tongue shot another bolt of lust through her.

She muffled a sound and took a better grip on his cock as she drew the top of it into her mouth, just the crown, and gave it several hard sucks.

Kyle growled low in his throat.

The noise was such a base sound of pleasure, hearing it got her wet. Just, *swoosh*, she was all slippery heat between her legs. She gave her thighs a quick squeeze, then suctioned her lips around his circumference and rode smoothly and slowly down his thickness. Up and down, up and down…she pumped her fist along with her mouth movements, each time taking him in deeper.

"Jesus," he hissed.

Never slowing, she angled her eyes up to check on him.

His nipples stood out like pebbles on his chest, his hands were fisted knuckle-white around wads of sheets, and he was breathing so heavily, his stomach was collapsing inward on each deep inhale.

He looked close to coming.

She rode down him again. The steady, bumping incursion of his cock into the back of her mouth had softened the muscles there and worked up a good amount of lubricating saliva.

Time to conquer.

On the next downward bob, she swallowed him down her throat.

He made a sharp "ah!" sound, and his hips bucked.

With a swift exhale from her nostrils, she deep-throated him again. And again.

"Max," he gulped out, threading his fingers into her hair. "I'm going to—" He stiffened and shouted as semen erupted from his cock.

She stayed in close and drank him down.

He moaned, deep and guttural, then his body lost all of its former rigidity. He sprawled limply on the mattress.

She released his softening cock, kissed his belly once, then crawled up to lie beside him.

He clutched her close to his side. "Fuck," he said between labored breaths. "That was awesome."

She snuggled closer. She was feeling quite proud of herself, actually—she hadn't been sure if she could do that.

"Give me ten minutes to rest." He shifted and seemed to sink deeper into the mattress, his eyelids sagging down. "Then I'll fully consummate our homecoming."

"Traditional sex is going to have to wait, unfortunately."

His eyes came open, and he turned his head to look at her.

"I'm on my period."

He levered himself up onto one elbow and stared down at her.

"See?" She tapped his chin with a forefinger. "I told you I wasn't ovulating in Pakistan."

He didn't say anything.

"So, uh, I bet you're relieved I'm not pregnant." *Question mark.* Was he? "Right?"

He glanced up, gazing across the room for a long moment—gifting her with a gnarly view of his jaw scar—then looked down at her again. "I'm kind of disappointed. Is that strange?"

"No." She crinkled her brow at him. "I kind of am, too."

CHAPTER FORTY

KYLE CONTINUED TO stare down at Max. The sight of her, in his very own bed no less, was such a miraculous, amazing, stupefying thing, he was still processing the reality of it. He'd been so afraid of losing her—to learn that she'd been maimed or killed or fail to locate her at all.

Although, funnily enough, he'd never considered *not* trying to look for her, like maybe she'd be better off without him in her life.

He hadn't reverted to his old Worthless Shithead recordings.

Max's belief in him was really starting to take hold.

"I suppose it's just as well," Kyle said about her not being pregnant, although he didn't entirely feel those words when he imagined creating a blue-eyed, tow-headed child with her. Then he totally felt it when he pictured that tow-headed kid sick in a hospital bed. "I still want to get some genetic testing done."

"Do what you need to do, Kyle." She briefly cupped his cheek with her palm, her eyes soft. "But I'm not worried."

There she went, believing in him again.

She combed her fingers through his chest hair. "Besides the fact that I just had an incredibly tasty meal, I'm starting to feel a little hungry after all."

He laughed softly. "Yeah, me too." He rolled out of bed and stood, shoving his pants all the way off, his shoes with them. "Pizza sound good?"

"Sounds perfect."

He balled up his pants with his shoes and tossed them in the direction of the hamper, then snagged a pair of maroon basketball shorts out of his dresser drawer and tugged them on. "I have some flyers in the kitchen for several local joints. You can pick."

"Okay." She grabbed his shirt off the bed and threw it to him, then hopped to her feet.

They went into the kitchen together.

He pulled out a stack of fast-food pamphlets from the cupboard where they shared space with his coffee mugs.

"Mugs!" she exclaimed. "Let's brew some coffee too."

"Freaking caffeine addict," he drawled, handing her the pamphlets. He made for the fridge, but then a loud knock sounded at the door. "A cannister of coffee grounds is at the back of the top shelf."

Crossing his living room, he opened the door on a small fist plowing his way. *Holy—!* The punch slammed into the left side of his chin and whipped his head sideways. *Ow!*

"What the *fuck* is your problem, Kyle!?"

He faced front again and went rigid.

Sienna.

His ex-girlfriend glared at him through glitter-coated blond eyelashes, her enormous breasts heaving beneath the tight stretch of a skimpy tank top. "Is it a sick, perverted joke of yours to make me fly out here from

Virginia every time I want to have the *simplest* conversation with you?!" She snapped her arms across her chest. "You *never* think I have anything important to say. Here you are back from deployment early, but once again you can't be *bothered* to respond to my text messages. Well, guess what? I do have something important to say! Something vital! Do you hear me, you fucking prick?"

"I'm not just *back from deployment*," Kyle retorted, a vein throbbing to life in his forehead. "You got your wish, Sienna, and I crashed in Pakistan. So excuse the fuck out of me if spending these last two weeks trying not to *die* superseded talking to your cousin Michael about the naval career he'll never have because he's a complete mullethead."

"This isn't about Michael!" Sienna yelled.

"I don't care what it's about," he shot back. "I want you out of my life." He shifted his weight onto the balls of his feet, poised for the Universe to roll its eyes and start in on a bunch of *yeah, right'ing*. Because he'd said those very same words to Sienna a thousand times in the past and had never owned the strength to mean them.

But that was before Max.

Now that Max was in his life, he was done with sabotaging. So, yeah, this time when he told his ex to get lost, he was met with only silence from the Universe.

He meant it this time.

"I have a new phone now," he told his ex. "So you don't have my number anymore. If you should ever manage to text me anyway, I'll automatically push the delete key." *Hell, yeah, I will!* "Got that?"

Sienna's cheeks bloomed bright red. "Fuck you, you

idiot bastard! I'm here for a reason!"

"Whatever it is, I don't—"

"Brodie's dead!" Sienna shrieked.

"Brodie—?" Kyle began, but then the world wiped out onto its side and went dark. *Dead?*

A wash of angry tears added extra shine to Sienna's glare. "The bone marrow transplant didn't work, you colossal asshole, and he died two days ago."

Died? Kyle was barely able to squeeze breath through the constriction of his throat. "I—But no." His guts slithered down to the floor and tangled around his feet.

"*That's* what I've been trying to get it touch with you about," Sienna said through her teeth. "And because my texts weren't *important* enough for you to answer, now you've missed the memorial service. Are you happy with yourself, Kyle?! That poor boy was put into the ground without his real father to see him laid to rest. You abandoned our son!"

Kyle felt all the blood drain from his face. He couldn't even lift an arm to protect himself when Sienna decided to punctuate her last remark with a hard slap to his face.

His head kicked sideways from the blow while the sound of flesh on flesh *cracked* out loud as a plate breaking. He shuffled sideways on unsteady legs, then slumped his shoulders and bowed his head.

You were going to leave Brodie's hospital room today, weren't you?

Oh, God. Kyle pushed his face into his hands. *I'm so sorry.*

"Excuse me."

Two words, spoken quietly but firmly, and everything stopped. Pain. Noise. Thoughts. Time.

Kyle lifted his head. Something trickled from his nose, and he dully identified it as blood.

Max was standing just inside the foyer, her complexion stark white, the pizza-delivery pamphlets shaking in her hand. She wasn't focused on him, though. She had a solid bead on Sienna.

"I'm very sorry for your loss," Max said tautly. "I understand that you must be in incredible pain right now, but I can't imagine a more cruel way to give someone bad news than what you just did to Kyle."

Sienna stared at Max, her wet lashes turning her eyelids into frowning slits. "Whoever the hell you are, this is none of your damned business."

"I'm Kyle's fiancée," Max returned, "which makes his welfare wholly my business." Max walked toward the door. "You need to leave."

Sienna's face stained a darker shade of red.

Max set her hand on the knob. "But please take a moment to calm yourself before you drive off, Miss Kelleman." Max's eyes narrowed. "I wouldn't wish a crash on *you*." She closed the door in Sienna's face, then turned to look at him.

It felt like spoiled globs of cottage cheese were in his throat when he swallowed. His barometer in life—the blue light in Max's eyes—was doused completely out. *This is bad...very, very...*

Brodie's dead.

Kyle smashed his eyes shut, squeezing his lids until he'd stopped all but the smallest bit of moisture from seeping beneath his lashes. He was snatching at control with grasping fingers...and losing the fight. Soon he was going to lose it completely. "I need you to go now too. I want to be alone."

"Kyle," Max implored gently. "You've just received a terrible shock. Let me—"

"Go," he ordered. "And...and don't come back."

"What?" She was astounded.

CHAPTER FORTY-ONE

KYLE ABRUPTLY TURNED away from Max and stalked across the room, giving her his back. "I thought I'd change," he rasped out, his voice coarse with this horrid, swelling need to weep. "I fooled myself into believing that my time with you in Pakistan made me over into a good man. But it didn't." He glared at the photo of him, LZ, Beans Vanderby, and Bingo Robbins skiing at Mammoth. "Deep down I'm still the guy you can't depend on, Max. Today, next month, two years from now—at some point, I'll let you down. So you need to get the fuck out before I do."

"Brodie didn't die because of anything you did or didn't do. You didn't screw anything up."

You were going to leave Brodie's hospital room today, weren't you?

He spun around, clenching his fists tight enough to knot the muscles in his forearms. "You're wrong. I should've stayed...given Brodie more bone marrow...something..." His throat clamped. "Anything."

She took a halting step toward him. "Kyle—"

"Go," he ground out. "I mean it." He shoved past her and flung open the front door. "Get out, Max. Now!"

Max's chest moved. "No," she said, soft, but adamant.

Kyle's heart banged hard enough to knock a couple of his ribs into his stomach. Max said something else to him, but it was as if her voice was coming at him from behind soundproof glass. Or maybe it was being drowned out by the dull roar rising in his ears, a tsunami of screams.

That poor boy was put into the ground without his real father to see him laid to rest!

You abandoned our son!

You're so undependable. Just like your father!

"Dammit!" Kyle bellowed. "GET OUT!"

Max paled another shade but didn't budge.

Jutting his chin, he quick-stepped around her and grabbed her in a full bear-hug from behind, his arms locking hers down.

The pamphlets sprayed everywhere.

Lifting her off the floor, he charged for the door.

Max made a sound deep in her chest, and swung her legs up, planting her feet on either side of the door frame. He continued forward, making her knees bend. He met resistance. Protesting wood barked.

Max snapped her legs straight, and her strong swimmer's muscles sent them both flying backward.

He hurtled through his living room until he was stopped by the abrupt meeting of the backs of his legs to the arm of his couch. He tumbled backward, his ass ending up, of all places, inside his open suitcase. He fell onto his back, the edge of his suitcase digging into his spine, and—*oh, fuck.*

Max's back!

"Jesus." He rolled sideways and set her on her feet as gently as possible. "Did I hurt you?"

She straightened and took two steps away from him, her face a blazing shade of red.

"Are you okay?" He scrambled to his feet.

"I just agreed to marry you," she snapped. "Do you think I'd make that kind of commitment, then just walk out during one of the most wretched moments of your life?" She scowled at him. "I will never leave you. Hear me on that. *Never.*"

Sweat beaded his brow like droplets of hot dew. "If you don't leave me, someday I'll bail on you. Guaranteed."

"Really?" She crossed her arms. "What guarantees it?"

A sock was draped over his shoulder. He snatched it off and hurled it to the floor. "My fucking past."

"Like what?"

"Like the day I visited Brodie in the hospital, it was too much for me. Too…painful, too hard. I nearly left right then and there. I even took a step toward the door before I stopped myself. And the day of our ambulance crash in Pakistan, after we ate those energy bars, I started to feel something for you, and it fucked with my head. I wanted to leave then too."

"But you *didn't* leave, either of those times." She exhaled a large breath. "Thoughts don't mean anything, Kyle. Everyone has stupid, crazy thoughts sometimes that they don't mean. Actions are what count."

"Okay, then what about the day of our cell-phone exchange, when you started asking me all those damned questions, trying to connect with me? I walked away then, didn't I? I didn't just fucking *think* about walking. I actually did."

"You didn't abandon me, for crying out loud. You just backed off because you weren't ready for where I was pushing you back then. But you are now."

"Am I?"

"You asked me to marry you, didn't you?"

"That was stupid."

"Why? Because you're an undependable schlub?"

He balled the muscles in his jaw. "Yes."

She threw her arms out from her sides. "Why are you so determined to see only the worst in yourself?"

"Because that's what there is to see," he clipped out. "You need to stop fucking believing in me."

"And you need to stop being so unfair to yourself."

"I'm not—"

She took him by the shirt collar. "You drowned yourself for me, Kyle—*that's* the kind of man you are!" She shook him. "*You drowned yourself for me!*" she repeated fiercely, huge pools of tears gathering along her lower eyelids, weighting them open into a Sailor Moon look. "There's no way to be more reliable than that."

She let go of him and lurched backward. "You're so afraid of becoming like your deadbeat dad you condemn yourself for every little piece of evidence, real or imagined, that you assume proves you *are* him. But I'm telling you now—and you'd better believe me—that you're the farthest thing in the world from a deadbeat."

Her voice lowered. "Remember the day in Pakistan when you told me I should give myself a break and let someone else carry the load? I said I couldn't because no one follows through. Well, do you think I *ever* would've agreed to marry you—would've fallen in love with you—

if I wasn't one hundred percent sure you were the man I could depend on?" Her tears tumbled over her lashes now.

He watched them make tracks down her cheeks and felt his throat jerk.

"You *didn't* leave Brodie; you endured an incredibly painful bone marrow procedure to try and help him. You didn't leave me the day of the ambulance crash; you saved me from terrorists. And you didn't leave me after your helicopter was shot down. You stayed with me even while the helo sank. You unstrapped my seatbelt, saving me then too. *That* is evidence from your past, Kyle. *See* it and own who you really are."

He stared her down, his eyes feeling so gravelly they had to be red-rimmed as hell. Her words played through his mind, and…something happened. The fists he had clenched at his sides went loose, and the Shithead recordings he'd started up again switched off.

He couldn't talk himself back into the shadows this time, because…everything Max had just said was true. He'd never *really* bailed on anything important. If something difficult or painful came along, he would punish himself for even thinking it was difficult or painful, then never give himself credit for actually facing down the difficulties.

But he did face down the difficult shit. He tried hard. He was okay.

He wasn't a worthless deadbeat.

He gasped in his next breath as a lifetime of self-destruction poured out of him all at once. It was so sudden and forceful, it took out his legs. He slammed down to the carpet onto his knees, and the need to weep totally overwhelmed him. Throwing his head back, he covered his face with his hands, his anguish purging from him hard as punches.

He cried for everything.

For Brodie, the son he'd never really known, and so maybe Kyle didn't have the right to sob for some boy who was all but a stranger, but what poor kid deserved to die at seven years old, anyway?

For Jobs—the friend Kyle hadn't grieved for yet...for the aviator and the man Steve would never have a chance to become now.

For all the women Kyle had used—including Max—on his mission to avoid intimacy, because he'd been too damned afraid to find out who he truly was.

And he cried for himself, for the father he'd wanted and needed so badly, but had lacked his whole life, and for all the soul-grinding sabotage he'd done to himself for too many years to count.

Who knew where he would've ended up if Max hadn't come into his life. Probably alone in a sewer, asphyxiated by his own vomit.

Max... She was on her knees, hugging him tightly.

He shuddered as his splayed-open self vomited out the last of the dark gorge. His hands lowered from his face on their own, and he dropped his brow to Max's shoulder, clutching her. "Well, that was a word-class cry fest," he said hoarsely. He should probably be embarrassed as fuck that she was seeing him like this, but truth was, he couldn't imagine having made it through without her. "Thanks for not letting me offload again you with my consummate sabotage skills."

She smoothed her hand down the back of his hair. "You know, the last time you tried was after we had unprotected sex." She leaned back. "Do you remember what I said to you during that argument?" She answered for herself. "That we're the two kids who've always been let down, but we're not going to do that to each other. Ever."

"Yeah." He cleared his throat and stood before he could choke up again. He helped her to her feet. "I need to quit being an idiot about that."

He and Max only had a whole lot of forever stretched out in front of them.

He hugged her close, staying like that for a long time.

Through one of the open living-room windows the far-off slap and whoosh of a gentle surf filled the passing moments, rhythmic and soothing and timeless.

CHAPTER FORTY-TWO

November, seven months later, Hotel Del Coronado

T HERE HAD TO be upwards of five hundred people at the wedding.

Held in the Crown Room at the Hotel Del Coronado, the reception was a class act, decorations done in white and gold, twinkle lights strung across every inch of the ceiling, and enough flowers stuck in vases along the walls to have cleaned out a commercial-sized greenhouse. An open bar and a champagne fountain kept the liquor flowing, and filet mignon was on the menu for later.

"Jeez," Max said, arriving on the other side of the champagne fountain from Kyle. "This place makes me feel like we got married in a barn."

The Hotel Del—as it was known to San Diegans—was one of the poshest hotels in the city. An architectural marvel, the pristine white main building was topped with a red conical roof that any aviator stationed in San Diego could recognize from the air in his sleep.

"Forget this." Kyle waved a negligent hand around the extravagant room. "Eric's a trust fund baby. Our wedding was great."

Six months ago he and Max had chosen the tradition- al military route for their wedding, first marrying in the Naval Air Station North Island base chapel, then celebrating afterward at the Officer's Club.

She twinkled at him. "It was." Slipping her glass under the cascading champagne, she glanced at him from beneath her eyelashes. "I'm ovulating, by the way."

"What?" He tucked his chin in. "Like, you mean, right here in the fountain?"

She chuckled. "Like, this morning." She sipped her drink. "Do you want to do something about it?"

"I thought we'd decided to wait." Although not from Kyle worrying about giving her a sick kid—within one month of being married, he'd received a clean bill of health.

They'd just both agreed it would be a good idea to spend a year as a married couple before adding a kid to the equation.

Strolling around the fountain with a sexy swing in her hips, Max reached up with one hand and straightened Kyle's black bow tie. "That was before I saw you looking so dapper in your mess dress uniform." She winked. "You're a whole lot of zowie, hubby."

He chuckled. "Dapper, am I?" He'd stuffed himself into the Navy's fanciest officer uniform today because he was doing the Best Man thing, a role Eric O'Dwyer had played at Kyle's own wedding—although Eric had been co-best man alongside Kyle's younger brother, Andy.

Eric had brothers, too—three of them—but he wasn't particularly close to them, so he'd asked Kyle to do the honors. Kyle had gladly stepped up.

Lights dimmed, and the live band switched to a love song.

Kyle listened to the lyrics for a moment, trying to

place the song. It was *Biggest Part of Me* by Ambrosia.

He glanced over to the dance floor. Eric and Nicole were facing each other on either side of it, both chuckling softly.

Max sighed. "Nicole looks so stunning," she observed, not for the first time.

Kyle had never seen the badass DEA agent put such solid effort into looking nice, and the effect was, yeah, absolutely astounding. Nicole's hair was half-up in a complicated style and partially covered with a down-the-back veil. Her makeup was done to accentuate her exotic features, and her wedding dress was a real gaga number, sleeveless, with a neckline that showcased her rack to an impressive degree, a lot of swirling beadwork hugging her athletic figure.

"Vera Wang," Max sighed again, like that was supposed to mean something to him.

Eric and Nicole walked toward each other, eyes locked, then embraced and started to slow dance.

Biggest Part of Me leaned heavily toward sappy, if you asked him, so he wasn't sure what the big deal was, but…

Now that he was a married man, sappy could work. "Would you care to dance, Mrs. Hammond?"

"I'd love to." Smiling, Max took the arm he held out to her and let him lead her to the dance floor. He pulled her close, and she linked her arms around his neck and swayed with him.

He gazed down at her with warm eyes. To him, Max outshone the bride.

She was wearing a dark pink—*rose*, according to Max—dress with thin straps that highlighted the delicate bone structure in her shoulders, completely camouflaging the nubile strength Kyle knew lay beneath her clothes. It was always a bit of a pulse-quickener, knowing he held the secret to just how hot her body truly was. "Have I told you how beautiful you look today?"

"Let's see…" Max made a pretense of thinking about it. "Only a hundred times."

"Consider this a hundred and one."

Her blue-on-blue eyes gleamed.

The sight had an immediate effect on the flow of blood through his veins. Most of it rushed south, and, with a hand on her lower back, he tugged her closer and leaned toward her ear. "So do you want to sneak off and find a closet somewhere, capitalize on that ovulation thing you mentioned a moment ago?"

She huffed air from her nose. "We're at a wedding, Kyle."

"Hey, it's nothing Eric didn't do at our wedding…in the *chapel*, no less."

An incredulous ripple of air escaped her. "You're kidding?"

"Nope. Remember the rock we spotted on Nicole's finger at our reception? Apparently a little shaboink went down with the proposal." He swirled Max around, moving to sweep her into a mini-dip, but then he accidently bumped shoulders with someone hanging out at the side of the dance floor.

"Oh, hey, man, sorry," Kyle apologized, then caught sight of who he'd collided with. "Whoa, Casanova!" He stepped off the dance floor with Max. "How are you doing? Fully recovered?"

Casanova's bird was the other helo that got shot down the fateful night near the Mangla Dam—it was the explosion Kyle saw in his helicopter's rearview—and Kyle had heard that Casanova spent a week afterward being chased by terrorists across northern Pakistan.

"I'm good for the most part, thanks," Casanova answered. "Just some lingering back issues."

"I can relate to that," Max said.

Kyle twisted his lips tight. Yeah, certain movements still pained her, and probably always would. It seemed really unfair that Kyle walked away from the crash without a single, lingering issue, and Max hadn't. But he supposed he should mostly be grateful.

The outcome of that crash could've been much worse, all the way around.

"My wife, Max," Kyle introduced.

Casanova shook her hand. "I remember you from Pakistan. *LA Times*, right?"

Max smiled. "Good memory."

"Kind of an unforgettable day." Casanova smiled back. "Nice to see you again."

No, no, no. Kyle did not want a guy of Casanova's looks smiling at his wife.

Kyle put an arm around Max's shoulders. "So, what are you doing here, Vanderby? I thought you were transferred to an East Coast squadron."

"Yeah, I'm with HSC-7 now. I'm back in town visiting Danny, so he brought me as his Plus One to LZ's wedding."

Eric had been in the Wolfpack before becoming an admiral's aide, so he'd invited all of his former squadron mates to his wedding today, and that included Casanova's brother, Beans.

A waitress came by with a tray of drinks. "Jack and Coke?" she inquired of Casanova.

"That's me." Casanova accepted the offered drink, then turned back to Kyle. "I'm glad I ran into you, actually." His expression sobered. "I've been wanting to tell you how sorry I am about your copilot. You lent me Steve Whitmore, and then he…" Casanova studied his drink.

"Yeah, it sucks big time that Jobs died," Kyle agreed. "But it wasn't out of anything you or I did wrong."

An Aviation Mishap Board had cleared the entire rescue team of all culpability in the crash.

"Still." Casanova's eyes raked back up. "It doesn't sit well."

No. It didn't.

Casanova took a long draw on his Jack and Coke. "Hey, I heard what you did at your wedding, leaving a man missing in the sword arch to honor Steve."

Kyle nodded. Nearly all Navy weddings concluded with the sword arch ritual, where squadron mates of the groom—who were decked out in their choker whites—formed two lines facing one another, then drew ceremonial swords and crossed them high overhead to create a passageway the newly wedded couple dashed through on their way to married life.

For Kyle and Max's sword arch, Kyle had arranged to have four men on one side and five on the other, leaving an open space for Jobs, who, if he'd lived, Kyle would've definitely asked to be a sword bearer.

Casanova lifted his cocktail glass in toast. "That was very cool of you."

"Thanks." Kyle paused, not sure what else to say.

An awkward moment passed.

Max stepped in, "So, how do you like your new squadron?"

Casanova took another swig of his drink. "I prefer the West coast, actually, and it's hard being so far away from my brother, but I was chasing down the woman I was trying to marry, and she lives and works in Norfolk."

"Oh, yeah?" Max's eyebrows arched. "Did you end up marrying her?"

Keeping reading for bonus material to ALLIED OPERATIONS…

IN 1988, MARK Eoff, a squadron mate of my husbands, and a good friend of both of ours, barely survived a helicopter crash.

While flying over the Pacific Ocean, a cable in the rear rotor of his aircraft wore through and failed. His helo suffered a catastrophic failure in the rear rotor system, and he and all his crew plunged into the sea.

Mark's death would've been a cruel loss to the world. He's a 6'3" teddy bear of a fellow, good-natured, with a dry wit, and I don't think I've ever heard an unkind word come out of his mouth. Considering all that happened to Mark, it's a miracle he made it through, but I'm thankful he did.

The crash Mark endured was one of the worst experiences of his life, but he is just the sort of generous soul who would openly share his experiences with me. With his consent, I have drawn liberally from his real-life account of the helicopter crash that almost ended his life in order to give Kyle Hammond's story as much realism as possible.

As you read ALLIED OPERATIONS, you may have thought some parts of the story were unbelievable. How could a man drown and not die? As impossible as it sounds, it really happened. As you will see…

The heart-wrenching story of Mark's horrible accident is copied below in his own words.

I received a phone call the other day from an old Navy buddy who found something I had written many years ago. It was a yellowed, dot-matrix, continuous-feed computer printout of my experiences following a tragic helicopter crash from 1988. I didn't even remember writing it, but here is the account of that incident.

August 10th, 1988.

IT'S COOL AND overcast in the morning with little wind. *Nice day for flying.* That's what I think.

I had no way of knowing it would turn out to be the worst day of my life.

Wednesday morning.

I'M ASSIGNED AS the HSL-35 Detachment 10 Maintenance Officer aboard *USS Reid* (FFG-30), and draw the dawn launch. The mission is routine: a simulated transit through the Straits of Hormuz off the shores of San Diego. The helicopter's mission? Stay within ten miles of the ship. *No problem. Can handle.*

There's nothing noteworthy in the mission brief. Winds light and variable. Estimated ceiling is overcast at a thousand feet. *Piece of cake.* A thorough preflight inspection of our bird reveals no problems. The sun is coming up, and we launch without incident, actually beating our scheduled 0700 launch time by six or seven minutes.

Things are going well. The aircraft is flying very nicely.

After we've completed the simulation, we soon discover that it doesn't take long to investigate virtually every square inch of a circle within a ten-mile radius. Our sole source of entertainment becomes the incredible variety of marine life packed into this small area. Huge schools of porpoises. And whales.

Another fuel check. There's 1+40 hours remaining on gas. It is 0845. About 45 minutes until our scheduled return time for fuel and crew swap. My copilot is flying, having a great time. I'm busying myself with fuel checks, monitoring gauges, and looking outside the cockpit for yet another whale, porpoise, or sunfish.

My fish-gazing activities are interrupted by a weird feeling in my butt, like the aircraft is sliding out from under me. I think my copilot has somehow lost tail-rotor authority, and maybe I'd better help him get the situation under control. I'd lost tail-rotor authority before and knew how to handle it. I turn to look at my copilot just as he's turning to look at me.

Walt's eyes are wide when he says, "Mark, I think you'd better take it."

By the time I take the controls, *whoa!* We've already rotated 180 degrees to the right! As we continue to rotate, picking up speed, going faster and faster, I look down—the left pedal is stuck all the way forward! I immediately attempt to gain forward airspeed in order to fly us into cleaner air.

My attempt is fruitless.

By now only three or four seconds have elapsed from the first indication of trouble, but the aircraft is already spinning violently. The noise and vibration are unbearable, and I know I have lost complete tail rotor thrust.

I yell, "ECLs, ECLs!!" into my microphone. I need to remove the torque from the rotor head to stop this spinning! The aircraft is whirling so violently, my glasses get ripped off my face, and the microphone is torn away from my mouth. I can't read any of the gauges, and the horizon is blurring wildly past my eyes.

All I can do is hold on (literally) and horse the stick around, trying to maintain a level attitude. I can't move my head…can't take in a breath…can't do anything but hold on. My mind is racing, trying to figure out what to do next. It seems as if I'm spinning for an eternity, when in reality it is probably more like five to ten seconds.

The crash comes as a total and utter surprise.

I hit the water with such force I can hear the aircraft explode into fragments. On impact, the helo continues to turn initially, but then rolls right. A feeling of spinal compression, as if I'm being crushed, overcomes me. Later I'll find out that I'd crashed with such force, I fractured my skull. I remember thinking, "Dammit! I did not want to do this!"

I'm dazed.

I'm shaken.

It occurs to me that somehow I'm still alive.

It's now very quiet, calm even. There isn't any sensation of cold water. I'm detached from my body, watching myself perform my egress steps.

I can see, but, as I sink, it gets darker by the second. I find and grab the door handle, a poorly designed metal rod, and try to open it. I use both hands. *No good.* I try to find the jettison handle, but it's blocked by wreckage. Performing my egress drill gives me purpose. I hadn't been able to take a breath prior to impact, and what I have is just about gone. My lungs are burning. No, scorching! I try to relax as I reach for my HEED bottle, a mini oxygen tank pilots carry in their survival vests. It's now too dark to see anything but shapes. I slap the pocket where my HEED should be.

It's not there!

I frantically search for it. My bottle is gone—lost during impact. I'm running out of time. Out of air!

I unstrap and make a move for the copilot's door. *No good.* The way is blocked. My last hope is to squeeze between the bulkheads and try to get out of the aft cabin. I can't see anything now. Feeling my way into the narrow space, I become lodged. I'm trapped in a sinking aircraft, going to die! I'm all out of air and ideas. My lungs are on fire, exploding!

It is the hardest thing I've ever done, but I take a deep breath. I just can't fight it any longer. As I ingest a lungful of seawater and JP-5 jet fuel, I feel a flash of pain and immediately lose consciousness.

Fade to black...

I had died in a helicopter crash.

Sometime later...

WHAT AM I looking at? Where is the helicopter? I slowly turn my head, first to the left, then to the right. I see nothing—the water around me is very dark green—but I can feel I'm clear of the aircraft. I glance down and find the toggles that activate my LPA: my life preserver. I grab them slowly and pull first the left, then the right. Nothing happens. I try them again. I lift my head and look up. I can see a lighter shade of very dark green water.

I raise my arms toward the light…

Black out again.

IT TURNS OUT that both my crewmen are lucky. At the moment of impact, their back window blew clear, and the aircraft immediately filled with water. First one man, then the other, egressed through the window, and kicked for the surface. Once on top, they checked each other for injuries, then proceeded to search for the pilots.

Some seconds later, I surface. My vest is inflated, but I'm floating face down. When the first crewman reaches me, my body has righted itself. I am blue in the face and so bloated and distended from all the water that he can't even tell which pilot I am. When he touches my neck to check for a pulse, it triggers me to vomit large quantities of water, JP-5, and blood. I start breathing, weakly.

The ship, only about three miles away when we crashed, immediately proceeds to the site. They reach the scene and have the surviving members of the flight crew aboard the motor whaleboat within seventeen minutes of the crash. My inert form is hoisted aboard *Reid* by horse collar, and the ship's medical corpsman is standing by to render aid.

At the same time, an H-3 helicopter, which happened to be airborne at the time, diverts to *Reid* to medevac me and my crewmen to Balboa Naval Hospital, San Diego.

The loud roar of rotor blades and the powerful downwash bring me up to a level of semi-consciousness.

I'm stretched out on a litter of some sort and being loaded into a helicopter. What is happening? The helicopter lifts off, and I feel cold. Inches from my vision is the face of the corpsman from the *Reid*. He looks very worried, and keeps asking me if I'm OK.

I say I am.

We are en route by 0930.

I shift onto my side, and cough. I look down and see blood. What's happening to me? Another man in the cabin holds a note in front of me: "10 minutes from Balboa." That's the name of the Naval Hospital. It hits me that I'm in some kind of serious trouble, but I can't make out exactly what, and, once again, I drift into unconsciousness.

THE NEXT SEVERAL hours are a blur of medical activity.

As soon as I'm at the hospital, a horde of specialists descends on me, trying desperately to coax a reaction out of my battered, barely alive body. It's a period of sensory overload, punctuated by moments of excruciating and profound pain, as I'm poked, prodded, and cut open.

Apparently, the squadron representative is told no fewer than three times I'm not going to make it. Everyone should prepare themselves; I'm not expected to live through the night.

Eventually, the drugs take effect, and, once again, I am without consciousness.

WHEN I WAKE up, I'm alone. Tubes are jammed down my throat, and the rhythmic rising and falling of my chest indicates I'm hooked up to a respirator. My arms are immobilized, and there is an astounding array of IVs protruding from my body. My neck is in a brace, limiting my range of motion.

I feel terrible.

Then I see a face come into view. My wife! She finds a small piece of skin not covered with tape or with something sticking out of it, and touches me as she gives me a kiss. I immediately feel a whole lot better.

Then, more faces.

I recognize them from my helicopter squadron. And it hits me—I've been in a helicopter crash. Memories come flooding back. My copilot! Where is my copilot…? I can't talk with the tube down my throat, so I try spelling out his name by waving my fingers.

Only much later did I find out he was never recovered.

SOMEHOW, BY SOME miracle, I end up living. The next day I'm transferred from Intensive Care to the ward. Three days after that, I go home.

To this day, I don't know how I got out of the helicopter after getting lodged in the bulkhead. I can only surmise that I simply floated through the hole where the pilot's windscreen used to be. I'll never really know. I do know one thing, though. Training saved my life. If I hadn't had the presence of mind to activate my life preserver during my brief period of consciousness, I probably never would have surfaced. Estimates put me at about sixty feet down, near the point of negative buoyancy. And once I did surface, only the quick, decisive action of my crewmen kept me alive long enough to be rescued.

I owe them. Big time.

IN TIME, ALL of my injuries completely resolved themselves, and I'm returned to full duty, including flying.

However, I have never fully recovered from the loss of my copilot. He was a good friend, the best. They say if you stay in this business long enough, you will lose a friend. I guess that's true. Flying is a dangerous business. I never forget that. It takes a special type of individual to put it all on the line every day. I don't consider myself a hero. Just an average guy doing a tough job.

But my friend and copilot, Walt…he's a hero. He gave everything he had for something he believed in.

I will miss him.

Walt Hogan, farthest right...

From left: Pat "Flash" McConnell, Tony "Steamer" Perez, Anthony "Alpha Tango" Tracy, Walt "Goat" Hogan. Picture curtesy of Anthony Tracy. Printed by permission.

My heartfelt thanks to both Mark and Tricia Eoff for sharing their story.

I'm a huge fan of romance novels.

I read for escapism, and I hate it when a story falls short of enthralling me.

If I've failed to do my job and didn't provide you with some much-needed escapism, then I deserve a review bomb.

On the other hand, if Kyle and Max's story swept you away, warmed you, and inspired you to turn the last page with a big sigh, then I'd love to know that.

Please tell me in a review.

I'd really like to know if this book about hot naval aviators met (or maybe surpassed!) your expectations.

Thank you.

Author Notes

The militant group Jaish-e-Mohammed, or JEM, is a real terrorist organization, and the events surrounding the American solider Bowe Bergdahl are drawn from actual news events. These aspects of the story were presented to the best of my research. The four American engineers who were taken by JEM as hostages are a fabrication.

Although Pakistan and India have suffered from a troubled past, these two nations were never in open conflict during the time period encompassed by ALLIED OPERATIONS. Other aspects of the Pakistani culture, government, and landscape I've tried to present as accurately as possible, with the exception of the area between the small town called Chhajja and Mangla Dam. There was actually much more than a few thousand feet between the two, providing ample room for the helicopters of the rescue operation to land. I couldn't have that!

The International Humanitarian Medical Relief organization is imagined.

Now Available!

MAN DOWN

Book 3 in the Wings of Gold Series

WINNER of the HOLT Medallion for outstanding literary fiction in a novel with Strong Romantic Elements
2017 Kindle Book Award Semi-finalist for Romance
Reader's Favorite Bronze Medal Winner for Romance

After being shot down by the Taliban on a Special Operations mission, a Navy pilot and Navy SEAL rescue a beautiful humanitarian doctor. While the three of them evade capture in a race for their lives across northern Pakistan, the two former boyhood friends heal a 10-year breach, and the pilot and doctor find a way to let go of their painful pasts to find love.

Don't miss a single book in Tracy Tappan's thrilling series!

Go to www.tracytappan.com and sign up for her author updates, and find out about FREE books today!

GLOSSARY

<u>Autorotation</u>: This is a state of flight in which the engine is disengaged from the main rotor system of a helicopter so that the blades are driven solely by air moving up through the rotor (in other words, the engine is no longer supplying power to the main rotor). The most common use of autorotation in helicopters is to safely land the aircraft in the event of an engine failure or tail-rotor failure.

<u>BUD/S</u>: stands for Basic Underwater Demolition/SEAL Training. This is the 6-month SEAL training course which starts with five weeks of indoctrination and pre-conditioning, then goes on to three different phases of training. The first phase is the toughest and includes Hell Week, where three quarters of the class will quit.

<u>Captain's Mast</u>: This is name of the Navy and Marine procedure used for dealing with non-judicial punishment (NJP). The accused will stand before his or her commanding officer and be judged on the facts. He or she may have a lawyer present, but usually doesn't, as this is a more informal hearing than a court martial.

<u>Chalk</u>: A chalk is a group of troops that deploy from a single aircraft—"chalk" is often used to refer to a platoon-sized unit being deployed on air assault operations. The

term was first coined in World War II for airborne troops, due to the fact that the aircraft number of the flight they were on was written on the troops' backs with chalk.

Daily and Turn: This is a series of special checks and inspections done on a helicopter in order to prep it for the next flight. Maintenance personnel usually perform these checks, except when away from home base, and then it is the duty of the AW.

FLIR: stand for Forward-Looking Infrared. The sensors on a FLIR camera use detection of infrared radiation, typically emitted from a heat source, to create a picture on a video output.

Geedunk: This is the slang term used to refer to the gift and snack store on board.

HM3: stands for Hospital Corpsman, Third Class. This is a rate of E4.

ISR: stands for intelligence, surveillance, and reconnaissance.

LSE: stands for Landing Signal Enlisted.

Mensurate: This is SPECOPS lingo referring to information supplied by intelligence personnel to the special operatives about all measurable aspects of a target. For the pilots, this information includes how large a landing zone is, if there are poles or telephone wires nearby, how tall buildings are, etcetera.

<u>RAST</u>: stands for Recovery, Assist, Secure and Traverse. This is the system that helps the H-60 Seahawk helicopter land on the back of ships. Based on a "bear trap" system, steel "claws" clamp shut around a probe at the bottom of the aircraft in order to stabilize the helo once it's on deck.

<u>Super JO</u>: This is a senior lieutenant who has been pegged early on in his or her career as a front runner in the aviation community. He or she is groomed for the best positions and early promotion, and are often given jobs generally reserved for officers above his or her rank.

<u>UNREP</u>: stands for Underway Replenishments, such as food, fuel, etc.